Neal Rankin had warned her to expect a cocky man in his mid-thirties. He hadn't warned her that the owner/manager of the T Bar K was also devilishly handsome.

Six feet of hard, lean muscle, eyes as green as a willow tree, hair the color of rich sable and dimples bracketing a perfectly masculine mouth. His looks were the kind most women swooned over. But not Isabella. She knew his kind all too well.

Yet once Ross Ketchum was standing directly in front of her, she was struck by the full potency of his presence. She'd never seen any male as masculine as this one.

"Isabella Corrales," he mused softly. "A beautiful name for a beautiful lady."

"I'm not here for decoration, Mr. Ketchum. I'm here to help you."

Dear Reader,

It's that time of year again...for decking the halls, trimming the tree...and sitting by the crackling fire with a good book. And we at Silhouette have just the one to start you off—Joan Elliott Pickart's *The Marrying MacAllister,* the next offering in her series, THE BABY BET: MACALLISTER'S GIFTS. When a prospective single mother out to adopt one baby finds herself unable to choose between two orphaned sisters, she is distressed, until the perfect solution appears: marry handsome fellow traveler and renowned single guy Matt MacAllister! Your heart will melt along with his resolve.

MONTANA MAVERICKS: THE KINGSLEYS concludes with *Sweet Talk* by Jackie Merritt. When the beloved town veterinarian—and trauma survivor—is captivated by the town's fire chief, she tries to suppress her feelings. But the rugged hero is determined to make her his. Reader favorite Annette Broadrick continues her SECRET SISTERS series with *Too Tough To Tame.* A woman out to avenge the harm done to her family paints a portrait of her nemesis—which only serves to bring the two of them together. In *His Defender,* Stella Bagwell offers another MEN OF THE WEST book, in which a lawyer hired to defend a ranch owner winds up under his roof...and falling for her newest client! In *Make-Believe Mistletoe* by Gina Wilkins, a single female professor who has wished for an eligible bachelor for Christmas hardly thinks the grumpy but handsome man who's reluctantly offered her shelter from a storm is the answer to her prayers—at least not at first. And speaking of Christmas wishes—five-year-old twin boys have made theirs—and it all revolves around a new daddy. The candidate they have in mind? The handsome town sheriff, in *Daddy Patrol* by Sharon DeVita.

As you can see, no matter what romantic read you have in mind this holiday season, we have the book for you. Happy holidays, happy reading—and come back next month, for six new wonderful offerings from Silhouette Special Edition!

Sincerely,

Gail Chasan
Senior Editor

Please address questions and book requests to:
Silhouette Reader Service
U.S.: 3010 Walden Ave., P.O. Box 1325, Buffalo, NY 14269
Canadian: P.O. Box 609, Fort Erie, Ont. L2A 5X3

His Defender

STELLA BAGWELL

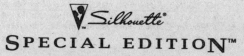

SPECIAL EDITION™

Published by Silhouette Books

America's Publisher of Contemporary Romance

With love to Dr. Z.

Thank you for your care and kindness.

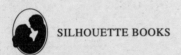 **SILHOUETTE BOOKS**

ISBN 0-373-24582-3

HIS DEFENDER

Copyright © 2003 by Stella Bagwell

Visit Silhouette at www.eHarlequin.com

Printed in U.S.A.

STELLA BAGWELL

sold her first book in Silhouette in November 1985. More than forty novels later, she still loves her job and says she isn't completely content unless she's writing. Recently, she and her husband of thirty years moved from the hills of Oklahoma to Seadrift, Texas, a sleepy little fishing town located on the coastal bend. Stella says the water, the tropical climate and the seabirds make it a lovely place to let her imagination soar and to put the stories in her head down on paper.

She and her husband have one son, Jason, who lives in nearby Port Lavaca, where he teaches high school math.

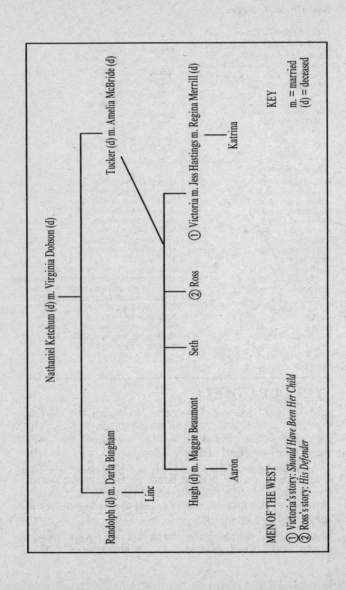

Nathaniel Ketchum (d) m. Virginia Dobson (d)

Randolph (d) m. Darla Bingham

Line

Hugh (d) m. Maggie Beaumont

Aaron

Seth

② Ross

Tucker (d) m. Amelia McBride (d)

① Victoria m. Jess Hastings m. Regina Merrill (d)

Katrina

KEY

m. = married
(d) = deceased

MEN OF THE WEST

① Victoria's story: *Should Have Been Her Child*
② Ross's story: *His Defender*

Chapter One

"I've never tried to kill anybody! Whoever says different is a damn liar!"

Ross Ketchum stopped pacing around the study of the T Bar K ranch house long enough to glare at his sister and her new husband.

"What about that time the city cops hauled you in for choking Lance Martin?" Victoria asked.

Ross threw back his head and laughed. "That was just a little high school prom fight, and Lance needed taking down a notch or two."

Victoria shared a wry look with her husband, Jess, who was sitting beside her on a long, leather couch.

"Okay," Victoria conceded, "so it was just a little squabble between two roosters. But other people around here remember the incident. And if this thing goes to trial—"

"It isn't going to go to trial, Sis," Ross said with confidence. "Not with me as the defendant."

With a helpless groan, Victoria turned to her husband. "I give up. It's your turn to try and convince him how serious this thing is."

Jess Hastings was not only Victoria's new husband, he was also the under-sheriff of San Juan County. And, more ironically, he was the person Ross had supposedly tried to kill.

Three weeks ago, right here on T Bar K land, someone had shot Jess in the shoulder. If the bullet had struck three inches lower, his brother-in-law would be dead now.

"Victoria is right, Ross," Jess spoke up. "The D.A. is making noises about pressing charges."

His jaw tight, Ross pulled the black cowboy hat from his head and tossed it at a rail of pegs hanging on a nearby wall. The hat hit one of the pegs, dangled wildly, then settled into place. Like his life, he thought wryly. Sometimes it seemed he was only hanging on by his fingertips, but after everything was washed and dried he was usually standing firmly on his feet. He had to believe things would turn out for the best this time, too.

"Well, obviously I've been framed," he said. "And that means we're all going to have to be careful around here."

Jess nodded in total agreement. "The way I see it, none of us can be too careful."

Ross turned a concerned eye on his sister. "You couldn't have married Jess and moved to the Hastings ranch at a better time. I'm glad you're not staying here now."

Once Jess had been released from the hospital, Victoria had been so eager to marry him, she'd forgone a big, splashy wedding for a simple ceremony in the judge's chambers. Ross didn't understand such love and devotion. At least, he'd never felt it for any woman. But he was glad his sister was happy at last. Her marriage was the only joyful thing that had happened around the T Bar K in years.

''I'll still be in and out,'' Victoria assured him, then, with a grateful glance at her husband, added, ''but Jess will be with me. In the meantime, Neal Rankin is expecting you in his office tomorrow morning at nine.''

Neal Rankin was the attorney the Ketchums used for all the legal business concerning the T Bar K. Along with being their attorney, he'd been a good friend to Ross and Victoria ever since their childhood days.

Frowning, Ross looked up from unbuckling his spurs. ''Rankin? What for? Don't tell me that something is wrong with the ranch's books?''

''No. It's not the books,'' Victoria told him. ''He wants to speak with you about this shooting incident.''

Ross snorted a laugh. ''Since when did Neal Rankin think he was a criminal attorney? He must be needing a vacation.''

''With friends like you, I'm sure he does need a vacation,'' Victoria shot back at her brother. ''But he wants to speak with you just the same. We—uh, he thinks we need to hire a defense attorney for you.''

Leaning down once again, Ross pulled the sundial spurs from the heels of his boots. He'd been in the saddle all day. He was tired. He needed a shower and bed. He didn't want to talk about, or even think about, attorneys and shootings and jail.

''Oh hell, I don't need a defense attorney.''

''Then you'd better tell Neal that in the morning,'' Victoria said flatly. ''Because he thinks you're in trouble.''

Grinning, Ross winked at her. ''Trouble is my middle name, Sis. Everybody in San Juan County, New Mexico, knows that.''

* * *

The next morning Ross drove into Aztec early and ate a leisurely breakfast of bacon and eggs at the Wagon Wheel Café. After his third cup of coffee, he walked down the sidewalk to Neal Rankin's small law office. Inside, behind a wide desk, a hefty woman with graying black hair smiled at him.

"Hello, Mr. Ketchum," she greeted cheerfully. "Nice day, isn't it?"

"Hello yourself, Connie. And any day that Neal calls me to the office is a grand day," he said drolly. "Is he in yet?"

Connie jerked a thumb toward the door behind her left shoulder. "Ten minutes ago. Better go in now before someone else gets in line."

Ross crossed the room and entered the small connecting office. A tall man with dark-blond hair was in the process of pouring coffee into a dark ceramic mug. He looked around as Ross helped himself to a chair.

"I guess you've never heard of knocking," he said.

"Not on your door, buddy," Ross told him.

With an accepting shake of his head, Neal held up the coffee cup. "Want some?"

"No. I just left the Wagon Wheel. The little waitress there never let my cup cool," Ross said with a cocky grin.

Neal took a seat behind his desk. "That's because she knows you're a rich man."

Ross chuckled. "And here I thought she was taken with my looks."

"You're crazy, Ross. You're thirty-five years old and you're not a bit different than you were at twenty."

"Why should I try to improve on a good thing?" Ross grinned, then got straight to the point of his visit. "Besides, you're the one who's crazy if you're thinking I need a lawyer to defend me."

The other man sipped from the mug before he settled

comfortably back in the leather chair. "I not only think you need one, I've already hired one for you."

Incredulous, Ross scooted to the edge of his seat. "No!"

"That's right," Neal said calmly. "She'll be here in the morning. And I expect you to be around the ranch when she arrives." ·

Ross looked even more stunned. "She?"

Neal nodded. "Isabella Corrales, Bella for short. She's very good. She worked for a time as a prosecutor for Dona Ana County."

Incensed, Ross jerked off his hat and slapped it against his knee. "You not only hire a woman, but you hire one who's a prosecutor! What are you trying to do to me?"

Accustomed to Ross's passionate outbursts, Neal smiled patiently. "Calm down, old friend. I'm trying to take care of you."

"Hmmph," Ross grunted. "Sounds like it. What do you do to your enemies, stake them out in a bed of fire ants?"

"This is serious business, Ross. You could be brought up on several counts, the most serious being intent to kill."

Ross mouthed a few curse words. "Yeah, my own brother-in-law, for Pete's sake. Come on, Neal, anybody with two eyes can see this is a frame job."

"Maybe. But with a murder already having taken place on the T Bar K, it makes you look mighty suspicious."

"Damn it, I had nothing to do with that murder!"

"I know that. But the law doesn't. Right now they're searching for clues, and everything they're turning up points to you."

"You're dramatizing this whole thing, buddy," Ross said, then dropping his head in his hand, he massaged the deep furrows in his forehead. "And you know how I feel about professional women," he added in a low, gritty voice. "What the hell did you go and hire one for?"

"To keep your neck out of jail. Is that a good enough reason?"

Lifting his head, Ross glared at him. "Fire her and hire somebody else! I don't have time for some stiff-necked female trying to make a name for herself in the court-room."

Picking up a pen, Neal began to doodle on an already scribbled-on ink blotter. "You don't know anything about this woman. How can you judge her?"

It was easy, Ross thought, when he'd had one just like her break his heart as though it was nothing more than an old chipped plate.

"Because I know her kind," Ross said gruffly.

For long moments, Neal studied his friend. "Get this straight, buddy, Bella is nothing like Linda."

Linda. Just the woman's name was enough to fill Ross with dark bitterness. Five years had passed since she'd walked out of his life, but time hadn't lessened the pain of rejection or the hard lesson she'd taught him.

"I sure as hell didn't come here this morning to discuss Linda," he said flatly.

"And I didn't call you in here to discuss one of your past women," Neal replied. "I just want to make sure you don't try to lump Bella in with her."

Ross drew in a deep breath and let it out. Neal was his friend. A good friend. He didn't want to have a war of words with the man.

"Okay. So I don't know the woman. And I'll take your word that she isn't like Linda. But that doesn't mean I want or need her as a lawyer."

Neal continued to regard him, then with a quick shrug, he said, "Okay, Ross, if you don't want her representing you, you're going to have to be the one to tell her so. As soon as she gets here in the morning, I'll send her out to the T Bar K.''

Feeling certain he'd just come out the winner, Ross smiled like a spoiled tomcat. ''And I'll be waiting.'

Isabella couldn't believe she was finally home. Well, Aztec wasn't exactly the Jicarilla Apache reservation, but it was much closer than Las Cruces, where she'd spent the past two years working in the D.A.'s office. And Aztec was just a temporary stay for her. She'd already rented a house in Dulce, and as soon as the construction was finished on her office building there, she would truly be moving back home.

But first she had to deal with the problem on the T Bar K. That thought had her full lips faintly twisting as she steered her car over the bumpy dirt road. Ross Ketchum wasn't exactly the sort of person she'd choose for a client. He certainly wasn't the type she'd worked through arduous hours of law school to represent. He was rich and spoiled. And from what her friend Neal had told her, he was both cocky and arrogant. But Ross needed her, Neal had said. And that had been the key word in her decision to accept this job. That along with the fact that Neal Rankin had helped Isabella's mother, Alona, at a time when she'd desperately needed it. The least Isabella could do now was to help his friend Ross.

The road ahead began to climb and twist through a mixture of spruce, pine and aspen trees. To her left, the Animas River flowed violently over huge boulders and ate at the red earth banks on either side. By July, a month away, the snow melt would end and the river would sink and crawl like a gentle baby. By that time, she hoped, she would be back on the reservation and this thing with Ross Ketchum would all be history.

A few minutes later, the mountains opened up and a smattering of barns and buildings begin to appear. Horses and cows were penned in several different spots, while everywhere she looked there seemed to be cowboys and pickup trucks.

Even though she'd never been on the T Bar K before, she'd heard of the ranch. She supposed everyone in northern New Mexico knew of the place. Over a hundred thousand acres, it boasted some of the best cattle and horses to be bought in all the western states. Plus, old man Ketchum had had a reputation that rivaled some of the state's more notorious outlaws, like Billy the Kid and "Black Jack Ketchum," whom Neal had assured her was no relation to Ross or his family.

Still, she knew firsthand that regular folks in the area liked to make the connection. She could only hope Ross hadn't followed the outlaw trail his father had supposedly taken.

Eventually, she made her way up to the ranch house itself, a massive log structure with long wings running from both sides of the main structure. After parking her car, she walked through a small yard gate, then onto a wide porch that ran for at least forty feet along the front of the house.

A large woman with dark-brown skin and graying black hair answered the door. From the blank look on her face, Isabella surmised she wasn't expected this morning.

"Hello," she said warmly. "I'm Isabella Corrales. I'm here to see Ross."

In spite of the wary look in her eyes, the older woman nodded. "I'm Marina. I cook for the Ketchums. Ross isn't in the house now. He's down at the barns. You like to come in and wait for him?"

Isabella glanced at her wristwatch. It was fifteen minutes past the time she was supposed to be here. Normally she wasn't late for appointments, but she'd not counted on the road to the ranch being so rough. Still, you'd think a man with trouble hanging over his head would be anxious to meet his new defender, she silently reasoned.

"Do you think he'll be back to the house soon?"

The large woman shrugged one shoulder. "He don't worry about time."

Isabella glanced thoughtfully away from the house. The working ranch yard was not that far back down the mountainside. Rather than wait for him to come to her, she'd go find the man.

"In that case, I think I'll walk down to the barns."

The cook eyed Isabella's pale beige dress and matching high heels. "It's dusty down there, *señorita,*" she warned.

Isabella smiled at the woman. "A little dust never bothered me. And please, call me Bella. I'm sure we'll be seeing a lot of each other in the coming days."

She could feel the cook's shrewd gaze on her back as she turned and walked off the porch. As she headed toward the cluster of barns and cattle pens, she wondered how much, if anything, the woman knew about the shooting that had taken place three weeks ago. Not much probably. With a property this massive, comings and goings could occur without anyone here at the ranch house ever knowing. A fact that could be both helpful and harmful to Ross Ketchum.

"Yippee! Ride 'im, Ross! Don't let 'im get his head down!"

"He's a devil, Ross! Watch out—"

Following the cowboys' shouts of encouragement, Isabella walked up to a round pen made of metal fencing just in time to see a big white gelding rearing straight up on his hind legs. In the saddle, a dark-haired man wearing a black cowboy hat and a pair of scarred brown leather chaps was doing his best to hang on.

"Excuse me," she quickly said to one of the spectators sitting atop the fence. "Did you call the man out there on the horse Ross?"

With a disinterested glance at her, the old, rail-thin cowboy nodded. "Yes, ma'am. That's Ross Ketchum."

Stunned that the owner of this ranch would be doing such physical work, she stepped closer to the fence and peered out at the battle going on between man and beast.

"Oh! Oh, no!" she cried suddenly as she watched the horse's back heels suddenly kick toward the heavens and her client land with a thump in the dirt.

"Don't worry, ma'am. He ain't hurt. Ross is like a cat with nine lives."

Isabella glanced in disbelief at the old cowboy, who continued to keep his seat on the fence. "Well, aren't you going to help him out of there?" she asked in total dismay.

"No, ma'am. He's not finished with old Juggler. He's gotta show him who's boss around here."

Isabella expelled a shocked breath. "You mean he's going to get back on that killer?"

For an answer, the ranch hand motioned toward the middle of the pen where Ross had gotten to his feet and was about to climb back into the gelding's saddle.

With anxious fascination, she watched the dark-haired cowboy clench a tight rein in his fist, then touch his spurs to the horse's sides. This time the animal walked obediently forward. After he'd traveled the complete circumference of the circle, Ross urged him into a smooth, short lope.

On the third lap, Isabella caught his eye and he reined the big horse to a skidding halt a few feet away from her.

Chunks of dirt flew up from the animal's hooves and splattered the front of her dress.

"Hey, Skinny," he called, "who's your new friend?"

The grizzled old cowboy glanced at Isabella. "Hadn't had a chance to ask her yet."

Isabella's lips pressed together in disapproval as she looked up at Ross Ketchum. Neal Rankin had warned her to expect a cocky man in his mid-thirties. He hadn't warned her that the owner/manager of the T Bar K was also devilishly handsome. Six feet of hard, lean muscle, eyes as green as a willow tree, hair the color of rich sable and dimples bracketing a perfectly masculine mouth. His looks were the kind most women swooned over. But not Isabella. She knew his kind all too well.

Lifting her chin, she said coolly, "I'm certain you know exactly who I am, Mr. Ketchum. You were supposed to have met me at the house thirty minutes ago."

He slanted an eye up at the morning sun. Isabella's gaze zeroed in on his wrists to see he wasn't wearing a watch. Apparently Marina's comment that Ross didn't worry about time was true. But running a place of this size surely forced him to keep up with time and schedules, didn't it?

Ross swept off his hat and held it against his heart. "I must apologize, Ms. Corrales. Time gets away from me when I'm having fun."

Her brows swept mockingly upward as she watched a wave of thick, dark hair plop onto his tanned forehead. "You call biting the dust having fun?" she asked.

The grin on his face deepened, as though he found her and the whole morning full of amusement. "Every good cowboy gets thrown from time to time, Ms. Corrales. It goes with the job." He reached up and affectionately stroked the white gelding's neck. "And if a horse isn't strong enough to throw a rider, he's not strong enough to be in the T Bar K remuda. Juggler here is one of the best.''

''In other words, a horse has to be part outlaw to work your range,'' Isabella replied.

A full-blown smile spread over his face, rewarding her with a flash of white teeth against his dark skin. Isabella found herself staring, completely mesmerized by his striking appearance.

''I couldn't have said it any better, Ms. Corrales.'' He swung himself out of the saddle and threw the reins at the old cowboy. ''Take care of him, will you, Skinny? Linc will probably want to use him later this morning.''

''Sure thing, Ross.''

The cowboy called Skinny climbed off the fence and took charge of the horse. Ross Ketchum ducked his head and climbed through the metal rails. Once he was standing directly in front of Isabella, she was struck by the full potency of his presence. She'd never seen any male as masculine as this one. Nor had she ever felt her heart doing such a pitter-patter race inside her chest.

Jerking off a leather glove, he extended his right hand to her. ''Hello, Ms. Corrales.''

Tough calluses scraped against soft skin as the warmth of his fingers wrapped around hers.

''Call me Bella,'' she said, while wondering why she suddenly felt so breathless. She'd met far more important men than Ross Ketchum.

''Isabella Corrales,'' he mused softly. ''A beautiful name for a beautiful lady.''

Isabella felt the scorching trail of his clear green eyes as it swept her face, then fell inch by inch down the front of her slim body.

Clearing her throat, she pulled her hand from his grasp.

"I'm not here for decoration, Mr. Ketchum," she said briskly. "I'm here to help you."

He pulled the glove off his left hand and stuffed the pair of them in the back pocket of his jeans. When he looked back at her, all amusement was gone from his face.

"I told Neal I didn't need you. He should have told you that. But he's stubborn. He wanted me to do it."

Her heart suddenly sank, which didn't make sense. She'd not really wanted this job in the first place. She didn't like men of Ross Ketchum's caliber. She should be glad he was giving her the boot. It would free her time so that she could get on with her moving. But she didn't like the idea of being fired before she'd ever started the job.

"So you're saying you don't want me for your attorney?"

"I'm saying I don't want *any* attorney."

She moistened her lips with the tip of her tongue as she tried to decide how to deal with the unexpected problem he'd just handed her.

"Oh. So you plan on defending yourself?"

He smiled then, but there was no humor about the expression. "I'm not going to need to be defended. The law will get this thing straightened out before it comes to that."

She studied his face as she tried to figure out if he was simply unconcerned about the trouble hanging over his head or if his attitude had something to do with her being a woman. An Apache woman, at that.

"And what if they don't?" she persisted.

He shrugged. "Then I'll hire somebody who will."

She bristled. "Do you think I can't do my job, Mr. Ketchum?"

He grimaced. "Look, Ms. Corrales, I don't want to turn this into something personal."

Her lips tilted into a dry smile. "But you just did, Mr. Ketchum, by firing me."

"I didn't fire you. I only told you I didn't need you."

Swatting at the tiny clumps of dirt on her bodice, she said, "I believe you need to rethink that decision."

Damn Neal Rankin, Ross silently cursed. His friend should have warned him that the woman was young and beautiful. Probably the most beautiful woman he'd ever seen. Straight black hair was clasped at the nape of her neck and fell like a shiny scarf to the middle of her back. Delicate brows arched over a pair of soft gray eyes, which were veiled with long, luxurious lashes. A straight nose that flared slightly at the nostrils led down to a set of dusky pink lips that were full and velvety. Her high, molded cheekbones and caramel-brown skin said she was a Native American, but the paleness of her eyes told Ross she also possessed white blood.

"What I think is that Neal got a little nervous," he drawled. "And jumped the gun."

Resting a hand on one slim hip, she looked away from him. Ross watched the earrings of cedar beads and chunks of turquoise brush against her neck. Right at a spot that would be so kissable, he thought.

"And you don't think you should be getting a little nervous yourself, Mr. Ketchum?"

The only thing that was making Ross nervous was being near her. She had an earthy sexiness about her that called to every male particle in his body. And the last thing he wanted was to be attracted to a career woman like Isabella Corrales.

"An innocent man doesn't have anything to be nervous about, Ms. Corrales. Now if you'll excuse me, I have work waiting on me."

Tugging the brim of his hat down low on his forehead,

he turned and started in a long stride toward one of the barns. Not to be deterred, Isabella followed.

"We haven't discussed your problem, Mr. Ketchum."

"I don't have a problem."

Grimacing, she skipped every other step to keep up with his long-legged steps. "But you could have a problem with the law at any given moment. That's when you'll need me."

Pausing, he turned to give her a droll look. "Let's set things straight right now, Ms. Corrales. There's not a woman on this earth that I'll ever need."

Although there was no outward bite to his voice, Isabella detected an underlying hostility that took her by surprise.

"Do you have a problem with women?" she asked bluntly.

"I love women," he answered, then grinned lecherously. "When they're in their right place."

Her mouth fell open as he turned and continued on his path toward the barn. Outraged, Isabella raced ahead to block his path.

Looking up at him, she said tightly, "Neal warned me that you were arrogant and possessed a temper. He didn't tell me you were also coarse and rude."

The goading smile fell from his face. "But at least I'm honest. That's probably more than you can say for most of your clients."

Once again her mouth popped open, then snapped shut. "I haven't had a client—until you. I'm a prosecutor. Or I was."

His brows lifted to a jeering arch. "Then I guess you're still a prosecutor. Because you don't have me, either."

Her teeth ground together. She should be telling Ross Ketchum exactly where he could go and stay for a hot eternity. But if a lawyer limited her cases to only those clients she liked, she'd quickly go to the poorhouse. And in her case, beggars couldn't be choosers. Plus, starting her private practice with a client as well-known as Ross would be a great advantage to her.

"Sorry, but Neal has already paid me a retainer."

He shrugged. "That's all right. Keep it for your trouble."

He was going to let her go. Just like that. The money meant nothing to him. But why would it? she asked herself. He had more than he needed. Getting rid of her was much more important to him. But why?

Her delicate jaw hardened to a firm line as she lifted her eyes to his. "Is your problem that I'm a woman? Or that I'm Apache?" she challenged.

Something flashed in his green eyes. She was trying to figure out exactly what it was, when he muttered, "Oh hell."

"Don't—" Before she could say more, he took her by the upper arm.

"Come here," he demanded.

For one instant she started to plant her heels in the ground and tell him he wasn't going to manhandle her. But she wanted answers and insulting him wasn't the way to get them. Besides, she thought, something was wildly exciting about having his strong fingers wrapped around her arm in such a totally masculine way.

She allowed him to lead her across the red dusty ground until they were standing under a wide overhang that shaded a row of horse stalls. Here the odors of alfalfa hay, horses and manure were pungent, but not nearly strong enough to drown out the uniquely male scent of Ross Ketchum.

"Look, Ms. Corrales, I—"

"Call me Bella," she interrupted.

With his hand still firmly gripping her arm, he drew in a deep breath and let it out. "All right, Bella. I think it's about time I set you straight about me. There are plenty of people around here who don't like me for one reason or another. Some say I'm hard. Maybe I am. I admit that I expect a lot from the men who work for me. I won't accept laziness and I don't make allowances for screwups. I won't tolerate whiners or shirkers. And I expect loyalty. If a man doesn't ride proudly for the T Bar K brand, then he won't ride for me. But most people who really know me will tell you that I'm also fair. So whether you're red, white or blue makes no difference to me.''

She was trembling. Whether it was from his touch or his words, she didn't know. She only knew that something about Ross Ketchum was affecting her in a way she'd never experienced before.

"Good," she managed to murmur. "Then there shouldn't be any problem with my being your lawyer."

The determined glint in her eyes must have convinced him she wasn't going to back down. After a moment he shook his head with fatal acceptance.

"You don't give up, do you?"

She smiled. "I'm loyal, too, Mr. Ketchum. When I take on a job, I finish it. Come hell or high water. And for what it's worth, I hope you never have to see the inside of a courtroom. But if you do, I want to be there with you."

He studied her for long, pregnant moments. "I think you actually mean that."

He appeared surprised, a fact that Isabella found strange. Surely the man had been offered help from time to time. Or maybe he just wasn't used to the help coming from a woman.

"I do mean it. So you're agreeing to let me stay on the job?"

Before he caught himself, Ross moved his hand sensually up and down her arm. When he finally became aware of what he was doing, he dropped his hold as though he was touching a hot iron.

"It looks as though I'll have to agree," he told her as he stepped back to put a measure of space between them. "Otherwise, I'll be standing around wasting my days arguing with you."

She smiled again and this time a dimple appeared in her left cheek. As Ross took in the beauty of her face, he realized he'd allowed her to manipulate him. But what the hell, she wouldn't be around that much. Surely he could keep his hands and his heart to himself. After all, he'd learned his lesson. He'd learned that women like Isabella and men like himself just didn't mix.

"Then I won't waste any more of your time today," she said and extended her hand to him once more. "Goodbye, Mr. Ketchum."

Ross took her hand and wondered why he had the silly urge to lift the back of it to his lips.

"You might as well call me Ross," he invited. Then blurted inanely, "When are you coming back?"

"Tomorrow. We need to talk over the details of the shooting. Will you have any free time tomorrow afternoon?"

"I never have free time, Bella. But I'll make it." *Just for you.* The silently added words in his head caused him to curse to himself.

"Good," she said with a smile. "I'll see you then."

Pulling her hand from his, she turned and walked away. Ross was watching her make her way to the big house when a male voice sounded behind him.

"Who was that, boss?"

Turning, Ross bristled to see Tim, a young ranch hand appreciatively eyeing Isabella as she climbed into her car.

"*That* is my new lawyer."

"Hmm. I wouldn't mind a little trouble coming my way if I had someone like her to help me out of it."

Trouble wasn't being framed for attempted murder, Ross thought. Trouble was a beautiful woman with raven-black hair and eyes the color of a gentle rain cloud.

Chapter Two

An hour and a half later, Isabella parked her car in front of a small frame house shaded by a huge ponderosa pine and an ancient cottonwood. On fifty acres of red, rocky land, the Corrales homestead was situated at the edge of a wide arroyo and hidden from the nearest neighbors three miles away.

Outside her car, Isabella breathed in the familiar scents of pine, juniper and sage as her gaze swept to the far north where the high, snow-capped peaks of the San Juan Mountains were visible, then to the south, where the landscape swept away to rocky red buttes and wide-open mesas.

For the past thirty-five years her mother had lived in this same spot. And throughout Isabella's childhood this tough land had been her magical playground. Unlike her half-brother John, who'd constantly hounded their mother to drive him in to Dulce for what little entertainment there was to be had there, Isabella had loved the outdoors and had spent her time with the neighbors' grazing sheep and climbing the nearby rocky bluffs.

Sighing with fond memories, she turned and walked toward the house. She was near the front steps when a black mongrel dog ran up behind her and barked.

Whirling around, she looked down to see Duke scurrying toward her. His happy whines and furiously wagging tail elicited a fond laugh from Isabella. No matter how long she stayed away from her home on the reservation, Duke never forgot her.

Squatting on her heels, she hugged the dog's neck and stroked his graying muzzle.

"Hello, my old buddy," she spoke softly to the dog. "How is Duke? Hmm?"

"He's a happy dog now that you're here."

The spoken words brought Isabella's head up to see her mother standing in the open door of the house.

Alona Corrales was a young forty-eight. Slim and tall, her black hair was threaded faintly with gray at the temples and worn in a long braid against her back. Her gentle brown features were still smooth and lovely. Each time Isabella looked at her mother or even thought of her, she felt immense pride and love.

"Mother!"

Rising from the dog, she ran the last remaining steps to the doorway and threw her arms around her mother.

Laughing softly, Alona hugged her daughter close to her breast. "You didn't tell me you were coming today! This is a wonderful surprise!"

"I finished my business earlier than expected today. And I couldn't wait to come home," Isabella explained.

Alona put her daughter aside and gave her a beaming smile. "I'm so glad. But I wasn't expecting you for a few more days."

"Well, I can only stay for tonight," she warned as she followed Alona into the modest house.

"Then we won't waste a minute. Come with me to the kitchen. I was just finishing up some strawberry preserves when I heard Duke bark. You can have a glass of iced tea while I work."

"Sounds great," Isabella said as the two of them made their way to the kitchen.

Inside the small, cozy room, Alona went directly to the stove and stirred the contents of a huge metal pot with a wooden spoon. Isabella opened the white metal cabinets where the glasses were stored.

"Do you want a glass, too?" she asked her mother.

"Please. It's getting hot in here from all this cooking."

While Isabella filled the glasses with ice and located the pitcher of tea, she said, "You should get air-conditioning, Mother."

"To use only two months out of the year? The cost is too much."

After adding sugar to both glasses, Isabella carried the drinks over to a small chrome-and-red Formica table.

"I would help you with the cost."

Alona shook her head as she lifted the pot from the gas burner and began to pour the cooked strawberries into small mason jars that were sitting in neat rows on a nearby countertop.

"You have enough expenses of your own right now to worry about helping me. By the way," she added as she concentrated on filling the jars, "I went by your office site this morning. The carpenters are getting up the framework. The one in charge told me they should have the outside completed by the end of the month. That is, if the weather holds fair."

Isabella eased down in one of the dinette chairs and

kicked off her high heels. As she massaged her feet, she said, "I drove through Dulce before I came out here. I wanted to see for myself just what the carpenters had been doing. When I look at how much more there is to do, it feels like the whole thing is going at a snail's pace. I'm beginning to wonder if I should have simply rented a building."

"You tried, remember? There wasn't anything vacant that would have been appropriate for a law office. And besides, renting is like throwing money out the window."

Isabella smiled faintly as Alona placed the dirty pot in a sink filled with soapy water.

"I am renting a house, Mother."

Frowning, Alona began to tighten the lids on the jars. "Only because you refused to live here with me."

Picking up her tea, Isabella took a grateful swallow before she replied to her mother's comment. "Mother, we've been all through this before. I love you very much, but we shouldn't live together. We both need our privacy, and I would drive you crazy with my messiness. And anyway, it will be nice to live only a few blocks from where I'll be working. I won't have to get up early and make a long drive."

"Maybe so," Alona reluctantly agreed. She left the cabinet counter and joined Isabella at the table. "And I can't gripe," she went on. "Not when I'm so happy that you're finally back on the reservation. These years you've been away getting your degree and working have been lonely for me."

Even though Isabella's life had been very busy the past few years, she'd been lonely, too. Friends were not the same as family. And the bustling city of Las Cruces was not the same as this land that was her home.

"You haven't heard from John?" she asked.

Alona's expression was suddenly shuttered as she sank into a chair across from her daughter. "Not in a couple of months."

Isabella felt a spurt of disgust. As soon as her brother had graduated high school more than fifteen years ago, he'd left the reservation for better things. She couldn't exactly fault him for that. She'd had to go away for a while, too, to get her education. But during that period she had continually visited her mother on a regular basis. John returned home only once or twice a year and even then it was only to stay for a few hours.

"Sometimes I think he's ashamed to be Apache," Isabella said with disgust. "He acts like it dirties him to come home to the reservation."

A pained expression crossed Alona's face. "Bella, that's an awful thing to say of your brother!"

Isabella made a palms-up gesture. "You don't see him around here, do you? He's a smart man. A doctor! He could be here helping his people. Instead he's living in California where he can make lots of money."

Alona sighed. "It's true John isn't happy here. But I'm not so sure it has anything to do with money. I think it's because of his father and how he was killed."

Isabella snorted. "Thousands of people have lost loved ones to a drunk driver. John is no different. And that happened thirty years ago! John was only a baby. He didn't even know his father."

"And you never knew yours," Alona added regretfully. "Both of my children were raised without fathers." A wistful look filled her eyes. "That's not what I would have chosen for either of you."

Alona's husband and John's father, Lee, had been killed when John was only two years old. Some time afterwards, Alona had become involved with Isabella's father, a rich, prominent white man, who'd refused, even until his death, to acknowledge his half-Apache daughter. Alona rarely ever brought up the subjects of Lee Corrales or Winston Jones. Isabella wasn't exactly sure why her mother had mentioned the two men today.

"Oh Mother, you've done your very best with me and John. And you're a good example of the fact that a woman doesn't need a man to survive."

Alona shot her daughter a reproving look. "Bella, I haven't chosen to be single all these years. I would have preferred to have a man at my side. But good men are hard to find."

"Amen to that," Isabella said with conviction before she tilted the glass of tea to her lips.

Alona rolled her dark eyes. "I guess this means you're not seeing Brett anymore."

Shaking her head, Isabella stirred the sugar up from the bottom of her glass. Thank goodness she hadn't been foolish enough to fall in love with the Dona Ana deputy before she'd learned exactly how he felt about her plans to return to the reservation.

There's no way I'd bury myself in some dirty, dusty little town filled with nothing but Indians.

Months had passed since she'd broken their relationship, but his words still haunted and sickened her. She was half-Indian, she'd reminded him. But he'd argued it wasn't the same. She was a civilized Apache. She was educated. She knew more about life than just raising goats and drinking whiskey.

Shaking away the awful memory, she said, "He was just a friend, Mother. And now that I've left Las Cruces, I doubt I'll ever talk to him again."

Alona made a tsking noise of disapproval. "A beautiful woman like you without a man. It's indecent."

Isabella wrinkled her nose playfully at her mother. Alona could pass for thirty-five and when the two of them were out together she turned as many male heads as Isabella. "I could say the same thing about you."

Alona chuckled. "Don't try being a lawyer and twisting my words back at me."

"But I am a lawyer," Isabella pointed out. "And that's what keeps me happy. I don't need a man hanging around me, trying his best to break my heart."

Sighing, Alona folded her fingers together and rested them on the tabletop. "So tell me about this new case you've taken on. I take it that's why you can only stay one night?"

Isabella reached back and pulled the beaded barrette from her hair. Once the shiny black strands were loose, she twisted the whole lot into a bun at the back of her head and refastened it with the barrette. The cool air blowing through the open window felt good against her bared neck.

"That's right. I've got to be back at the T Bar K by tomorrow afternoon."

Concern suddenly shadowed Alona's dark eyes. "I've heard about that ranch before. It's enormous and those people who own it are rich. They also have a reputation for being rough."

Ross Ketchum's outward appearance might be described as rough. He was certainly a physical man. But Isabella figured if she looked beneath the chaps and spurs and battered cowboy hat, she'd find he was as slick as a snake and more clever than a wily coyote.

"Neal assures me that the Ketchum family is upright. Otherwise, I would have never agreed to help Ross."

Alona's eyes narrowed as she studied her daughter. "Have you met this man yet?"

She'd more than met Ross Ketchum, Isabella thought.

She'd collided with the man. All through her drive here to the reservation, he'd pestered her thoughts. And she had to admit, if only to herself, that she'd never encountered any-one like him.

"Yes. Today."

Alona sighed. "Well, I understand that once you decided to become a defense attorney, you'd eventually be rubbing elbows with all sorts of people. I guess I just didn't expect you to jump feetfirst into a murder case."

Isabella smiled. It wasn't like her mother to dramatize anything. "It's attempted murder, Mother."

"Yes, but I hear that a dead man was found on the T Bar K about a month ago. And they're saying his death was a murder."

"It's amazing how news travels," Isabella remarked with dismay. "Especially bad news."

"I saw it on the Farmington evening newscast."

There wasn't any point in trying to hide the disturbing information from Alona. Especially when it was already being spread through the media. "Okay, you heard right," Isabella admitted. "But the specifics of that case haven't been made privy to me yet. And anyway, I'm not at all certain that the under-sheriff's shooting has any connection to the homicide."

Alona looked completely befuddled. "How can you say that? It looks pretty obvious to me that the incidents are connected."

"Sometimes things are too obvious, Mother. That's why I plan to do a lot of investigating. To see what's hidden underneath all that obvious stuff."

"What is this Ketchum man like?" Alona asked curi-ously.

Isabella drummed her fingers on the tabletop. She wasn't about to let her mother know the man had left her trembling, literally. Alona would take the tidbit of information and run with it in all the wrong directions. For years now her mother had wanted her to get married and produce a brood of children.

Shrugging one shoulder, she said, "Oh, he was nothing special. Just a typical cowboy."

Alona eyed her skeptically. "Is that why you're all dressed up today? Because you met with this typical cowboy?"

Isabella glanced down at her dress. At least she'd managed to brush away the specks of dirt that had flown up from the hooves of Ross's horse once she'd gotten back into the car.

"I'm an attorney, Mother," Isabella said primly. "I have to dress accordingly."

A wide smile spread across Alona's face. "Of course you do. And I'm sure that typical cowboy thought you were very beautiful."

Had he? Isabella wondered. He'd called her beautiful, but he'd probably mouthed those words to dozens of women. Especially when he wanted one to agree to his terms.

"Ross Ketchum doesn't care what I look like. In fact, I had to do some fast talking just to hold on to this job." Quickly, before her mother could say any more, Isabella rose to her feet. "I'm going to get my things from the car and change clothes. I thought I might drive over and see Naomi before dark. Want to come along with me?"

"I'd love to." Rising to her feet, Alona walked over to the sink full of dirty dishes. "I'll finish up here while you're getting ready."

Isabella started out of the kitchen, then paused at the door to look thoughtfully back at her mother. "Do you think we should call and warn her that we're coming?"

Alona laughed. "Knowing Naomi, she's already sensed that we're headed her way."

Isabella's godmother considered herself a medicine woman. And at seventy-five, she wasn't going to hear differently from Isabella. Besides, she loved hearing the older woman's stories and chants. A godmother was a very important role model to a young Apache girl and Naomi had always been there to give Isabella support and advice. She'd been the primary attendant at Isabella's Sunrise Ceremony, an arduous four days of prayers, chants and dancing that young Apache girls go through as they enter womanhood. Since then, Naomi had taught her about many things, especially courage and tenacity—two things she fully expected to need when she dealt with Ross Ketchum.

The next afternoon Ross was in the T Bar K study, growling into the phone as he waited for his new attorney to arrive. "Neal, if I had one good excuse to drive into town, I would. Just to kick your ass."

Laughter came back in Ross's ear. "You might try it, buddy. But I doubt you'd get it done."

Ross chuckled as he leaned back in the chair and propped his boots on one corner of the polished oak desk.

"You'd have a hell of a time stopping me," he told his friend.

"So what are you all revved up about this afternoon?" Neal asked. "You should be out selling cattle instead of sitting inside on the telephone."

Normally, Ross was never inside the ranch house at this time of day. There were always plenty of things to be done at the barns or out on the range. It was spring and Linc was working overtime breeding the broodmares. His cousin could have used his help this afternoon. Instead, he was here in the study waiting on Isabella Corrales.

"Oh, I don't expect you have any idea what I'm doing, do you?" he drawled sarcastically. "You're the one who sicced Ms. Corrales on me yesterday."

There was a long pause before Neal said, "You told me you were going to get rid of her."

"Damn it! I tried."

"Apparently you didn't try hard enough."

The smile he heard in Neal's voice galled Ross to no end. "She insisted that I need her," Ross muttered. "I need her like I need a new pair of spurs!"

"Running low on spurs, are you?"

Ross lifted his green eyes to the beamed ceiling of the study. "Hell, no! I've got at least twenty pairs."

"About the same amount as you have women," Neal mused aloud. "Well, one more shouldn't hurt you."

Jerking his boots off the desk, Ross shot straight up in the chair. "Don't clump Ms. Corrales with my women," he warned.

"I wouldn't dream of it," Neal countered. "She's much too nice for the likes of you, old buddy."

Nice? Surely a woman who was that beautiful and sexy couldn't be nice, too. Could she?

Curiosity suddenly replaced his irritation. "What's the story on her anyway?"

"What do you mean?"

"You know. Is she married? And what is she doing up here in this neck of the woods?"

"Why Ross, you must be slipping," Neal said dryly. "I assumed you'd already gotten all that information from her yesterday."

Ross had spent the past twenty-four hours trying to forget yesterday and his meeting with Isabella. But so far he'd not forgotten anything about his new attorney. "Ms. Corrales and I had words. But not that kind."

"Okay, I'll take pity on you," Neal told him. "She's not married. Never has been. And she's in the area because she's going home to the reservation."

"Which reservation?"

"The Jicarilla."

Ross frowned with disbelief. "Surely not to practice law."

"Why not?"

"Because there's nothing there!" Ross exclaimed.

Neal chuckled. "I think you'd better take that debate up with Isabella."

There were plenty more questions Ross would have liked to ask his friend about Isabella Corrales, but he noticed Marina had suddenly appeared in the doorway of the study.

Placing his hand over the receiver's mouthpiece, he looked at the woman who'd worked as the Ketchums' cook, housekeeper and nanny for the past forty years.

"*Señorita* Corrales is here," she announced. "In the living room."

"Show her back here, Marina. And when you're finished, would you make us a fresh pot of coffee? And bring some cookies or something sweet with it."

"The *señorita* might not like coffee."

Ross's nostrils flared. "But you *know* that I like it," he said with exaggerated patience. "You can ask the *señorita*—I mean, Ms. Corrales—what she'd like to drink."

Nodding, the older woman turned and disappeared into the hallway. Ross directed his attention back to Neal, still waiting on the other end of the phone.

"Sorry, Neal. My visitor has arrived. I've got to go."

"Bella isn't your visitor. She's your attorney. And you'd do well to remember that, *amigo.*"

"Don't worry, Neal. That's something I'm in no danger of forgetting."

He hung up the telephone and leaned back in the chair to wait. Hardly enough time had passed to twiddle his thumbs before Isabella entered the room.

The moment Ross laid eyes on her, he felt a swift, hard blow to his gut. He'd thought she was beautiful yesterday, but today she was even more lovely. A powder-blue dress of some soft, gauzy material draped her breasts and hips, while the hem fluttered against her slim calves. Her glossy black hair was braided into a thick coronet atop her head. Hammered silver in the shape of small crescent moons swung from her ears, while dusky pink hues on her cheeks and lips added to her already vibrant face.

As he rose to his feet to greet her, the sinking feeling in the pit of his stomach worsened.

"Good afternoon, Bella," he said as he extended his hand to hers.

The contact of his callused hand was like grabbing hold of a hot branding iron. Isabella tried to hide the sudden jolt with a wide smile.

"I'm glad you decided to meet with me today," she said warmly.

He smiled back at her and Isabella struggled not to be charmed by the dimples in his cheeks or the sparkle in his green eyes.

"I'd never be guilty of standing up a lady twice in a row," he said, then gestured to the opposite side of the long room where a burgundy chesterfield couch and matching chair were positioned for a view of the mountains. "Have a seat."

Isabella took a seat on the couch, while across from her Ross sank into the armchair, stretched out his long legs and crossed his boots at the ankles.

She drew in a long breath and told herself to relax. He

was only a man. It didn't matter that he was rich and sexy and could charm a bird out of a tree.

"I understand you're a busy man and you value your time," Isabella began. "But as I told you yesterday, it's important that you be prepared. Just in case the D.A. decides to arrest you."

His narrowed eyes surveyed her in one slow, sweeping motion. "Before we go any further, I'd like to know one thing."

Her brows lifted warily. "What?"

"Do you think I'm innocent? Or do you even give a damn about that?"

A knowing smile tilted her lips and Ross felt something stir deep in his gut.

"Does what I think make any difference to you?" she asked.

"You answered my question with a question," he pointed out.

She shifted slightly on the leather couch, thinking that the cost of this one piece of furniture would probably pay for every stick of furnishings in her mother's entire house. And the lizard boots on Ross's feet would certainly buy several air-conditioning units. The man had money, all right. But he also had troubles.

"Okay," she said. "For what it's worth, I don't believe you tried to kill your brother-in-law."

He grimaced. "Why? You don't even know me."

Shrugging, she allowed her eyes to meander over him. This afternoon he was without a hat. His thick dark hair waved back from his forehead and tickled the back of his collar. If she were to get closer, she expected she would see a few threads of gray at the temple. But then, she didn't have any business getting that close.

"I don't know much about the incident, either," she told

him. "At least, not yet. But I like to think I'm a good judge
of character. And besides, Neal assured me that even
though you're hot-headed, you're not a killer."

His lips twitched. "And you believe whatever Neal tells
you?"

"I know from experience that he's an honest man."

Jealousy waltzed in from nowhere and kicked him in the
midsection. "You've known Neal a long time?"

She smiled and Ross could see genuine fondness in her
eyes. The next time he saw Neal, he promised himself that
he was going to sock his friend in the jaw.

"Long enough."

She was as smooth and cool as gourmet ice cream, he
thought. But he'd bet the whole T Bar K that underneath
her poised exterior, he'd find a wicked hot streak.

"What did he tell you about the shooting?"

"Very little. That's what I want you to do."

He rubbed a restless hand against his thigh. "Jess is the
person you need to talk to. He's the one who was shot."

"I plan to talk to your brother-in-law and your sister,"
she assured him. "But before I do, I want to hear what you
have to say."

He started to respond, but Marina chose that moment to
enter the study. He waited until the older woman had left
a tray holding an insulated carafe of coffee and a plate of
thick, golden-brown cookies on his desk before he rose to
his feet. He walked over to the tray and quickly filled two
cups with coffee.

He glanced at her. "Cream or sugar?"

She shook her head and he carried the cup over to her.
As she leaned up to take it from him, he caught the sweet
scent of lilac on her skin. The last time he could remember
having smelled the old-fashioned fragrance was when his

mother, Amelia, had been alive. She'd been serene and beautiful, too. Just like Isabella Corrales.

"What about a cookie?" he asked. "They're full of coconut and chocolate chips. Marina makes them herself. And trust me, they're delicious."

A dimple appeared to the left of her mouth. "I'll have to try one now. Just to test your honesty."

The teasing lilt in her voice got to him more than her beauty, more than the sensual lure of her body, more than anything. It was an invitation for friendship, something that Ross Ketchum valued far above that sentimental notion called love.

He fetched her a cookie and a napkin. After he'd helped himself to a couple of the sweet desserts, he returned to his seat in the armchair.

"So," he said after biting off a hunk of one of the cookies. "What do you want to know?"

She wanted to know lots of things about Ross Ketchum, she realized. Things that had nothing to do with him needing an attorney, or his brother-in-law being shot.

Disgusted with her own weakness, she said, "Just start with the day of the shooting. What were you doing that day?"

"First of all, I'd been away on a business trip," he said, "and I didn't get here to the ranch until noon. After I ate lunch, I got a call from an acquaintance about a stallion he wanted to sell, so I drove over to his place to take a look at the horse."

"Where?"

"About twenty minutes west of Aztec," he answered quickly.

"Will this person verify that you were at his place?"

"No doubt about it."

Isabella put herself back into prosecutor mode. "And when did you leave there?"

"Around four," he told her, then grinned impishly. "And I didn't buy the stallion. He had a big ankle. He might have gone lame later on."

"Four," Isabella repeated thoughtfully. "The shooting took place when?"

Ross shrugged. "Victoria wasn't sure. She said dusk was falling."

"Hmm," she mused aloud. "If that's the case, you had plenty of time to drive back here and get out to the arroyo where the shooting occurred."

"That's right."

She sipped her coffee and tried a bite of the cookie. As Ross had promised, it was delicious.

"You don't seem a bit concerned about that," she accused.

The corners of his mouth turned downward. "Why the hell should I be? I didn't do anything."

"Yes, but can you prove that?" Isabella asked the pointed question.

He made a dismissive gesture with his hand. "The burden of proof should be on the state, not me. Or has the law that a person is innocent until proven guilty changed?"

"Nothing has changed. But if you had a solid alibi, you wouldn't have any need for a lawyer." A tiny frown creased the middle of her forehead. "So where did you go after you looked at the horse?"

He swallowed more of the coffee, which reminded Isabella that hers was getting cold. She reached for her cup and took a dainty sip.

"I went to another ranch. The Double X, just north of here. Someone had told me that the owner thought he'd spotted my missing stallion a few days before."

"Did you talk to him?"

Ross shook his head. "No. No one was home. So I drove back here, saddled Juggler and went to check on the cattle in the south flats."

"Who went with you?"

"No one. I went alone."

Her eyes widened at this bit of information. "Is that normal? For you to ride out alone?"

He chuckled as though he found her question inane, but Isabella knew it wouldn't be so funny if he found himself on a witness stand.

"Look, Bella, the T Bar K is a big spread. And though I've got a bunkhouse full of hands, we're still sometimes spread thin. If I can do a job alone, I do it."

As Isabella watched him pop the last piece of cookie into his mouth, she felt certain that Ross Ketchum was being honest with her. But her opinion didn't count in a court of law. He needed an alibi.

"I'm sorry, Ross, but I'm merely asking you what any good prosecutor would want to know."

He left his seat and placed his empty cup on the serving tray. Then turning to face her, he looped his thumbs over the wide leather belt at his waist. "Okay," he said, "I can't account for my whereabouts. But that doesn't make me guilty."

"No," she agreed. "It just makes you unlucky."

"What are you going to do about it?"

Rising from the couch, she walked over to where he stood by the desk. After placing her coffee cup next to his, she looked up at him.

"I'm going to figure out who really did this thing."

Ross couldn't help it, he burst out laughing. "Sure. One little woman is going to do what the whole San Juan County sheriffs' department can't seem to accomplish."

She didn't allow his laughter to get to her. After all, her boast probably did sound ridiculous. But he was a white man. He wouldn't understand if she tried to explain that Naomi had told her that the truth would appear to Isabella. And her godmother had never told her a wrong thing.

"I'm Apache," she said with solemn pride. "We're tenacious hunters. We don't give up until we get our prey."

Humor creased his cheeks and danced in his green eyes. "Okay, so where do you intend to start on this great hunting trip?"

A provocative smile suddenly curved the corners of her lips. "I think the best place to start would be your bedroom."

Chapter Three

"My bedroom!"

The shocked look on Ross's face told Isabella he'd taken her suggestion all wrong. Which didn't surprise her that much. Next to ranching, women were probably his favorite entertainment. And now he was thinking she wanted to be his tidbit for the afternoon.

Heat swarmed her face as she tilted her chin up at him. "Yes, your bedroom," she answered primly. "That is where you keep your firearms, isn't it?"

"Oh," he said inanely. "Yeah. I have a gun cabinet in my bedroom. Is that what you want to see?"

Turning her back to him, she licked her dry lips. "Among other things."

His hand suddenly rested against the small of her back and Isabella had the absurd urge to close her eyes.

"It's at the other end of the house," he told her. "I'll show you."

Isabella mentally shook herself and quickly started toward the door. Ross followed at her side while his hand remained at her back. Once they were out of the long study and in the hallway, he guided her to the left.

"How many people live here in the ranch house now?" she asked, while wondering why she didn't make a move to pull away from him.

"Only me. Victoria moved out three weeks ago when she married Jess. Marina lives in a small house of her own on the property."

The two of them had already passed several doorways. Too many rooms for just one man, Isabella thought.

"There's another wing on the opposite side of the house," he added, as though reading her thoughts. "Victoria did use those."

More curious than ever, she glanced up at him. "Why did your father build such a huge house?"

"Well, he had four children. And when Mother was still alive he did a lot of entertaining. Cattle and horse buyers might come and stay a whole week while they looked over the ranch's livestock. That's when the ranch was really hopping," he added, his voice full of wistful pride.

She gave him a sidelong glance. "And it isn't hopping now?"

He smiled faintly. "Sure it is. We just do things differently nowadays."

"You mean you don't invite people into your home anymore?"

Ross frowned. "You're trying to make me sound inhospitable."

"Not really. You just don't seem the sort of man who'd enjoy playing host for very long." Not without a wife around to play hostess, she thought.

With a sly smile, he reached out and pushed open a door to his right and motioned for her to go in.

"This is it," he announced.

A bedroom said a lot about the person who slept there, and as Isabella looked around the spacious room, one thing kept coming to her mind. Ross Ketchum was all man.

The king-size bed was sturdy oak with short, fat posts at the head and foot. It was covered with a rich burgundy-colored spread that matched the drapes on the windows. Paintings and sketches of the old west were scattered here and there on the whitewashed walls. To one side of the doorway a row of pegs held an assortment of felt and straw cowboy hats, a leather holster for a six-shooter, and a brown, oiled slicker. Along the end of the room, a tall gun cabinet made of varnished cedar and glass sat next to a shorter chest of drawers.

Several steps away to her right, one lone photo sat atop an otherwise bare dresser top. The distance between it and Isabella made it impossible to see who or what was in it.

"No TV?" she asked.

His lips twisted wryly. "A man has better things to do in bed."

She should have seen that coming, Isabella thought with a measure of irritation at herself.

"Is that where the rifle was kept?" she asked, inclining her head toward the gun cabinet. "The one that was fired at Mr. Hastings?"

Ross nodded. "That's it. I've had that particular 30.30 for years. Dad gave it to me for my fourteenth birthday. We used to take deer-hunting trips back then, before his heart got too bad."

There it was again, she thought. That faint wistfulness in his voice that said he missed his parents and missed the way his home life used to be.

The notion softened her in a place that was far too private to be letting thoughts of Ross Ketchum inside.

"When did your parents pass away?" she asked gently.

"Dad died nearly two years ago. Mother passed on quite a while before that. Probably five or six years, I'd say. I've pushed the dates out of my head. They're not ones I want to remember, if you know what I mean."

She knew all too well. When her grandmother Corrales had died, she'd felt such an intense loss, she'd not been able to eat or sleep for days.

"I'm sure your father is riding another range now. And your mother is probably with him."

Her remark reminded Ross that she was Apache; she viewed spirituality and the afterlife in a slightly different way than most white folks. The Apache believed that once a loved one died, he or she simply journeyed to another world where life continued in much the same way.

"I hope you're right. But I doubt Amelia is with him."

Her brows lifted. "Why do you say that? Surely your parents would want to be together."

He chuckled. "Dad was a tough old codger. I can't see any woman wanting to live two lives with him."

Isabella wanted to ask him why he hadn't followed his father's example and filled the empty ranch house with a wife and children. From the information Neal had given her, she knew he was thirty-five. Well past the settling-down age. But questions of that sort would be getting away from her reason for being here, she told herself. And anyway, it didn't matter why Ross Ketchum was without a wife. She wasn't interested in him in such a way. She doubted she would ever be *that* interested in any man again after Brett.

Leaving his side, she walked over to the gun cabinet and

peered through the glass doors. There were four rifles and a pump shotgun resting in the velvet holders.

"Is this where you store all your firearms?" she asked thoughtfully.

"Yeah. There's a couple of pistols in the drawer at the bottom."

"Did you have the cabinet locked up the day of the shooting?"

Ross cursed. "No. I never lock the thing. It would be pretty useless when anybody could knock the glass out. Besides, why should I lock it? There's no children around, except my nephew Aaron, who lives about a mile on up the mountain. And he never comes into this room. Even if he did, the guns are never loaded."

She could see his point, even if she didn't agree with it.

Turning away from the cabinet, she studied the layout of the room. "What about those sliding glass doors? Where do they go?"

Ross walked over and pushed the drapes completely to one side to expose a view of a rocky, pine-dotted bluff.

"And if you're wondering, I never lock the doors, either," he told her.

"So in other words, anybody could have walked through those doors and taken the 30.30 from the gun cabinet," Isabella reasoned.

"That pretty much sums it up." Moving over to where she stood, he looked down at her, his expression slightly daunting. "Still think you're going to catch your prey?"

His closeness set her heart to pounding like the heavy beat of a war drum. "Yes."

"I'm interested to hear how you plan to do it."

His eyes were crinkled at the corners, she realized. And there was a tiny scar running through the line of his upper lip. Heat radiated from his body and washed through Isabella in palpable waves. She'd never reacted so physically to any man before, and it disturbed her that a man like Ross had such a strong effect on her.

"Easy," she said, as she struggled to keep her mind on her business and off of the potent man standing next to her. "We make a list of all the people who dislike you and go through it one by one until we find our man."

Laughter rumbled deep in his chest before it spilled into the quiet bedroom.

"Oh, honey, if you have to make a list of all the people who dislike me, you're going to be here for a good long while."

The man could very well be charged with attempted murder and all he could do was laugh. She wanted to stomp his foot, whack her fist against his chest, anything to wake him up and make him realize that simply being a Ketchum wasn't enough to keep him out of jail.

Her nostrils flared. "Then all I can say is that you'd better get used to my company," she said coolly. "Because right now you don't have much defense."

The humor suddenly fell from his face. "Now look, Bella, I don't care how you go about handling this thing. Just don't expect me to spend my days playing Hardy Boy with you."

His arrogance was unbelievable. "To be honest, I expect very little from you," she clipped, then turned and walked out of his bedroom.

He caught up to her in the hallway and her lips pressed together as his hand closed tightly around her elbow. Did he have to put his hands on her every time he got within a foot of her? she wondered. She'd never had a man touch her so much. Especially a man she'd known for little more than twenty-four hours. To make matters worse, she'd never wanted a man to touch her the way she wanted Ross to touch her.

"Wait a minute," he muttered roughly. "Just what was that crack supposed to mean?"

"It means that—" she paused and drew in a fierce breath. "It's obvious you're not interested in clearing yourself. You don't even see a need to get to the bottom of this suspicion hanging over your head. Maybe if you'd been the one with a bullet in your shoulder, you might be showing a little more concern!"

"Oh, hell," he spat with disgust.

She breathed deeply and told herself she would refuse to be intimidated by this man. "That's right."

"There's nothing right about it," he blasted back at her. "Jess is a part of the family. I don't want him hurt any more than I do my sister!"

Isabella shook her head as she tried to hold on to her temper. "I really can't figure out why I agreed to take on this job."

"I've been wondering the same thing myself."

A teasing glint had returned to his eyes and she didn't know whether to throw up her hands or laugh. Maybe it wouldn't hurt her to lighten up just a bit.

"Does anything ever worry you?" she wanted to know.

Only women like you, Ross thought. When a man started needing, wanting, loving, that's when he was in real danger of being hurt.

He urged her on down the hallway. "Worry is useless, Bella. It changes nothing."

Back in the study, he invited her to sit again, but she shook her head. "I need to be going. I have things to do in Aztec. And I'm sure you've had enough of my company."

Actually, he hadn't. Just looking at her pleased Ross in

a way that nothing had before. And to his great surprise, she intrigued him. There were many things he'd like to know about her. Particularly why a beautiful woman like her wasn't married.

Because she's married to her career, you fool. Just like Linda was.

"What about the list you were talking about?" he asked. "Don't you want to hear all the people who dislike me?"

She cast him a wry smile. "I'm going to let you have a little time to think about that. I don't want you to leave anyone out."

"All right, I'll do that," he agreed, then once again took hold of her arm.

Isabella looked pointedly to the spot where his fingers were wrapped around her flesh, then up to his face. "What are you doing now?"

The testiness in her voice caused a dimple to appear in his cheek. "I'm going to walk you to the door. My mother did try to raise my brothers and me as gentlemen. Why? Is it against the law for a client to touch his attorney?"

It was definitely a crime when it felt like this, Isabella thought. She opened her mouth to give him a reply at the same moment Marina knocked on the open door.

Turning away from Isabella, Ross looked at the cook. "What is it, Marina?"

"I wanted to see if the *chica* is going to stay for supper."

"No," Isabella spoke up quickly. "I have to be going."

"That's too bad," Marina replied, "I'm making smoked ribs. One of Ross's favorites. And chocolate cake."

"It sounds delicious," Isabella told her. "But I really do have things to do in Aztec."

"You could drive back when you're finished," Ross quickly suggested, then wondered what the hell he thought he was doing. He didn't need to be having dinner with this woman. Even if they managed to keep things strictly business, she was lethal. Spending time with her was going to keep him on a tightrope.

Marina smiled at her boss's suggestion.

Isabella turned a hopeless expression on him. "I could drive back," she reasoned. "But I'm not keen on driving the mountain road here to the ranch after dark. And it would be dark by the time we finished supper."

"You are right, *señorita*," Marina spoke up. "The road is much too rough and dangerous for a woman to be driving after dark. You should stay here on the ranch. We have plenty of rooms."

It was all Ross could do to keep his jaw from dropping. Marina never took it upon herself to invite people to stay on the ranch. On top of that, she was usually slow to warm up to strangers. But here she was treating Isabella better than a long-lost relative.

"Thank you, Marina, but I wouldn't dream of imposing on you," Isabella assured her. "My motel room has most everything I need."

Ross looked at her in surprise. "You're staying in a motel?"

Isabella made a palms-up gesture. "Yes. Why? Is there something wrong with that?"

"Well, no. I just—Neal said something about you going home to the reservation. I thought you were staying there."

"While I'm working on your case I need to be in this area. And it's too far to drive from here to the reservation every day," she explained.

The last thing he needed was to have Isabella Corrales underfoot, Ross thought. But a motel room was costly. He didn't want her to be out that much money. Not on his account. And she did make for a very pretty decoration.

"Did Neal make any arrangements to pay your expenses while you worked for me?" Ross asked her.

Isabella shook her head. "No. But don't worry, I'll tack it on the final bill," she added teasingly.

With sudden decision, he said, "You can't continue to stay in a motel. With this big house full of empty rooms, it would be senseless. Once you finish your business in Aztec this afternoon, pack your bags and drive back out here to the ranch. Marina will have everything ready for you."

The cook's brown face creased into a satisfied grin. "That's right."

Stay here on Ross Ketchum's ranch? Isabella asked herself. She'd be putting herself in the way of danger. Not the sinister kind that had taken place out on T Bar K range. No, she was thinking of a more subtle sort of danger. The kind that sneaked up on a person's heart.

"But I need—"

"A phone, a fax, a computer? The ranch has all of those things," Ross assured her.

"I—" she looked awkwardly at Marina who was waiting to hear her decision. "I think I need to discuss this with Ross. Would you excuse us, Marina?"

With a nod of understanding, the cook left the room. Isabella turned back to Ross, who was studying her with a bemused expression.

"All right. What's the matter?" he asked before she could utter a word.

"I'll tell you what's the matter," she clipped out concisely. "Yesterday you didn't even want me as your lawyer. And not more than fifteen minutes ago, you made it very clear you didn't have time for me. That doesn't sound like a man who's eager to have me staying in his home."

As his eyes lazily scrolled her face, his arms crossed his

broad chest. "I admit it's bad business to put a beautiful woman in close proximity to me. But I'm making an exception with you."

Close proximity to him? As far as she was concerned, it would *definitely* be bad business. But that didn't stop her from wondering what it would feel like to have those big, strong arms circled around her or to have her cheek resting against his broad chest.

"Oh?" she asked. "Because you've finally realized you're in a bit of a jam with the law?"

To her disgust he chuckled. "No. I'm making an exception because you're not my type. So you'll be perfectly safe in my company. And I won't be threatened by yours."

Not his type. Isabella should be relieved. Instead, she felt insulted. Lifting her chin, she said, "I appreciate your offer. But I don't think it would be wise to…stay here on the T Bar K."

His brows lifted with an innocence that belied the glint in his eyes. "Why not? You planned to do some investigating, didn't you?"

Her heart continued to thud at a pace that was quickly draining her. "Yes."

"It pretty much stands to reason that whoever framed me is here on this ranch. Don't you agree?"

"Yes. But—"

"But nothing," he countered. "This is where you need to be doing your hunting, Isabella. Not in Aztec."

Reluctantly, she had to agree that he was right. Staying here on the ranch would make her job far easier and possibly give her some insights into the case that she might not get elsewhere. Besides, it would be foolish to pay a bunch of money for a motel room when this huge house was virtually empty.

"You know, you're making a good point," she said after a moment. "And besides, I've realized something else."

"What's that?" he asked with a smug smile.

"You're not my type, either."

The smile on his face deepened and instead of taking hold of her elbow, he curled his arm around the back of her waist.

"Come on. I'll walk you to the door."

Oh, she was slipping badly, she thought. Not only had the man talked her into staying on his ranch, he'd also managed to turn her knees to rubber. She was going to have to toughen up if she ever expected to survive this job.

Later that evening, Isabella arrived back at the T Bar K with her bags and an uneasy feeling she couldn't shake. The more she'd thought about it these past few hours, the more she'd realized it had been a mistake to accept Ross's invitation. But it was too late to change things now without looking ungrateful.

Marina met her at the door and the older woman's smile chased away some of Isabella's misgivings.

"Do you have more bags?" she asked, inclining her head to the three nylon duffel bags on the porch floor. "I'll get one of the men to help you."

"No. This is it, Marina. If you'll just show me where to take them, I can manage."

Marina bent down and picked up two of the bags. "You get that one, *chica,* and follow me," she ordered.

Isabella stepped into the house behind the cook and followed her through the massive living area, then down a wide hallway similar to the one that had led to Ross's room, only this corridor lay in an opposite direction.

"This is where you stay," Marina told her as she pushed

open a door to her right. "This was Victoria's room. Pretty, no?"

It was a beautiful room filled with varnished pine furniture and decorated in shades of pink, beige and white. Sliding glass doors looked toward the west and a wide mesa filled with gray and purple sage, tall yucca and an occasional sphere of red rock.

"This is absolutely lovely, Marina. Much better than a motel room."

The woman dropped Isabella's bags onto the queen-size bed. "I'm glad you like it. And I'm glad you come."

Isabella cast the woman a gentle smile. "I'm not sure Ross would have invited me if you hadn't brought up the subject."

Marina shrugged one thick shoulder. "Ross don't think. He's too busy buying and selling cattle and horses. He don't think about women. Not like he should."

It was clear the T Bar K cook wasn't regarding her as Ross's lawyer, but as a romantic diversion. Isabella silently let out a weary sigh.

"What do you mean? Does Ross not have anything to do with women?" The question seemed ludicrous. Especially when he couldn't seem to keep his hands off her and everything out of his mouth intimated at something sexual.

The other woman frowned. "Oh, he likes women. Too much. He goes out and has his fun. But he don't bring them home here to the T Bar K."

Isabella dropped the bag she was carrying onto the bed with the other two and unzipped it. "Well, that's probably because he's not serious about them."

"Serious?" Marina made a noise somewhere between a snort and a cackle. "Ross is never serious about a woman. He thinks it's enough to take them places and buy them things. He don't care if he breaks a heart. 'Cause he don't feel anything in here.''

Isabella watched Marina's large hand press against her ample bosom. "That's a sad thing to say, Marina."

"Sad but true," Marina retorted. "I tell Ross that some-day he will ache for love. But by then he will be like his daddy. He won't have anybody. Unless he change."

Feeling a little uncomfortable with Marina's personal ex-posé of Ross, Isabella cleared her throat. "Well, right now I've got to keep the man from going to jail."

Marina's hand moved from the region of her heart to her wrinkled forehead, as though a picture was turning in her mind. "This is bad, Isabella. There is an evil one on the ranch."

Isabella unzipped the remainder of her bags and pulled out a stack of underclothes from one of them. As she carried them to a nearby dresser, she asked, "What do you know about the shooting?"

"Nothing. Except I told Victoria not to go to the arroyo that evening. I told her that place was bad. Someone would be hurt. But her and Jess went anyway."

It didn't surprise Isabella to hear that Marina had been spouting warnings and prophecies. As Naomi's goddaughter, she'd heard all sorts of visions and predictions. Surprisingly most came true, but there were times nothing happened. Too bad that hadn't been the case when Victoria and Jess had ridden out to the arroyo.

Placing her things in one of the drawers, Isabella went back to the bed for another armload. "Was Ross aware that the two of them were headed out to the arroyo?"

Marina pondered for a moment, then shook her head. "Ross was gone from the ranch, I think, when Victoria and Jess rode off. He'd been out hunting Snip."

"But do you know if someone had told him beforehand

where his sister and brother-in-law were going?'' Isabella persisted.

Marina frowned as she weighed Isabella's question. ''Could be. There's plenty of men down at the barn to tell him things.''

''That's true.'' She glanced thoughtfully at Marina. ''Just how did Ross feel about Jess at the time of the shooting?''

Marina glanced regretfully toward the sliding glass doors. ''He didn't like Jess. 'Cause he thought he'd done his sister wrong. But he didn't shoot him, *chica*.''

Isabella smiled. It was more than obvious that Ross held a very special place in Marina's heart. ''No. I'm sure he didn't.''

The cook suddenly reached out and patted Isabella's shoulder. ''You're gonna fix things for Ross. And then we'll all be glad.''

It felt nice for someone to have confidence in her, but it also weighed her with a heavy responsibility. Ross might not think he was in a sticky situation, but from what Neal had told her, the rest of the Ketchum family was very worried. They were depending on her to keep Ross out of jail.

''I hope you're right, Marina.''

The older woman smiled with confidence as she headed toward the door. ''You finish unpacking. Supper will be soon.''

Nearly an hour later, Isabella was in the living room, studying what she assumed to be a family photo when Ross walked up behind her. The faint scent of musky cologne mixed with another scent, which she'd come to recognize as uniquely his, drifted to her nostrils and warned her that his muscular body was only inches away.

''That was when my older brother Hugh was still alive,'' he said quietly.

Isabella bent at the waist to look more closely at the framed picture resting on a small end table. Three men were standing next to a wooden corral. All of them were rigged out in boots and chaps and hats. All were dark-haired, muscular and ruggedly handsome. No doubt Tucker Ketchum and his wife Amelia had been proud of their three sons.

"Which one is Hugh?" she asked.

"The one on the left. I don't know if anyone told you, but he was gored to death by a bull about six years ago."

Isabella nodded. "Neal mentioned it. Hugh's widow, Maggie, lives here on T Bar K property, doesn't she? I think you said something about your nephew living nearby."

As she asked the question, she turned around to face him and was immediately relieved to see he was still wearing the jeans and yellow cotton shirt he'd had on earlier this afternoon. She'd sensed that he wouldn't be one to dress for the evening meal, so she'd changed from her dress into a pair of black capri pants and a black sleeveless top.

His eyes slipped over her face, then downward to where her top V'd between her breasts before he finally met her gaze. "That's right. Maggie is still single. She's had a hard time getting over Hugh's death."

"What about you?" Isabella asked softly.

"Oh, hell," he muttered impatiently. "That's a stupid question. A man never gets over losing his brother. I think of Hugh every day. Sometimes several times a day."

She suddenly thought of John and how she might react if something were to happen to him. It would devastate her to lose the only sibling she had. But on the other hand, there were times when days went by without her thinking about John. She supposed it might be different if the two of them were close. But they weren't, and, she thought sadly, she doubted their relationship would ever change.

"So you two were close."

Even though she'd stated a fact more than asked a question, Ross nodded and grinned. "Hugh was more like me than Seth ever was. Don't get me wrong, I'm close to Seth, too. But he's always been a lawman at heart. Hugh liked punching cattle and riding broncs. He was good at it, too. A damn sight better than me."

The compliment to his late brother surprised Isabella. She'd expected Ross to be the sort that thought of himself as the best.

"I'm sorry Hugh's not here to help you through this," she said.

He looked at her, and she could feel his eyes traveling over her hair, which she'd let down from its braid and tied back with a black scarf.

I'm sure that cowboy thought you were very beautiful.

Faint color seeped into Isabella's cheeks as her mother's words suddenly waltzed through her mind. She had no idea whether Ross thought she was beautiful, but she did know he looked at her in a way that no man had before, a way that made her feel as though he could see right through her clothing.

"Hugh wouldn't like what's been happening on the ranch here lately," Ross said, his expression suddenly turning grim. "Not even a little bit."

"What about your other brother?" Isabella asked curiously. "Does he know Victoria's husband was shot with your rifle?"

"No. He doesn't even know Victoria and Jess have gotten married. You see, Seth is a Texas Ranger and sometimes he goes off on undercover assignments. When that happens we can't get in touch with him." He shook his head. "That's not entirely right. I expect we could. If it was a dire emergency we could contact his captain down in San Antonio. But this isn't dire enough…yet.''

Isabella wondered how bad things would have to get before the Ranger was called in. Attempted murder to their brother-in-law wasn't exactly a minor squabble. Aloud, she said, ''Well, I hope it doesn't become any worse than it already is.''

Grinning as though he didn't have a worry in the world, Ross turned and walked to the other side of the room where a small bar quartered off one corner. ''Would you like a drink before we go into dinner?''

''No. I don't drink.''

''It doesn't have to be alcoholic. You can have juice or a soft drink,'' he offered.

''All right. Just make it small. I need to save room to try out Marina's cooking.''

She moved toward the front of the room as he filled two glasses with crushed ice.

''You're in for a treat,'' Ross said. ''Nobody can cook like Marina.''

After filling the squatty tumblers with cola, he carried them both to where she was standing by a huge picture window. Beyond the wide glass, dusk was falling, merging the shadows of the distant ranch yard. Lights streamed from the log bunkhouse and horses quietly milled in nearby pens. It was a heavenly sight.

''Twilight and a cowboy's day is done,'' he murmured.

She took the glass he offered and as she looked up at him, the contentment she found on his face revealed more to her about Ross Ketchum than anything he'd said so far.

The T Bar K wasn't just a ranch or a job to him. It was his love, his life. Without it, he'd be a lost man. Just as she would be lost if she couldn't fulfill her dream of helping her people.

"How long has Marina worked for your family?"

"Oh, about forty years probably. She was here before I was born. And that was thirty-five years ago."

Isabella watched him tilt the glass to his lips while thinking those thirty-five years had turned him into a prime male specimen. Just looking at him took her breath.

"She must feel like family to you."

Ross nodded. "After Mom died, I guess Victoria and I both looked to Marina to take her place. 'Course, she couldn't. Not entirely. But she made the empty hole feel not so empty. If you know what I mean."

Something about his words tightened her throat and forced her to look away from him. Up until tonight, he'd projected the picture of a cocky man, indifferent to the wants and needs of others, confident that nothing and no one could touch him. But now she was seeing a different side of him, a side that said he loved and needed and hurt just like any other man.

"Yes. I believe I do know what you mean," she murmured.

He smiled at her over the rim of his glass and she felt her heart kick into overdrive, a reaction that irritated her greatly. What was the matter with her? Had she forgotten the white father who'd rejected her? The white lover who'd shunned her people? Ross might not be prejudiced, but he was an admitted playboy. That should be enough to keep her senses on the right track.

"We've been doing a lot of talking about me and my family," he said. "Why don't you tell me about yours?"

Turning her head away from him, she stared out the window as night fell over the foothills of the San Juan's. "There's not much to tell. I was born on the Jicarilla Apache reservation and I guess I'll probably die there."

The faint rustle of clothing warned Isabella he was moving closer. Her breath caught in her throat.

"Is your family still living there?" he asked.

She released the trapped air and sucked in another long breath before she answered. "My mother, a grandfather and a godmother."

"Do you have any siblings?" he asked.

She stifled a moan as she felt his fingers touch her hair ever so slightly.

"An older half brother. He's a doctor and lives in California."

"Do you see him often?"

With him standing so close, she could hardly think. Heat from his body radiated into hers and warmed her with the unbidden urge to turn and touch him. But the wary, sensible side of her realized that a touch would lead to a kiss, and a kiss would lead to…she couldn't think about that. She couldn't ever allow herself to imagine Ross Ketchum as a lover.

"Not really," she answered as she tried to shake away the sensual thoughts. "He has his own life in California and rarely ever sees his family back here on the reservation."

"You sound a little bitter. Do you two not get along?"

One of her shoulders lifted and fell. "We don't argue, if that's what you mean. We just have different priorities in life."

"What about your father?" he asked, his voice dropping to a husky note.

Isabella fought the urge to shiver as his fingers began to slide through her hair in much the same way she'd seen him stroke the horse's mane yesterday. Never in her life had she been so completely aware of a man.

"He's dead," she said bluntly.

There was a pause, then he said, "Sounds like we have something in common. We've both lost our fathers."

No, Isabella thought bitterly. He'd lost his father. She'd never had one. His father had left him a legacy. Hers had left her illegitimate.

"Not really," she said thickly.

His fingertips brushed her neck, sending rivers of fire across her skin. Her eyes wide, she turned sharply toward him.

"What are you doing?" she demanded.

One corner of his mouth crooked upward. "I'm just trying to find out if you're really as soft as you look."

Isabella wanted to be angry with him, but something inside her was melting and she couldn't seem to do a thing to stop it.

"I'm not here for your amusement," she said as primly as she could manage. "I'm here to keep you from ending up behind bars."

His brows lifted and the grooves at the side of his mouth deepened. "You didn't have to remind me of that."

"Maybe I should remind you that I'm not your type."

With a soft chuckle his arms slid around her waist, his head bent down to hers. "I'm beginning to think I made a mistake about that," he murmured.

And he was about to make another one, Isabella thought wildly. Or was she the one who was about to make the mistake? She couldn't let this man kiss her! Everything about him said he was a heartbreaker. But everything inside her was yearning to see if the sizzle from his hands would match the taste of his lips.

Her gaze was settling on the object of her thoughts when a knock sounded behind them. Muttering a curse, Ross quickly lifted his head to see Marina standing in the open archway leading into the living area.

The woman's smooth expression didn't falter as she eyed Ross's hand resting possessively against Isabella's back.

"Supper is ready," she announced.

An odd mixture of disappointment and relief swirled through Isabella, leaving her weak and confused.

"We'll be right there, Marina," he said, then smiling down at Isabella, he offered her his arm.

Because her knees were like two pieces of cooked spaghetti, she gratefully curled both hands around the hard muscles of his upper arm.

"Ready?" he prompted.

For you or supper? Isabella bit her tongue to keep from asking as she nodded and allowed him to lead her out of the room.

Chapter Four

"I guess I should apologize," Ross said to her moments later as they walked through the quiet ranch house.

Isabella gave him a sidelong glance. He didn't seem the sort of man to apologize for anything. "For what?" she asked warily.

"We won't be eating in the dining room. Since I'm the only one living in the house anymore, it saves Marina a lot of steps. And the dining room is just too formal for my taste, anyway. I hope you don't mind eating in the kitchen."

The fact that he was considerate of Marina both surprised and touched Isabella. Even though he'd intimated that the cook was like family, he was a man after all, and men were often times blind to all the work it took to run a household. Apparently Ross Ketchum could be thoughtful.

"I've lived ninety percent of my life on the reservation,

Ross. Believe me, I'm not accustomed to being formal. The kitchen sounds nice,'' she told him.

And cozy, Isabella thought as they entered the room with a low ceiling supported by huge beams and Spanish tile shining on the floor. The long table was made of varnished pine planks and took up a good portion of the space. A few steps away from the table, a row of potted succulents grew near a wide window.

At one corner of the table, Ross pulled out a chair for her. Once she was seated, he took the chair at the end.

''Where's Marina?'' Isabella asked as she glanced over to the part of the room where a gas range, refrigerator and a working countertop took up one solid wall.

''She goes home about this time every evening. Her house is a quarter mile on down the mountain. Past the ranch yard.''

So Marina lived on the T Bar K, Isabella mused. Obviously the Ketchums made sure their employees were well cared for. ''I didn't notice another house when I drove in. Can you see Marina's place from the road?''

Ross handed her a platter heaped with smoked ribs. She placed three on her plate and handed the platter back to him.

As he took it from her, he said, ''No. Marina's little house is hidden by a stand of pines. Dad had it built for her years ago.''

''He must have been a generous man,'' Isabella remarked.

His expression turned wry. ''In some ways he was generous. But in Marina's case, he was selfish. He wanted to make sure she was always around to do the cooking and to help Mom.''

''Well, from what I can see, Marina wouldn't be any

where else but here on the ranch. Though it does surprise me that she leaves you with the dirty dishes.''

He grinned. ''She leaves them. But I don't clean them up. She'll be back at four in the morning to do all that and get breakfast ready.''

Isabella stared at him. ''Four! You get up at four?''

He passed her a bowl of coleslaw. ''No. I get up at four-thirty.''

Isabella was amazed. The man didn't have to punch a time clock. He owned this place. He could do as he pleased. ''But why so early?''

He shot her a look of disbelief. ''To shave, shower, dress, drink coffee, eat breakfast. The things a normal man does before he goes to work.''

''And when do you go to work?'' she asked curiously.

Her question appeared to amuse him. As if she should already know the answer. ''Daylight, Isabella. A cowboy starts at daylight.''

''Oh. So what about reading the newspaper or watching the morning news? You don't do that before you leave the house?''

He chuckled. ''How could we get a daily paper this far out? And I don't try to keep up with the news, local or otherwise. I have too much on my own plate to try to re-member other people's problems. Once in a while I'll listen to the market report on the radio. But that's a waste, too. Once your cattle go into the sale ring, you're going to find out real quick what they're really worth.''

She glanced at him as she continued filling her plate with the vegetables Marina had prepared. ''So what do you do for entertainment? Or is the ranch your entertainment?''

One corner of his mouth twisted upward as his eyes scanned her face. ''Oh, I like to break horses. I enjoy a good hunting trip now and then. And I like to read.''

"Read?" That was the last thing she'd expected him to say and the surprise must have shown on her face, because he suddenly frowned at her.

"Yeah, read. Just because I wear a hat and spurs doesn't mean I'm stupid or uneducated."

She frowned back at him. "I wasn't implying anything of the sort. I just can't imagine you doing something so…sedentary."

A playful grin returned to his lips. "Well, a man has to rest sometime."

The image of him lying in bed, a book propped against his naked chest, was not the sort of thing she needed in her mind right now. Especially with the two of them alone and her heart beating an eager little tap dance against her ribs.

"What do you read?"

"Some fiction. But mainly American history. Most people don't understand that the past and how our nation was molded and built affects the way we live today. Take this ranch, for example. When my father and uncle first began to run cattle here, they had to deal with rustlers on a regular basis."

She picked up a rib and bit into the juicy beef. "But you don't have to deal with them now, do you?"

"Hell, yes! You've got to keep every cow and calf branded, tagged and earmarked. And some son-of-a-gun stole my stallion! That ought to tell you how much rustling still goes on these days."

"I think I remember you mentioning something about a stallion," she said. "When was he stolen?"

"I can't give you an exact date. Because I'm not exactly sure when he might have been taken. Nearly three months ago, I turned him out to pasture. Something I don't often do. But Snip had cut his hock and I wanted him to rest that leg."

"So you don't know the exact day the stallion went missing?"

Ross shook his head. "No. He'd usually show up around the ranch yard every two or three days to mooch a bucket of grain. When I realized he hadn't made his regular appearance, me and some of the boys rode out to look for him. That's when they found the John Doe remains."

Isabella's brows drew together as she tried to connect all the information she'd been given. "Neal told me that the coroner has already ruled that a homicide."

"That's right," Ross said grimly. "That's why Jess and Victoria were out there at the arroyo that evening. They were searching for evidence when someone took a shot at him."

She looked at him as her mind began to click and turn. "I can't help but wonder if your missing stallion has anything to do with the murder. Or the shooting."

"Jess thinks there might be a connection. But I don't see how."

"How many people knew about Snip?"

The rib in his hand stopped halfway to his mouth. "Hundreds of people have been here on the ranch to buy cattle or horses. Any of them could have seen the horse and admire him. But I can't imagine any rancher stealing from me that way. It just isn't done. Besides, the horse is registered and an identification number is tattooed inside his lip. Whoever stole him can't sell him for money. At least, not in a sale ring. They'd be caught. None of it makes any sense," he added.

"The horse could have simply died out on the range somewhere," she suggested. "Did that ever cross your mind?"

"I've thought about that. But then one of us here on the ranch would have found his carcass."

"The T Bar K goes for more than a hundred thousand acres, I was told. You couldn't possibly search every foot of it."

"That's true," he agreed. "But Snip never roamed that far from the ranch house. If he was killed by lightning or died from colic we would have seen the buzzards circling."

"That's a horrible thought," she said with a shudder.

He looked at her as though her softness was out of place in his world. "No, it's just a fact of nature, Isabella. Everything has to eat."

She breathed deeply through her nostrils as she pushed the image he'd painted out of her mind. "Dear Lord, you must be a hard man to talk that way about your own pet."

He shrugged one shoulder. "You grew up on the Jicarilla. You ought to know that this land is rough. A man has to be hard to survive."

Physically yes, she thought. But what about emotionally? Had this place made him so tough he no longer had any feelings?

"My life on the Jicarilla was hard, too," she reasoned. "But it didn't make me heartless. Just stronger."

He frowned at her. "Who said I was heartless? I loved Snip. I want him back. And God help the man who took him. But if the forces of nature got him, I'll have to accept the fact and go on."

And if circumstantial evidence eventually put Ross on trial, how would he accept that? she wondered. Then her mind just as quickly shied away from the image. To Isabella, Ross being unjustly tried was even worse than the idea of buzzards making a luncheon of his beloved Snip.

They finished the remainder of the meal with bits and pieces of small talk. Once they'd eaten the last bite of dessert, Ross suggested they carry their coffee out to the back porch.

Since it was still relatively early and she didn't want to appear unsociable, Isabella agreed. But the moment they took a seat together on a cushioned glider, she doubted the wisdom in joining him.

The night was like purple velvet wrapped warm and soft around the mountains. Stars winked like glittering jewels in the wide, western sky and the only sound to be heard was the far-off trickle of a stream falling over a bed of boulders.

Beside her, Ross's thigh and shoulder pressed warmly against hers and his gravelly sigh was a husky note that beckoned to every womanly particle in her body.

"This is heaven," he murmured.

Heaven? There wasn't anything angelic going through Isabella's mind at the moment. But the pleasure of being this close to him certainly felt like paradise.

"You must be a happy man," she quietly remarked.

He glanced at her from the corner of his eye. "Why shouldn't I be? I love this place. I love my job. I'm healthy and I'm wealthy. What more could a man want?"

Isabella supposed he was right. But she sensed that underneath his devil-may-care attitude, he was a man who shunned anyone who tried to get too close to him.

"So there's nothing you need."

There was a smile in his voice when he answered. "Other than getting Snip back, I can't think of a thing."

Her gaze slipped to his strong, tanned forearms, then farther down to where his hand rested against his thigh. What would it be like to be his lover? she wondered wildly. To be stroked by such tough hands, to be crushed against his hard body? The mere thought made her inwardly shiver.

"What about a woman?" she asked huskily.

He gave her a sidelong glance. "I can have a woman. When I want one."

If she'd thought he'd been simply crowing, she would have gotten to her feet and walked off. But there hadn't been a note of arrogance in his voice. Besides, she thought ruefully, it was most likely the truth. He could probably have most any woman he wanted, anytime he wanted. Except her. She might let herself do a little fantasizing about Ross Ketchum, but she wasn't about to let herself fall victim to his charms.

"I don't mean on a temporary basis, Ross. I'm talking about someone to live here with you. To share your life."

His head twisted around so that he was looking at her squarely. Isabella's heart thumped even faster as her eyes met his.

"Why don't you just come out and ask me why I'm not married?" he dared.

"Okay. Why aren't you?"

He let out a rough sigh. "I like women, Isabella. But not that much."

"Maybe you've never met the right one," she suggested softly.

Oh, he'd believed he'd met her, Ross thought. He'd fallen hard for Linda. She'd been pretty and sweet and everything Ross had ever thought he wanted in a woman. But he and the T Bar K hadn't been enough to satisfy her. She'd wanted to be a reporter. Not just a reporter for the local newspaper in Aztec, but a noted journalist for a major news media outlet. The minute she'd been offered a prestigious job at a leading television station in Denver, she hadn't hesitated to tell him goodbye.

"Look Isabella, I don't want to get married," he snapped. "Now or ever. I'm not the marrying sort."

Her prying had obviously irritated him. Apparently he believed his private life was none of her business. But the more she knew about the man, the more it enabled her to help him. And she wasn't going to lie to herself. She wanted to know how his mind worked, and also his heart.

"So, you don't intend to follow your father's footsteps?"

A puzzled frown touched his forehead. "How do you mean?"

Turning her gaze away from him, she sipped her coffee. "Well, he married and had children."

His reaction to that was a mocking snort. "Some folks say I'm just like Tucker. And maybe I am in some ways. He loved women. And he was a horse trader at heart. He made certain he always bought everything low and sold it high. But those are the only ways I'm patterned after him."

Curious, she glanced at him. "You say Tucker loved women. Yet he was married to your mother. Are you telling me that he had affairs?"

Shrugging, Ross glanced away from her. "Sure he had affairs. I don't think Victoria ever realized he was unfaithful to our mother. But I did. I'm fairly certain Seth and Hugh were probably aware of it, too."

And what, pray tell, had that done to the three brothers' young impressionable minds? Isabella wondered.

"What about your mother?" she asked. "Surely she didn't know. She didn't divorce him, did she?"

"No. Up until Mom died, they were married. Whether she knew about Dad's philandering is anybody's guess. She was a quiet woman. She kept herself busy here on the ranch with raising us kids and keeping the household running. I don't think I ever heard her raise her voice to Dad. If she'd been aware of his cheating, she never showed it."

His parents had lived together as a family, Isabella mused. Yet Ross had known that all had not rung true in the marriage. How sad that must have been for him and his brothers.

"Is that why you don't want to get married? Because of your father's infidelity?"

He let out a laugh so harsh that Isabella outwardly cringed. "Not hardly. That was his life. I've got sense enough to know I don't have to be like him. Unless I want to be."

Isabella's head swung back and forth. "I can't imagine you cheating on a woman that you loved."

He placed his coffee cup on the floor of the porch, then turned to face her. "Now see, Isabella, that's where you've got me all wrong. 'Cause in the first place, I'd never love a woman."

She felt sick. Although, she wasn't exactly sure why. His words weren't directed at her personally. And she wasn't concerned about his ever loving her. It was the whole notion that he wanted to be a man with an empty heart.

Quickly, she rose from the seat and walked to the end of the porch. As she looked out at the steep bluff rising above the house, she told herself she was going to make a mess of things if she didn't get control of her emotions. This was her first real case since she'd left the D.A.'s office in Dona Ana County. She couldn't get all caught up in her client's life. She had to keep her mind clear and that meant keeping her emotions detached.

"What's the matter?"

His voice was just inches behind her left ear and even though there was space all around her, she felt suffocated by his nearness.

"Nothing," she lied. "I just needed to stretch."

"You left the glider like a scalded cat," he softly accused. "Did you leave because of what I said? About not ever loving a woman?"

She straightened her shoulders and continued to stare out at the bluff. "Whether you ever fall in love has nothing to

do with me,'' she said as casually as she could manage.
''Just as you said about your father's adultery: that was his
own business. This is your business.''

''Well now, let's not lump the two issues together,'' he
gently scolded. ''They're hardly the same.''

She breathed deeply, then turned enough to enable her
to see his face in the semidarkness. ''But equally sad.''

''You're way too serious for a woman of your age.''

''I'm twenty-eight,'' she retorted. ''And it's my job to
be serious.''

His hand suddenly settled on the top of her shoulder.
''You've been asking me all these questions, Isabella, but
you haven't given me a chance to ask you many. So why
don't you play fair and tell me why you're not married?''

Shaken by his question and the touch of his hand, her
lips parted as she looked up at him. ''Because I…haven't
found the right man.''

One of his dark brows lifted to mocking proportions.
''Maybe you haven't been looking in the right places,'' he
murmured.

She could feel her breaths growing short, her fingers curl
into her palms. She didn't know why he was making her
angry with his prying questions, after all, he was only giving her a little of her own medicine.

''Love isn't something a person can look for. It simply
comes to you. And so far it hasn't found me.''

''Do you want it to find you?''

Of course she wanted love to come her way. And for a
while with Brett she'd believed it had. But just as she'd
started to think he was the man who would give her the
children and home she'd always wanted, he'd shown his
true feathers and demanded that she forget about the reservation, forget that she was half Apache. Just thinking
about Brett filled her with bitterness and continued to

make her doubt her own judgment about people. Particularly men.

"I want a home just like any other woman, Ross. Now if you'll excuse me, I'm going inside—to my room."

Bending her head, she started to step around him, but his hand on her shoulder tightened to prevent her from walking away.

"Wait a minute," he said. "I only got to ask you one question and you've asked me several."

Isabella peered up at him. She'd already been in this man's company too long this evening. She was beginning to think things, feel things that were totally forbidden.

Putting as much frost to her voice as she could, she said, "That's because you're the one who's likely to be put on trial. Not me."

Her ice-cube attitude heated Ross as nothing else could have, and before he realized what he was doing, he yanked her forward and against his chest.

She landed against him with a soft plop as air from her lungs whooshed past her lips.

"You think you're a real ice princess, don't you?" he drawled softly.

His hands were searing her shoulders and the contact of his chest was causing her nipples to harden and tingle. The erotic reaction to him swamped her with helplessness.

"I don't think like that. Now let me go," she ordered between gritted teeth.

He grinned down at her mutinous face. "Not yet. Not until I find out something."

His hands slipped down her back, then tugged her even closer to his hard body. Fire flamed in her lower belly as he nestled her hips against his.

"Find out—what?" she whispered breathlessly.

His head began to lower toward hers. "Whether you want me as much as I want you."

"No!"

Isabella wasn't sure if she'd shouted the word or simply thought it. Either way, it did nothing to stop Ross's lips from closing over hers.

Mindlessly, her eyes closed, her hands clutched the front of his shirt as wave after wave of heat washed over her.

Kissing Ross was the most reckless, thrilling and stupid thing she'd ever done in her life. But she couldn't seem to stop herself, or gather the energy to try to stop him. He tasted wild and wonderful. Like all the things she'd ever wanted or needed. And the fact shook her in a way that nothing ever had.

"So," he murmured when his lips finally lifted away from hers. "You're not an ice princess after all."

Somehow she found the will to pull out of his embrace, but her face flamed with lingering desire as her eyes dared to meet his. "I'm not a fool, either. Good night, Mr. Ketchum."

No, he was the fool, Ross thought, as he watched her turn and walk away. He'd been crazy to invite her to stay on the ranch, to think he could keep his hands off her, and most of all he was an idiot for believing he could kiss her and not have his world turned upside down.

The next morning Isabella slept later than she'd intended, but by the time she'd fallen into a deep sleep, it was time for the rest of the ranch to be waking. She tried to blame her restless night on the strange bed and the rich food she'd consumed for supper, but who did she think she was fooling? she asked herself as she stood beneath the spray of the shower.

The kiss she'd shared with Ross Ketchum had caught

her totally off guard. She'd expected it to be pleasant. After all, he was a very sexy, very masculine man, and she'd felt the tug of physical attraction from the first moment she'd seen him in the horse pen. But last night when his hands had pulled her close and his lips had made a thorough search of hers, she'd felt a sense of homecoming. As though Ross Ketchum was the only man she was supposed to kiss and like it!

Dear Lord, what was happening to her? she prayed. Was this the way her mother had fallen victim to Winston Jones? Maybe there wasn't that much comparison between the two men, Isabella considered, in an effort to be fair minded. After all, Ross wasn't married or cheating on a wife as Winston had been. Yet she couldn't ignore that, like her father, Ross was a rich, prominent man. He was well-known in this area. He probably wouldn't want to have an Apache wife any more than Winston had wanted an Apache child.

Wife! The thought was like a slap in the face and Isabella quickly turned off the water and stepped out of the shower. As she roughly dried the water from her skin, she mentally upbraided herself for letting her thoughts get so far astray. One kiss didn't have anything to do with marriage. She didn't even want to be a wife! Not with a man like Ross. No, if she ever found enough courage to marry, it would be to a man of her own people, a man who would be proud of her and want her children.

After dressing in a white cotton dress splattered with sunflowers, Isabella applied a light amount of makeup, then tied back her hair with a white scarf.

In the kitchen she ate a flour tortilla spread with butter and honey and drank two cups of coffee while Marina puttered back and forth between the gas range and the sink full of dirty pots.

By the time she was finished eating, she'd managed to turn her thinking back to the problem at hand. Who had tried to kill Jess Hastings and why had he used Ross's rifle?

Rising from the table, Isabella carried her empty cup and dirty plate over to the sink. "Marina," she began thoughtfully, "on the evening the shooting took place, did you hear or see anyone around the house? Someone who normally doesn't come around?"

The cook continued to shuck fresh corn as she considered Isabella's question. "No. I didn't see anybody. I was here in the kitchen, cooking. Victoria had told me she was going to ask Jess to stay for supper, so I was making some extra things for him." She frowned with frustration. "Ross's bedroom is too far from here to hear anything."

That much was true, Isabella silently agreed. Ross's bedroom was on the far end of the south wing. There was no way Marina could have seen or heard anything from this part of the house.

"I need some clues, Marina. Something that will point me in the direction of who really shot at Jess."

The older woman sniffed. "I think you should talk to the ranch hands."

Isabella leaned her hip against the cabinet counter as she watched Marina peel the green husks from the corncobs.

"Ross tells me he's particular about the men who work for him," Isabella said. "Surely he would know if one of them had an evil streak or was holding some sort of grudge against Jess or the Ketchums."

"Not if the man kept his feelin's hid."

Isabella sighed. Marina was right. The crime committed against Jess had been a sneaky ambush. If any of the men started badmouthing Ross now, it would point a guilty arrow straight at him.

"You're a wise woman, Marina. Have you ever thought

about becoming a detective instead of a cook?" Isabella teased.

Marina laughed and waved away the compliment. "Ross would just as soon be in jail if he couldn't eat my cookin'."

Smiling, Isabella thanked Marina for the breakfast then went down to the study to use the telephone.

Victoria Hastings's receptionist answered after the first ring. "Dr. Hastings's office, Lois speaking."

"Hello, Lois. This is Isabella Corrales. I was wondering if I could possibly see Dr. Hastings today?"

"For a checkup or are you having a problem?"

She was having a problem all right, Isabella thought. But it had nothing to do with her health. Unless she wanted to call the intense physical reaction she felt for Ross an ailment. "Neither. I'm her brother's attorney. Her brother Ross," she further explained.

The news must have taken the receptionist by surprise because there was a long pause before she finally spoke. "Oh. Can you hold just a minute, Ms. Corrales?"

"Sure."

Classical music suddenly filled the line, but rather than listen, Isabella used the time the woman was away from the phone to study the room around her.

It was mostly a masculine room with heavy furniture, a wide rock fireplace and deer and elk heads hanging from several walls. On the corner of the desk where she was sitting, there was a small framed photo of a man and woman posed with a beautiful black horse.

Isabella assumed the couple was Tucker and Amelia Ketchum.

The man somewhat favored Ross with his dark hair and broad-shouldered physique. And, like his son, there was a faint grin on his face that said he had the world by the tail and nothing could stop him from getting what he wanted.

As for Amelia, her sober expression and reserved clothing seemed to make her the exact opposite of her husband's lively appearance. But then what woman wouldn't look somber if she was living with a man she knew to be unfaithful? Isabella grimly asked herself.

"Ms. Corrales? Are you still there?"

Isabella pulled her attention back to the telephone. "Yes."

"Dr. Hastings would like you to meet her for lunch. If that suits your schedule."

"Just tell me when and where," Isabella told her.

"Be here at the office at twelve-thirty. She should be finished by that time. Barring any emergencies between now and then."

"I'll be there. Thank you."

Isabella hung up the telephone, then glanced at her wristwatch. She had a couple of hours to kill before she needed to be at the doctor's office. She'd use the time to make notes, and perhaps when she met Ross's sister, she'd have a mental list made of all the things she needed to ask the woman.

More than two hours later, Isabella entered Victoria Ketchum Hastings's medical clinic. Except for a blond, middle-aged woman seated behind a low counter, the waiting area was empty. The receptionist looked up at Isabella and smiled.

"You must be Ms. Corrales?"

"That's right."

The woman rose to her feet. "We just finished with the last patient. I'll tell Dr. Hastings that you're here."

Close to five minutes passed before a tall woman with shoulder-length dark hair and pale skin pushed her way past a pair of swinging doors to enter the waiting area. A white lab coat covered most of her red blouse and white slacks.

After stuffing a stethoscope into the pocket of her coat, the doctor smiled and extended a hand to Isabella.

"I'm sorry to keep you waiting, Ms. Corrales. A patient was on the phone," she apologized. "I'm Victoria Hastings. Please call me Victoria."

Isabella immediately liked the woman's strong, warm handshake and direct eye contact. "Call me Bella," she invited with a smile. "And I should be the one apologizing for interrupting your work."

Victoria Hastings quickly pulled off her lab coat and hung it on a nearby coatrack. "You're not interrupting anything. I have to eat lunch at some point and this gives me a good excuse to go to the café. Would you like to walk? I thought we'd go to the Wagon Wheel. It's my favorite."

"Sounds good," Isabella agreed.

The two women left the clinic and walked down the street to the nearby eating place. Inside, they found a booth located next to a plate-glass window. Once they were seated and Isabella was facing Ross's sister, she had no problem coming to the conclusion that Victoria Hastings was a beautiful woman. Like Ross, her hair was a shade off black and her eyes were green. However, beyond that similarity, their features were different. Victoria resembled the woman in the photo Isabella had been studying back at the T Bar K, whereas Ross appeared to have inherited his father's rugged facial traits.

"I really appreciate you taking time from your busy schedule to meet with me today," Isabella told her.

Victoria smiled with pleasure. "Oh, it's no problem. In fact, this morning when Lois told me you were on the phone, I was thrilled. Ever since Neal told me he'd hired you, I've been wanting to talk to you. I love my brother very much and I'm sure you can understand how worried I've been about this whole mess.''

A wry smile touched Isabella's lips. ''It's a good thing Neal hired me. Otherwise, your brother would still be without a lawyer.''

Victoria nodded as though she understood completely. ''I know. Hiring you was my and Neal's decision. Ross doesn't think he needs a lawyer.'' She let out a little mirthless laugh. ''But then Ross doesn't think he needs anybody.''

Especially a woman, Isabella thought grimly.

Concern marked Victoria's features as she looked at Isabella. ''Is Ross—does this thing appear serious to you?''

A waitress appeared at their table and for a moment their conversation was interrupted as the two women both ordered the blue plate special and glasses of iced tea. After the young waitress had left, Isabella carefully answered Victoria's question.

''Well,'' she began, ''it seems that what the sheriff's department has against Ross is mostly circumstantial evidence. And there's not a whole lot of that. Except that the rifle belonged to Ross.''

''And that his fingerprints were on it,'' Victoria added ruefully.

''That isn't all that damning,'' Isabella pointed out. ''The rifle was his. His fingerprints should have been there.''

With a weary shake of her head, Victoria leaned back in the booth. ''I just wish he could account for his whereabouts at the time of the shooting. Then there wouldn't be any doubt or suspicion by the D.A.'s office, or anyone else for that matter.''

Isabella studied her closely. ''Do you think he's capable of shooting at your husband? Of trying to kill him?''

"Capable?" Victoria's features twisted as she contemplated the question. "I'm sure Ross would be capable of shooting at a man in order to defend himself. But to dry-gulch someone? No. It would take a cold-blooded person to do that and believe me, there's nothing cold about Ross."

Isabella could certainly attest to that, she thought wryly. The man was passionate. Not only about women, but also about the T Bar K and his beliefs in general.

"Tell me about that evening," Isabella urged.

Victoria gave her a quick rundown of what had taken place in the arroyo before and after Jess had been shot. Just hearing the woman describe the fear and horror of the incident sent shivers down Isabella's spine.

"So you believe whoever took a shot at Jess escaped on horseback," Isabella said.

Victoria nodded. "At first I thought it might have been Dixie or Chito running away. But then—"

"Wait." Isabella pulled a small notepad and pen from her purse. "Who are Dixie and Chito?"

"Our horses. Jess's and mine."

"Okay." She scribbled down a few notes in shorthand, then smiled across the table at Ross's sister. "Sorry. I've often been accused of being meticulous. But believe me, in my business the smallest detail sometimes pays off."

"Oh please, don't apologize. I'm just so relieved you're here to help Ross," she said gratefully. "I've had this awful feeling—ever since the John Doe was ruled a homicide—that something terrible was going to happen. And I'm still not over it. I believe those galloping hoofbeats I heard were the shooter riding away. I also believe he had to be someone on the ranch. Someone who knew about Ross's rifle and where to find it."

"I think you're right on that count."

The waitress returned with plates of sliced roast beef, mashed potatoes with brown gravy and baby English peas. After she refilled their tea glasses and placed a basket of hot rolls on the table, she moved on to another group of customers and the two women began to eat.

After a few bites, Victoria asked, "Have you been out to the ranch yet to question the men?"

For some reason a hot blush stole over Isabella's cheeks. "Uh…yes. Actually, I'm staying out at the ranch. In your old room."

The pretty doctor's eyes widened with complete surprise. "Really? I didn't know."

Isabella tried not to squirm on the bench seat. "I was staying here in Aztec in a motel room. But Ross seemed to think it would make things easier for me to stay on the T Bar K."

Victoria was now staring with open disbelief. "Ross invited you? This is a bit of news."

As Isabella surveyed the surprise on the doctor's face, Marina's words suddenly came back to her. *He likes women. But he don't bring them home. Here to the T Bar K.* But she wasn't one of his "women," Isabella mentally argued. And after last night, she was even more determined not to be anything more to Ross Ketchum than his lawyer.

"Uh, yes. Why? Is something wrong?"

Victoria suddenly began to chuckle with sheer pleasure. "No. Not a thing."

Isabella frowned with puzzlement. "Look, I don't know what you're thinking, but just so we get things straight, your brother doesn't like me. It's not what you're thinking!"

The doctor's chuckles stopped, but there was a huge smile on her face as she looked across the table at Isabella. "Oh, I'll bet he doesn't like you. I'll bet the very sight of you does all sorts of things to him."

Chapter Five

"I beg your pardon?"

Victoria laughed again, then made a negligible wave with her hand. "Forgive me, Bella. I'm not making a joke at your expense. I'm just…amazed, that's all."

She gave Isabella another quick grin and her green eyes twinkled in much the same way Ross's did.

"You'd have to know Ross to understand," she went on before Isabella could think of any sort of sensible response. "He doesn't like women like you. So it—"

"What do you mean, women like me?" Isabella swiftly interrupted. "Because I'm Apache?"

Victoria's expression was suddenly contrite. "Oh, no! Not at all! I'm talking about you being a career woman."

Well, at least he'd been honest when he'd told her that her being a Native American didn't bother him, Isabella thought. At least that was one thing he didn't have in common with Winston Jones or Brett Tabor.

"A career woman?" Isabella asked her. "Does Ross have something against working women? I thought that went out with the dark ages."

"Uh—" Victoria paused as though she'd decided she needed to take a moment to choose her words carefully. "He's not against women working, actually. I think—you'd better get the full story from him. It's his business, after all, not mine."

Isabella couldn't see herself asking the man about his female preferences. But if the opportunity arose, she might put the question to him.

With a dismissive wave of her hand, she said, "Forget I even asked the question. I don't want to pry into your brother's personal life. I'm not here to do that."

Victoria's brow puckered with confusion. "But, don't you need to know personal things about him? I mean, someone framed him for murder, or at the very least, attempted murder. If you ask me, that's getting pretty personal. And for all we know, this thing could have been done because of a woman."

Isabella thoughtfully pushed her fork into the mound of mashed potatoes on her plate. "Has your brother made many enemies?"

"Over women? Or just in general?"

Isabella sighed. "Let's start with the women."

Victoria rolled her eyes. "I'm sure there's been plenty." She shook her head slightly. "But in all fairness, Ross doesn't go looking for women. He just attracts them. And sometimes he doesn't know that she's attached to someone else."

Incredulous, Isabella looked up at Victoria. "Doesn't he ask beforehand?"

"Of course he does. But he doesn't always get an honest

answer. Not until he gets a visit or a phone call from an angry man.''

It was no wonder the man shied away from marriage, Isabella thought grimly. ''This complicates matters.''

''In what way?'' Victoria wanted to know.

Isabella leaned her shoulders against the back of the booth. ''It widens the possibilities. I've been thinking the shooting had to be connected to one of two things—the murdered John Doe or the stolen stallion. Now I have to broaden that prospect to include jealous husbands and boy-friends.''

Victoria nodded ruefully. ''I see what you mean. And it makes Ross sound…well, a bit irresponsible, doesn't it? But he's really not that way. He's a very hard-working, dedicated man.''

''Yes, I can see that about him.''

Victoria swallowed several bites of food before she spoke again, and this time her face was reflective. ''This is probably going to sound like a poor-little-rich-girl thing, but I'm not sure you understand what it's like for Ross. He's not only a physically gorgeous man, but he's also rich. That means he never knows if it's him or the money that women are after.''

''I'm sure there's a lot of men out there who would like to have Ross's problem,'' Isabella pointed out.

''That's true. But money and power are sometimes hard to deal with. Believe me, I know. It kept Jess and I apart for four long years. And, I believe, it's…isolated Ross in many ways.''

If Victoria was trying to make her feel sorry for Ross, it wasn't working. He was not the sort of man who elicited sympathy. ''He owns one of the largest, most prestigious ranches in northern New Mexico.''

Victoria nodded. ''And it's not easy to keep it going,

keep it in the black, make sure the hands are happy and willing to do their work. After Hugh was killed, Ross was handed a heavy load.''

''He could hire a manager rather than do all that work himself,'' Isabella suggested. Yet she knew, without Victoria having to tell her, that Ross Ketchum would rather die than have someone else running the T Bar K.

Victoria responded with a soft laugh. ''Are you kidding? Ross is just like our late father, Tucker. There wasn't anything more important to him than the ranch.''

In the past few moments, Isabella had become aware that the conversation had taken a personal turn. And she'd not only allowed it to follow that direction, she'd encouraged it. Because the more she learned about Ross Ketchum, she realized, the more she wanted to know.

''Did Ross and your father get along?''

A faint smile touched Victoria's face. ''Oh yes. Tucker thought the sun rose and set on Ross. He had two other sons, but Ross was his favorite. Maybe that was because he was his youngest son. Or maybe it was because he saw himself in Ross. Whatever the reason, they were a pair. And even though we all knew it was coming, Ross was devastated when our father died of heart failure.''

Isabella reached for her tea glass as she tried to push away the image of a grieving Ross. She didn't like to think he'd ever hurt that much. He was too alive, too vibrant and happy to be forced to feel that much pain.

''What about your mother? Was Ross close to her?''

Another faint smile crossed the doctor's lovely face. ''Ross was always respectful with our mother. He loved her. But he was closest to Tucker. After all, they had so much in common—the horses and cattle, the ranch.''

''I'm sorry,'' Isabella apologized sheepishly. ''This has nothing to do with the present problem. It's not like me to veer off the point. I guess staying on the ranch has made me a little intrigued about your family.'' And a whole lot intrigued about Ross, she had to admit to herself.

Victoria studied her closely. ''I didn't find your questions out of line. After all, it's your job to ask questions. Do you have a large family?''

Picking up a steak knife, Isabella began to slice off a bite of roast beef. ''No. Just a mother, grandfather and godmother.''

''No siblings?''

Isabella thought about John and all the times she'd tried to get close to him while the two of them had been growing up. He'd always backed away from her and their mother. He'd never wanted to be a part of the family, and, after a while, Isabella had given up trying to include him in their lives.

''I have a half brother who lives in California. He's a doctor, a general practitioner like yourself. But we're…not all that close.''

''That's a shame. I don't know what I'd do without my brothers. With Hugh gone and Seth living away in Texas, Ross is the sibling I lean on. He and I have always been close. Of course I love Seth, too. It's just that Ross is always right here and he'd do anything for me.'' She put down her fork and looked desperately at Isabella. ''You can't let anything happen to my brother, Isabella.''

''Don't worry,'' Isabella told Victoria. ''So far the sheriff's department has formally questioned Ross only once. The fact that they haven't called him in again tells me he's not their prime suspect or the evidence they have against him is too minor to enable the D.A. to prosecute.''

Victoria released a small sigh of relief. ''I hope things stay that way.''

''So do I. But if not, I'll be around to represent him.''

To Isabella's surprise, Victoria reached across the table and warmly covered her hand with hers.

"And while you're around," she said, "you can think of us Ketchums as your family, too."

That was exactly what she shouldn't do, Isabella thought later as she drove back to the T Bar K. It would be a mistake to allow herself to think she could be anything more to the Ketchums than a lawyer. Especially to Ross.

And she didn't come to that conclusion just because he was rich and had a fondness for the ladies. In the first place, he wasn't interested in her. And in the second, she had her own plans. Soon her office building in Dulce would be completed. She'd be moving there to set up her law practice and to make herself available to anyone on the reservation who needed legal representation. Even the ones who couldn't afford it.

For years now, ever since she'd been a young girl, that had been her hope and plan. It was the reason she'd worked her way through college and then law school. She wasn't ready to set those dreams aside for any man. Even Ross Ketchum.

Back at the ranch, Isabella compiled the notes she'd taken so far about the case. Once that was finished, she changed into a pair of worn blue jeans and a cool cotton blouse.

Carrying her small notepad with her, she went outside and surveyed the area around the house. Particularly the part of the yard that accessed the sliding glass doors leading into Ross's bedroom.

Outside the doors, the ground had been laid in red brick in a ten-by-twelve square. A cushioned lounger and a matching lawn chair shaded by a juniper, were blocked

from outside view by several large clumps of bloom-
ing sage.

Isabella directed her gaze to the right, toward the barns
and cattle pens. The area of activity was at least fifty to a
hundred yards away and could not be seen all that well
from this vantage point. If someone had walked or ridden
a horse to this side of the house, he more than likely
wouldn't have been seen.

And once he'd taken Ross's rifle, he would have headed
west, away from the ranch, she deduced. Apparently he
wasn't seen. Or if he was, no one on the T Bar K was
willing to speak up.

Slipping the notepad into the back pocket of her jeans,
Isabella headed purposely down the hillside to where the
cowboys were at work. Maybe if she asked the right questions here and there, she'd glean a few more clues.

She was at the horse stalls, introducing herself to Linc
Ketchum, Ross's cousin, when her client suddenly came up
behind her.

"What are you doing down here?" he asked abruptly.

Her lips parted as she turned to face him. "I'm—" she
paused as her eyes met his and the memory of their kiss
filled her with heat. "I'm trying to find the man who shot
your brother-in-law," she stated bluntly.

His lips twisted as he inclined his head toward the
T Bar K's head wrangler. "Well, you don't think it's Linc
here, do you? He wouldn't hurt a fly. Unless it was irritat-
ing one of the horses. The only time Linc ever gets riled
is when someone messes with his remuda."

Isabella glanced at the quiet man behind her, then back
to Ross. "You cousin is not on my lists of suspects. I
thought he might have overheard something, someone talking against you, or threatening you perhaps."

Ross laughed and Isabella's jaw tightened. Apparently

he still thought this whole thing was funny. Or was this just his way of covering up a deeper worry? she wondered. The notion faded some of her irritation.

"Linc would be here all night if he told you all the bad-mouthing he'd ever heard about me. Isn't that right, Linc?"

Isabella turned slightly so that she could see the man's response.

Linc grinned briefly as his gaze traveled back and forth between Ross and Isabella. "Half the night, at least," he admitted. "But I haven't heard anything here lately."

"Do the hands like Mr. Ketchum as a boss?" Isabella asked him.

"Yeah, most of them. There's a few who gripe about him being a slave driver. Those are the young ones, the ones who come to the ranch with the idea that being a cowboy is a lazy man's way of making a living. Ross doesn't waste any time setting them straight on that count."

From the corner of her eye, she could see Ross grinning. Obviously he was getting a kick out of his cousin's observations about him. And obviously the two men were closer than she'd expected them to be.

Back at the café, before their lunch was over, Victoria had talked a little more about her family and how the ranch had first started out with her father, Tucker, and his brother, Randolf, Linc's father, having joint ownership. But eventually Randolf had developed heart problems and sold his portion to Tucker. Later, after Randolf passed away, his wife, Darla, headed for the east coast, but young Linc had chosen to stay here on the ranch.

From what she could see, Linc didn't seem to harbor any resentment against Ross for being the one who'd eventually wound up with the T Bar K. In fact, she could feel genuine affection flowing between the two men.

"The evening of the shooting, did you see anyone ride a horse up to the house?" she asked Linc.

Linc shook his head. "I was here at the stables saddling Victoria's mare, Dixie. About the time I finished, Jess walked up and the two of them left. By then it was already getting late and I'd had a hard day. I headed to the bunkhouse to eat. If anyone had ridden toward the house, I wouldn't have seen him."

She hid her disappointment. "Well, thank you, Linc. If you do happen to think of anything or overhear anything, please let me know."

"I sure will, Ms. Corrales. Now if you two will excuse me, I think I just spotted the farrier driving up."

Isabella watched as the head wrangler walked out from beneath the shade of the shed row and headed over to greet a man climbing down from a black-and-gray pickup truck.

"I think you like my cousin," Ross said, his voice full of amusement.

She turned her gaze on him and tried not to think about last night and how it had felt to be crushed against that broad chest of his. "Why do you say that?"

One corner of his mouth turned upward. "Because you weren't sniping at him, like you do me."

She breathed deeply. "Maybe that's because he wasn't insulting me, the way you do."

Ross chuckled, then his expression turned sober. "I missed you this morning."

The unexpected remark caught Isabella off guard and for a moment, as a warm feeling spread over her, she hardly knew what to say.

"I don't get up at four-thirty. That's still the middle of the night to me."

His eyes meandered up and down the length of her. "I

would call you a city girl. But you don't look like one. Not like that.''

She glanced down at her jeans and boots and pale yellow blouse. ''I'm not a city girl. I was raised on the Jicarilla, remember?''

''You could have lived in town, in Dulce.''

''Dulce is hardly big enough to call itself a town, much less a city,'' she told him. ''But that's beside the point, because my family home is in the foothills. I grew up herding goats and sheep and trying to climb high enough to find a hawk's nest.''

''A regular little tomboy, sounds like,'' he said, a dimple grooving the side of his mouth. ''What, no baby dolls or tea parties?''

It surprised her that he even knew of the things little girls played and her thoughts went a step further as she imagined what sort of father he might be. Stern, but loving. Somehow she knew that. And somehow she also knew he would think it important to instill deep morals into his children, to motivate and fill them with ambition. But then this man was already thirty-five. He would probably never have children. Not when he was so dead set against marriage.

''Not really,'' she answered. ''I just happened to like the outdoors.''

''What about now?'' he asked curiously. ''Don't you want babies, a home and family?''

She turned away from him as yearnings deep inside pushed their way to the surface of her heart. From the moment she'd learned about Winston Jones, she'd longed for him to be her father, a real father. Not just the man who'd genetically helped to create her. But his refusal to be a part of her life had crushed her. As a young child she hadn't been able to understand why he hadn't wanted or loved her. Ultimately, she'd come to the conclusion that something had to be wrong with her. That she wasn't lovable. Especially to men. Consequently, as the years passed, she'd been very reluctant to try to have any sort of lasting relationship with a man. And then when she had tried with Brett, she'd wound up with nothing but a broken heart.

"Maybe. Later on," she said stiffly. "Right now I have my law practice to think of."

There was a pause, then he said, "Now why does that not surprise me?"

His sarcasm caused her to twist her head around to look at him.

"Am I supposed to understand what that means?" she asked.

His eyes raked her face in a way that said she was a great disappointment to him. Which didn't make sense. Whether she wanted a husband and children now or fifteen years from now had nothing to do with him, she thought.

"You're a career woman. Women like you always put their job before a husband or children."

He doesn't like women like you.

Victoria's words swiftly came back to her and instead of being angry with him, Isabella was too busy putting together the clues of this man's attitude. He'd been hurt by some woman, she thought with sudden dawning, a woman who'd chosen her career over him. And he believed she was no different. The notion sickened Isabella. Yet at the same time she was amazed that this man had ever cared that much for any woman.

"I could never do that," she replied. "I am Apache. Family is more important to me."

Suddenly he let out a long breath and the tension around his mouth eased.

"Forget I said that, Isabella. It was out of line."

His swiftly changing moods perplexed her. They also

warned her that there was far more to him than just a handsome face and sexy body.

Deciding it would be better for both of them if she changed the subject, she told him, "I had lunch with your sister today. She's a lovely woman."

A fond light filled his eyes. "She's the best. I'm glad to see Sis and Jess finally happy."

"She's very worried for her husband and for you. You were both targeted by the shooting. Just in different ways."

He frowned. "Now that Jess has gone back to work, I'm sure Sis is even more worried. But Jess is a lawman through and through. He'll watch his back."

For the first time since she'd taken this job, the very real threat to Ross's life struck her hard. His work here on the ranch made him a very vulnerable target. If someone really wanted to do him harm, it wouldn't be difficult. For the most part, Isabella's task was to make sure the court didn't wrongly accuse or convict him. But the more she thought about it, the more she realized that risk was far less than him being harmed by the evil person lurking about the ranch. And that person was on the ranch. Isabella was feeling more and more sure about that.

"And what about you?" she asked him. "Are you watching your back?"

He presented her with a wide grin and Isabella realized he was once again in his laid-back mode.

"I'm leaving that up to you, Isabella."

She tried not to smile. After all, this whole thing was a deadly matter. But he had an infectious charm about him that got to her and she found herself smiling back at him in spite of herself.

"Looks like I'd better hurry up and find the person who did this. 'Cause I don't have the time or energy to follow you around all day."

Still grinning, he looked out to where Linc and the farrier were examining a hoof on a bay horse.

"Speaking of following me around, what are you doing for the next couple of hours?"

Instantly on guard, she studied his profile. "I've been trying to organize my notes. I thought I'd look around a little more here at the barns, then go back to the house and try to put together what I have so far."

"Forget about that for now. I'm going to ride fence and I thought you might like to come along."

His suggestion couldn't have surprised her more. "Ride? Me?"

He latched his thumbs over his belt and rocked back on his boot heels. "Yeah, you. Do you know how to ride?"

"My grandfather owned horses for years. I grew up riding them."

Her answer prompted a nod of approval from Ross. "Good. Then I won't have to give you a quick lesson before we take off."

This is not a good idea, she silently warned herself. Last night had already shown her what could happen when she was alone with Ross. But she liked to think she wasn't totally without self-control. Surely she could keep her distance from the man for two hours.

"I thought you were a busy man," she commented.

"This is work, Isabella. It's riding an area I covered not too long ago, but it was some of Snip's favorite stomping ground. I'm hoping there might be a chance he could still be hanging around there. And I thought it would be an opportunity for you to see more of the ranch. That is, if you'd like to see more of it," he added.

Why did she get the feeling he was talking about him instead of the ranch? Don't be stupid, she quickly scolded herself. Ross didn't have to play subtle games to get a woman to spend time with him. And if he was simply after female company, he wouldn't be looking to her for it.

"Sure. It would be nice to see more of the ranch," she told him. "When did you plan to go?"

"In about fifteen minutes or so." His gaze ran up and down the length of her. "You're already dressed for riding. But you need a hat. Go up to the house and tell Marina to find you one of Victoria's old ones. Then meet me back down here."

Isabella agreed to his plan, then quickly strode off toward the house. Along the way her heart began to sing a happy little tune and, by the time she entered the kitchen in search of Marina, there was a smile on her face.

"I'm going riding, Marina, and I need a hat. Ross says Victoria has some old ones around here somewhere."

From her seat at the long table, Marina looked up from the paperback book she'd been reading. Surprise arched her brows. "You're going riding? With Ross?"

Isabella nodded. "He's hunting his stallion."

Marina grunted as she rose to her feet. "Hmph. That horse has caused a lot of trouble around here. Ross needs to forget about him."

She motioned for Isabella to follow her to a small mud-room located just off the back of the kitchen. Inside the cluttered space, she went over to a shelf jammed with hats, boots and rain slickers. From the jumbled items, she pulled out a cream-colored hat with a long stampede string made of braided horsehair.

Marina handed the hat to Isabella. "The brim is a little bent in the back, but it should shade you all right."

Isabella pulled the hat down on her head. To her pleasant surprise it fitted, and she smiled as she tightened the stampede string beneath her chin.

"I'm sure Ross won't ride fast enough for me to need

this," she said of the string, "but it makes me look like a cowgirl anyway."

Marina's expression softened as she studied the picture Isabella made in the hat. "Ross won't be looking for his stallion. He'll be looking at you."

Color bloomed in Isabella's cheeks. "Not really, Marina. From the impression I get, Ross thinks much more of that stallion than he does any woman."

Marina made another snort of disapproval. "One of these days that will change."

Isabella didn't think so. Ross Ketchum appeared to be the perfect definition of a confirmed bachelor. But Marina wasn't a woman to argue with, especially over the Ketchum family, whom she'd known for forty years.

"I'd better head back to the horse barn. Ross will be waiting for me," she told the cook.

The two women left the mudroom, but before Isabella could leave the kitchen, Marina turned a stern eye on her.

"Where are you going to ride, *chica?* You're not going out to that evil place, are you?"

Not certain she'd heard the older woman right, Isabella repeated, "Evil place?"

An anxious shadow crossed Marina's features. "Yes. The place where Jess was shot—the place where that poor soul was found."

"Oh. No. Ross didn't mention anything about going there. Why?"

Marina shook her head as though she couldn't believe Isabella had to ask such a question. "Why? Because it's a dangerous place! You two don't need to go there. You see what happened to Jess! It could happen to Ross. Or you."

Seeing the woman was clearly distressed by the notion, Isabella patted her shoulder. "Don't worry, Marina. We're only going looking for Snip. Not for murder clues." She smiled softly. "But thank you for being concerned about me."

Marina sniffed, then ambled over to the cabinet counter where she'd laid out lard and tortilla flour. "I like you, *chica,*" she mumbled awkwardly. "I wouldn't want to see you hurt."

If Isabella got hurt, it wouldn't likely be by a killer. It would be by her own foolish behavior. That's why she couldn't let her guard down around Ross. Or any man, for that matter.

Thoughtfully, she walked over to where Marina was measuring out lard into a crock bowl. "Marina, do you have any family around here?"

Her eyes on her job, Marina shook her head. "Not close family. I had a husband once. But he ran off and left me when things got rough. We had a little girl who got sick and died. After that he didn't much care if he was around me or not. That was years ago. I don't think about him anymore. But I think about my little girl. She was pretty and dark like you. And always happy. Always."

Isabella's heart winced at the suffering this woman must have gone through. "I guess this was all before you came to work for the Ketchums?"

"Yes. Seth was a baby then. And Hugh was just a little *nino.* I helped Amelia take care of her boys and that helped me forget."

"And you've stayed all these years," Isabella added with quiet contemplation.

Marina gave her a sidelong glance. "The Ketchums are my family, *chica.*"

Isabella would have liked to hear more about the older woman's life here with the Ketchum family, but she didn't have time to ask further questions. Not with Ross waiting for her.

Patting the woman's shoulder once again, she said, "Don't worry, I won't let Ross take me to that bad place."

Marina blinked and Isabella was surprised to see a sheen of moisture in her dark eyes.

"That's good. 'Cause if there ever was a man who liked to take chances, it's Ross."

By the time Isabella arrived at the barn, Ross had saddled a horse for her. She was a black-and-white spotted mare named Trixie. A sister to Victoria's mare, Dixie, he informed her.

The mare was sleek and shiny and possessed a beautiful little face and head. Isabella immediately fell in love with her as she stroked the animal's velvety nose.

"She won't buck, will she?" Isabella asked warily as Ross offered her a hand up in the saddle.

He shot her a dry look. "Do you honestly think I'd put you on a wild horse?"

She wrinkled her nose at him. "You were riding a bronc the first time I ever saw you and you proclaimed him to be one of your finest horses."

He chuckled at her reasoning. "Yeah, but that was me. And this is you. I wouldn't risk that pretty neck of yours. Besides, you can ride Juggler anytime you want. He'd never buck with a woman on him. He has good manners. So does Trixie. I promise."

She rolled her eyes, but in actuality his compliment about her being pretty had filled her with a warm flush of pleasure.

"It won't take long to see if you're telling me the truth," she assured him as she stuck the toe of her boot into the stirrup.

With Ross's hand on her left elbow, she grabbed a handful of Trixie's mane. At the same time, her right hand latched on to the back of the saddle's seat and pulled.

Halfway up to the horse's back, she felt a hand flatten against the middle of her bottom and give a mighty push upward. Isabella landed in the saddle with a hard thump and a red face.

Her jaw tight, she asked, "Did you have to do that?"

He laughed up at her lofty perch. "I was only trying to help," he said with an innocence that made her teeth snap together.

"You can keep that kind of help to yourself," she told him, then carefully clutching the reins, she pressed her heels to the little mare's sides.

As she rode away, Ross quickly untethered his own mount and swung himself into the saddle. Trotting alongside her, he said, "Do you know where you're going?"

She looked over at him while wondering if her face was still as red as it felt. "I'm planning on you showing me."

He jerked his head to the left toward a rise of rugged mountains. "We're going this way," he said, then with another grin, he shook his head. "Have you always been this way?"

"How's that?" she asked.

"Prim and proper."

Her face forward, she arched her back as she settled into the rhythm of the mare's walk. "I've always been a lady, if that's what you mean."

"I didn't think any differently. I just wondered if there was ever a time that you let your hair down."

"My hair is down. But that doesn't mean I let a man— manhandle me!"

"Oh, Isabella."

Her name came out on a groan of disbelief and the sound brought Isabella's thoughts up short. What was she doing making such an issue over something she would have normally laughed off? The way she was behaving, Ross was going to get the idea he was getting to her. And that was the last thing she needed.

But he was getting to her, she mentally argued. When he touched her, it felt like a major event. It left her both sizzling and scared. And that was something she couldn't let him know, Isabella quickly decided. If he somehow discovered the effect he was having on her, he would probably laugh himself silly. Or even worse, he might take it in a different way and put up a defensive wall between them. That wouldn't do, either. As client and attorney, they had to have a comfortable relationship.

"Sorry, Ross," she said as lightly as she could. "I'm not normally so stiff. I...just have things on my mind."

Grimacing, he turned his face away from her. "I'm sorry, too, Isabella. I wasn't really trying to offend you. But it looks like I did."

"No," she quickly countered. "You didn't. Now let's talk about something else, all right?"

"Sure." He shot her a quick grin. "How do you like Trixie?"

"So far she's a real sweetheart." She patted the mare's neck as she inclined her head to the far distance ahead of them. "Looks like we're going to ride up in the mountains."

"Not up very high. We're mostly going to ride through the draw between them. Think you're up to it?" he challenged.

"I haven't ridden in quite a while, but I think I can manage."

The afternoon was sunny, the heat relieved only by a soft breeze wafting down from the northwest. Pine scented the air and wildflowers bloomed along the dim cattle trail they were following.

Isabella drew in a deep breath of appreciation as she tried to remember the last time she'd had the chance to spend an afternoon outdoors, much less on a horse. Her life in Las Cruces had been hectic, with nearly every waking hour of her day spent getting ready to work or actually working.

During that time she'd garnered an immeasurable amount of experience in the courtroom and behind the scenes knowledge of investigating and trying a case. But her personal life had suffered from the dedication she'd given to her law career. Other than the her ill-fated relationship with Brett a few months ago, she could probably count on one hand the dates she'd had in the past five years. And those had been little more than casual conversation over dinner.

But she had to be honest with herself. That fault wasn't entirely to blame on her job. No, it was more to do with downright fear than anything else. Fear that if she hung around any one man for more than one outing, she might get to liking him. And if she started liking him, then she'd have to start asking herself if she was really on the right track to love or headed down the forsaken road her mother had taken. In the end, it had been easier to avoid men entirely. Until Brett had come along and persuaded her that she was lonely.

Too late she'd learned he was not the loving, genuine man she'd believed him to be, and the mistake she'd made by getting involved with him had reinforced her determination to never let her head be turned by another fast-talking man.

But Ross appeared to be shooting holes in that strategy and she wondered how long it would be until she regretted ever stepping a foot on the T Bar K.

Chapter Six

Forty minutes later they had ridden deep into the crease of the mountains. Here the trail narrowed and was canopied by huge ponderosa pine. Long shadows, mottled with sunlight, dappled the ground and spread into the surrounding woods.

Every now and then a chipmunk could be seen racing over rocks and the cushioned carpets of pine needles. But other than those furry little varmints, there wasn't an animal as large as a horse to be found.

"This doesn't exactly look like grazing area to me. I don't know what your stallion would be doing here," Isabella spoke up as her little mare followed directly behind Ross's mount.

"You'll change your mind in a minute or two," he promised.

"I don't know about my mind," she said, "but I need to change my seat. I'm starting to get saddle sore."

He twisted his head around in order to look at her. "There's a good place to stop and rest just right up the trail here. Can you make it a couple more minutes?"

She nodded and drew up her sagging shoulders. "Sure. I'll be right behind you."

The two of them slowly continued on through the woods until suddenly the pines disappeared and they entered a huge mountain meadow. The grass was as high as Trixie's knees, a sea of green, broken only here and there by the orange-red blossoms of an Indian paintbrush.

"This is beautiful!" Isabella exclaimed as she drew the mare to a halt beside Ross.

A pleased grin grooved the sides of his mouth as he looked over at her. "I thought you might like it." He urged his horse forward and motioned her to follow. "Come along and I'll show you something else."

He was like a little boy, she thought, showing her his secret hideout. The idea left Isabella feeling honored and far closer to him that she should be.

Ross directed the gelding he was riding to the left, what Isabella assumed was a westerly direction toward the sun. After a few moments, they merged once again with the shaded edge of the woods.

She heard the trickle of water long before she spotted a wide stream tumbling down the rocky slope of the mountain.

"Let's get off here," he suggested.

Relieved to finally take a break, she pulled Trixie to a halt next to his gelding. "I'm more than ready."

"Stay where you are and I'll help you down. Your legs might be a little wobbly," he warned.

Once he'd dismounted and was standing on the left side of her, Isabella put the reins down on the mare's neck and pulled her right foot from the stirrup, then arced her leg over Trixie's rump.

Just as she made the move to lower her boot to the ground, Ross's hands tightly circled her waist. With no effort at all, he lifted her up and away from the saddle, then set her solidly on the ground in front of him.

He looked down at her with concern. "How's the legs?"

She laughed softly. "Like they want to fly out from under me. But I'll be fine once I walk around a bit."

Nodding, he said, "Go ahead. But be careful. I'm going to tether our horses."

While Ross safely secured their mounts, Isabella walked gingerly down to the stream. At the edge of the swiftly flowing water, she squatted on her heels, pushed her hat to her back and splashed a handful of the icy water onto her face. The cool rivulets running down her throat and onto her shirt felt good against her heated skin. She splashed again and used her palm to smooth the cold drops over her forehead and into her hair.

"Don't drink it."

The order swung Isabella's head around and she frowned at him. "Why not? It's pure mountain water."

"That's true. And it's probably perfectly fine to drink, but you never know when a dead animal might be lying in the water upstream. I would hate for you to get sick."

She started to tell him that growing up on the Jicarilla, she'd always taken drinks from streams and never gotten sick. But times had changed, even in her short life. Advanced technology had brought pollution. And anyway, she found she rather liked Ross's protective attitude toward her. It made her feel special and wanted.

Rising to her full height, she said, "Well, I'm not that thirsty anyway."

Turning, Ross walked a few paces back to his horse and

lifted a canteen from his saddle horn. When he returned to her side, he took off the cap and handed it to her.

"It's not very cold," he warned. "But it's wet."

She thanked him as she took the canteen and tilted it to her lips. After a long drink, she said, "I didn't realize you'd brought water along."

"Always. You don't ever want to break the rule of carrying water with you when you're out in the wilderness. Your horse could get away from you or go lame—anything can happen. A long trek on foot without water wouldn't be fun."

"I'm Apache. Of all people, I should have remembered that bit of wisdom," she said sheepishly.

A lopsided grin twisted his lips. "Well, Apaches are known for traveling long distances on a small amount of water. You'd probably make it back to the ranch without a canteen a lot better than I would."

She laughed at his reasoning. "Don't bet on it. I'm just as soft as any white girl."

His brows peaked with amused curiosity. "Really? Let me see."

Before she could make any sort of move, his fingers were sliding seductively against her bare arm, sending a sensual shiver throughout her body.

As her senses tumbled in all directions, her gaze drifted downward to the middle of his chest where a pearl snap joined the denim fabric of his shirt. "I don't mean that sort of soft," she murmured.

His fingers paused their movement and the spot where they lingered on her arm began to burn.

"Well, I already know about the inside of you," he said.

Isabella's eyes fluttered up to his. "You do?" she asked skeptically.

Her hair was as dark as midnight and her eyes—oh Lord,

her eyes were soft and beautiful. Like the wing of a gray dove, Ross thought.

"I think so. You want me and everyone else to believe you're as tough as rawhide. And you probably are when you need to be. But otherwise you're as soft as a cupcake." *And most likely just as delicious,* he wanted to add.

Her heart began a rapid pitter-patter inside her chest. "I'm too jaded to be soft, Ross. Working in a courtroom— I've already seen too much of the bad side of people."

His eyes slipped over her face and throat where drops of water glistened against her honey-brown skin. From the moment he'd seen her up close, he'd wanted to touch her, he realized. And since then, that wanting had only increased. "You're only twenty-eight. You're too young to be jaded."

With a dry little laugh, she stepped around him. "A person can experience a lot of things in that length of time," she tossed over her shoulder.

For a few moments he watched her amble upward, alongside the stream, then he carried the canteen back to his horse and hung its strap securely around the saddle horn.

A few steps away, a huge boulder at least twenty feet high sprang from the ground. In a crevice halfway up, a lone pinon pine grew out at an angle to form a roof of green needles above the ground. Easing his long frame down in the shade, he leaned his back against the boulder and patted the ground next to him.

"Come sit beside me," he called to her. "You need to rest before we start back."

She eyed the spot beside him with faint misgivings before she finally shrugged and moved to join him.

"I've been sitting on Trixie for the past forty minutes. I don't need to sit," she pointed out, but she eased down next to him anyway.

"This is a different kind of sitting," he said. "You can stretch your legs out in front of you."

She settled herself a few inches to the right of him and the lilac scent of her perfume drifted to his nostrils, reminding him even more of her femininity. He'd not ever taken a woman riding like this and he was surprised at how pleasant it was to have her company. But then, just looking at Isabella filled him with a joy that made him feel about fifteen again. He had the whole world before him and couldn't wait to sample it.

"Are bears in this area?" she asked as her gaze scanned the meadow and the woods surrounding it.

"Sure. Browns and blacks. There's also elk and mule deer."

"My grandfather Corrales used to be a big hunter. He has a bearskin tacked to his wall in his home. When I was a little girl I was completely fascinated with it—the fierce claws and teeth." She smiled with fond remembrance. "Maybe that had something to do with the wild hunting stories he often told me."

Ross looked at her thoughtfully. "Your grandfather is still living, but your father is dead?"

Isabella focused on the meadow to the right of them and the sea of green grass softly bending in the breeze. "My grandfather is still living on the reservation. But he's not really my grandfather in blood, because his son, Lee Corrales, wasn't my father. Lee had been dead a couple of years before I was born. A drunk driver ran into his truck one night and killed him."

He took a moment to assemble the information she'd given him. "So your mother remarried after her first husband died."

A bitter laugh passed her lips before she could stop it. "That would be the logical conclusion. But no. Winston

Jones never married my mother. He was already married when I was conceived.''

"Oh.''

Disgust was etched into her frown as Isabella turned her head to look at him. "My mother knew he was married. But she thought it was ending and that he was getting a divorce. I don't know why she was so gullible as to believe him.''

"Maybe she was in love and she desperately wanted to believe him,'' Ross suggested.

Isabella looked at him with wide, disbelieving eyes. "In love? I'm surprised you would say such a thing. I thought you didn't believe in the emotion.''

His green eyes held on to her gray ones. "I never told you that. I just told you that I'd never be guilty of being in that drunken state of vulnerability.''

He watched her breathe deeply through her nostrils and knew that, just as the last time he'd mentioned love, he'd made her angry. The fact that the word agitated her so intrigued him.

"Well, my mother was definitely in that weakened state of mind for a while,'' Isabella told him. "Until she realized Winston had been lying to her all that time.''

"And by then she must have been pregnant with you,'' he added knowingly.

Isabella nodded grimly. "That's right. And once she understood he planned to remain married to his wife, she severed all ties with him.''

Ross's brows lifted. "What about you? Wasn't he a part of your life before he passed away?''

Her head bent as she leaned forward and absently fingered a blade of grass growing near her boot. "I never saw the man. Never spoke to him.''

He stared at her. "But he was your father! Didn't he—''

Her face jerked up and her gray eyes were hard as they met his. "I said I neither saw him nor spoke to him. He didn't care that I was his daughter or that he was my father. I was an embarrassment to him. One that he never intended to acknowledge."

Men could be real bastards. Ross had always known that. Even his own father had been one from time to time. And he supposed he'd been one, too, on occasion. But he couldn't imagine any man rejecting his own child. Especially one as beautiful and bright as Isabella. Winston Jones must have been snake-belly low.

"What about financial responsibility? Did he help your mother with that?"

Isabella smiled as though the mere idea of Winston giving Alona money was laughable. "The man was rich, but he never offered my mother one penny. He tried to tell her that I wasn't his child, that she'd been seeing other men at the same time she'd been seeing him." She paused long enough to let out a rueful sigh. "You see, Winston's wife was a prominent woman in Pagosa Springs—that's where they actually lived. According to my mother, this woman had stacks of money and Winston didn't want to lose that in a divorce court."

"How did she ever get involved with the man anyway?"

Isabella plucked a blade of grass and brought it to her lips. "After Lee was killed, my mother—her name is Alona—had my half brother, John, to support. So she took a job in Dulce waiting tables in a small restaurant. Winston did a lot of traveling with his real estate business and he sometimes stopped in Dulce for a meal. He took notice of Alona and asked her to come to work for him. About that time, he'd extended his Colorado office to an office in Chama, and she believed doing clerical work and answering the phone would be easier than waitressing. And I guess by then she was a little infatuated with the man. The way she described him, he was a striking figure. Unfortunately, he didn't have any substance on the inside.''

A sorrowful pain smacked Ross right in the middle of his chest. He'd been a far from perfect son, but no matter what, his father had always loved him. Why, even the ground they were sitting on was now his because his father had loved and cared for him. But Isabella had never known her father, much less shared a close bond with him. She hadn't deserved such rejection. And if Winston Jones hadn't already been a dead man, he would have taken great pleasure in applying a little fist work to his face.

''If Alona went to Chama to work for the man, that meant she left the reservation,'' Ross reasoned out loud.

Nodding, Isabella said quietly, ''Mother says that was the biggest mistake of her life—leaving her home and the people who'd always protected her.''

''Did she ever remarry?''

Isabella shook her head. ''No. She says it's not because of Winston. But I know better. He ruined her life. After she became pregnant and learned that Winston already had a wife, her own parents deserted her. They were so ashamed of their daughter's behavior that they left the reservation and shunned her until they died.''

Incredulous, he stared at her. ''Bella, that's incredible! You mean her own parents didn't help her?''

''They not only didn't help her, they broke all ties with her. I never knew that set of grandparents, and it's obvious…they didn't want to know me.'' She tossed away the piece of grass and turned her head to look at him. ''Mother has photos of them, but she keeps them hidden.''

Her eyes were full of dark shadows and Ross found himself wanting to pull her into his arms, to assure her that her family had been wrong, that none of it had been her fault.

He wanted to see her gray eyes smiling, not filled with bitter pain.

"Have you looked at the photos?"

Her lashes fluttered downward, her jaw tightened. "Yes."

"What was it like, looking at your grandparents?"

She sighed. "Like looking at two strangers," she said starkly, then with a shrug of one shoulder, she cast him a brief smile. "I don't grieve over them, Ross, if that's what you're wondering. My mother's father-in-law and mother-in-law, the Corrales, were wonderful grandparents to me. And even though their son was no longer living, they remained close and helpful to his widow."

At least there were some people in her family who'd been loving and accepting, Ross thought. "Does Alona live on the reservation now?"

"Yes, in the same house she lived in with Lee before he was killed."

As Ross studied her face, he wondered why her life, her family and future interested him. Normally when he was with a woman, he never had the inclination to learn those sorts of things. He didn't have to know about a woman's family or what was in her heart to enjoy an evening of her company. But when he was around Isabella, everything seemed to be different and important to him. The notion was damn scary.

"Do you plan to live with your mother when you return to the reservation?"

Isabella laughed softly. "No. I love my mother, but we couldn't live together. I've rented a house in town—in Dulce."

Ross couldn't remember the last time he'd been through that small community of Apaches. Probably when he'd driven up to Pagosa Springs to do some elk hunting more than a year ago. Except for the gambling casino that had been built nearby, he doubted the place had grown all that much from the few stores and houses that he could recall. For the life of him, he couldn't figure why Isabella would want to settle in such a desolate place. Not when she wanted to practice law.

"Uh...when do you think you'll be moving there?"

A sly grin parted her lips and exposed her beautiful white teeth. "Already getting tired of having me underfoot?"

"No," he said, and was surprised at how much he meant it. If Neal could only hear him now, he'd be shaking his head, Ross thought. The lawyer would probably want to know how Ross had gone from wanting to fire Isabella to inviting her to be his houseguest on the T Bar K. Actually, Ross wasn't sure himself how that had happened. He just knew he wasn't at all ready for Isabella to leave.

"You're welcome to stay," he added, "as long as...need be."

His quietly spoken words were as warm and seductive as the curl of a finger inviting her closer. She tried to tell herself that he was a practiced charmer, that he knew just what to say to a woman and the perfect moment to say it. Yet she couldn't deny that the interest he'd shown her was a sweet treat for a woman who'd purposely starved herself of male companionship.

"I'm...not sure when I'll be moving to Dulce. Right now I'm still waiting for the carpenters to finish the work on the building I'm going to use as an office."

He smiled. "That's good. That means you'll have more time to focus your attention on me—uh, on my case," he quickly corrected as he saw her brows pull together in a faint frown.

Rising to her feet, Isabella brushed the dirt and twigs

from the seat of her jeans. "As I told you before, Ross, I'm not here on the T Bar K for your entertainment."

Ross climbed to his feet and Isabella glanced up at him as his hand closed around her upper arm.

"I'm not flirting with you, Isabella," he said starkly.

The corners of her mouth turned downward as she gazed at him with obvious skepticism. "Really? It sounds like it to me."

"Maybe it does. But I—" Frustrated, he shook his head. "Oh, hell, I never was good at being subtle. I guess what I'm trying to say is that I like you. I like having you around. Is there anything wrong with that?"

Everything was wrong with it, she thought. He wasn't the type of man she could have a casual relationship with. He wasn't a man who would be satisfied simply holding a woman's hand. He'd want more and Isabella wasn't prepared to give it. Not to a man who would clearly break her heart if she gave him half a chance.

Nervously, she moistened her lips. "I'm glad you like me, Ross. But—"

He tugged on her arm, urging her closer. "But what?" he prompted. "You're afraid I'll get to liking you too much? Well, honey, I'll let you in on a little secret. I'm afraid of that, too."

Isabella's palms flattened against his chest as she attempted to prevent her body from making contact with his.

"Then maybe we'd better keep our distance from each other," she countered, her voice taut.

One corner of his lips twisted upward as his gaze traveled over her soft features. "We probably should do just that, Isabella. But I can't stay away from you. Not now. In fact, I can't forget about kissing you last night. I've wanted to do it again. And again," he added in a low whisper.

Isabella could see his head lowering toward hers, and

she realized what was about to happen, but she couldn't seem to make herself do a thing about it, except wait for the touch of his lips on hers.

When it happened, she moaned helplessly and pushed ever so slightly against his chest. But her feeble protest went unheeded as his hands splayed against her back and slowly drew her up against him.

The scent of horses, soap and leather clung to his clothes and mixed with the musky male scent of his body. Isabella breathed it in as her lips parted for him like a sweet flower opening for raindrops.

Her welcome response stunned him with longing and he thrust his tongue between her teeth and tasted the intimate contours of her mouth. It was like dark, rich honey, he thought. Incredibly rich, and he was unable to resist.

The boldness of his kiss should have shocked Isabella, should have sent alarm bells clanging in her head. But it felt too perfect, too right to do anything except give him her lips any way he wanted them.

As he feasted on their softness, she moaned softly in her throat and instinctively arched her body against him. Ross complied with her needy reaction by bringing his hands to the front of her shirt and cupping his fingers over her small, firm breasts.

Shaken by how much she wanted his hands on her bare flesh, she groaned and strained to get closer. Ross quickly parted the top two buttons on her shirt and slipped a hand inside her bra until his fingers came in contact with her nipple. It was rigid and her whole breast seemed to swell against the palm of his hand.

Desperate to taste her, he tore his mouth from hers and bent his head. Isabella cried out with sheer pleasure as he took her lace-covered nipple between his teeth and lips and rolled it around his tongue.

Oh dear heaven, he was making her crazy. If he didn't stop—if she didn't make him stop, she was going to wind up making love to him right here on the grass!

With all the strength she could muster, she pushed herself away and quickly turned her back to him. As she refastened her clothing, she realized her heart was beating out of control and the pine boughs above their heads seemed to be whirling as if a tornado had just swept past them. Her body was as hot as a furnace and she could feel a trickle of sweat slowly coursing a track between her breasts.

"Bella," he murmured thickly as his hands closed over her shoulders. "I—wasn't expecting that to happen. I didn't bring you out here to—seduce you."

She breathed deeply and prayed that her head would clear. But how could she hope for that, she wondered desperately, as long as he was touching her, as long as his body was pressed against the back of hers?

"No," she said hoarsely. "But that doesn't make what we were doing...very wise." She twisted back around to face him and was instantly shocked at how much she wanted to taste his lips again, to feel their hard warmth and the magic they created with her senses.

"If a man only did what was wise," he said lowly, "he'd be living a boring life."

Her fingers curled into his chest as desire raced through her veins like a potent narcotic.

"Maybe," she whispered. "But at least it would be a safe life."

He chuckled as he lowered his lips back to hers, and Isabella could no more resist him this time than she could have seconds ago.

Her eyes fell shut as his mouth angled possessively over hers and his hands explored the curves and contours of her back. Hot blood sang in her ears, deafening the whisper of the wind in the pines and the grass around their feet. And with each passing moment, Isabella felt herself slipping to a place where nothing existed except Ross and the heated pressure of his lips, the tight band of his arms and the rock-solid wall of his chest crushed against her breasts.

Frightened by the headlong rush of pleasure and the notion that this time she wouldn't be able to stop him or herself, Isabella managed to tear her mouth from his and pull out of the embrace.

This time she walked several steps away from him and with her back to him, she gulped in ragged breaths and pressed her palms to her heated cheeks. She'd never felt so shameless, so out of control in her life. But, oh my, it had felt so good in his arms. Too good, she thought desperately.

"Isabella, are you—" Once again, his hand came down on her shoulder and the gentle touch went straight to her heart. "Are you all right?"

Her throat tightened, forcing her to swallow. "Yes. I'm just…a little angry at myself."

His fingers smoothed back and forth across the slope of her shoulder. "Why? Because you were enjoying what we were doing?"

Did he have to put it so bluntly? she wondered crossly. *I never was good at being subtle.* Quickly, his words came back to remind her that, if anything, he was honest. That meant she had to be equally honest with him.

"I was enjoying it, Ross," she murmured thickly. "Too much. But that's not why I'm angry at myself. I—"

Desperate to make him understand, she turned and looked up at him with somber gray eyes. "I swore I would never make the same mistake my mother made. And if I let myself get involved with you, that's just what I'd be doing."

As soon as her words were out, a myriad of emotions paraded across his face. Surprise, anger and frustration.

"You think I'm in the same caliber as Winston Jones. Is that what you're telling me?"

Did she? Not really. But he was still a man who dallied with women's affections and, like Winston with Alona, he didn't have a serious intention toward her.

"Not exactly. But—"

"You think I'd desert my own child?" he asked, his voice incredulous.

"No. I think you'd probably be a wonderful father. Given the chance. But—you don't want to be a father. Or a husband. You said so yourself."

An irritated frown creased his forehead. "What's that got to do with me kissing you or you kissing me?" he wanted to know. "Do you think you should only kiss men who have intentions of marrying you? Is that it?"

Hot color swept up her neck and face. "No—oh, you don't understand, Ross," she said impatiently. "And it doesn't matter anyway."

Quickly, she turned away from him and headed to where the horses were tethered. She was untying Trixie's reins when Ross came up behind her and put a staying hand on her arm.

"I want to understand, Bella. Tell me."

Her head dropped as a sinking weight seemed to fill her heart. "I don't want to fall in love with you, Ross. We're two completely different people. And you're the very last man on earth who could give me what I want."

His fingers tightened ever so slightly on her arm as he studied her bent head. "That makes me feel real good, Bella."

The sarcasm in his voice made Isabella's heart wince. Forgetting the bridle reins, she twisted her upper body around to face him. "I'm not trying to insult you, Ross. I'm just speaking the truth. You have no desire to become a family man. And I—"

Suddenly all the hopes and dreams she'd ever had for herself swept through her and filled her with so much emotion she couldn't go on.

"You what?" he prompted.

Isabella turned her gaze toward the green meadow that stretched to the right of them. "I want a man who will give me a home and children, who will support my job. I don't want to be like my mother who had to raise an illegitimate daughter alone, who had her heart so broken she can't even think of marrying a man."

Gently, he took her by the shoulders and turned her toward him. "Bella, you're getting a little carried away. We only kissed and you start worrying about having an illegitimate child."

More hot color seeped into her cheeks. She knew she sounded like some sort of rigid spinster, but the desire she felt for this man was so great she knew it was going to be a constant struggle to keep from touching him, inviting him to kiss her again. And again.

"One thing leads to another," she murmured.

Shaking his head, he let out a disappointed sigh. "I would never put you in such a predicament."

"I never believed you would. It's just that I...can't be this close to you anymore." It was too dangerous to her heart, her mind, her sense of well-being, she thought. "Please don't...ask me to be," she added hoarsely, then before he could reply, she jammed on her hat and turned to collect Trixie's reins.

Once she'd tossed them around the mare's neck, Ross could see she was intent on leaving, and, though he wasn't ready, he helped her into the saddle, then mounted his own horse.

Silently they rode across the western edge of the secret meadow, then back onto the shaded cattle trail that would return them to the T Bar K. Deeper into the woods, the path narrowed down to single file and Ross automatically took the lead. Behind him, Isabella's shoulders slumped wearily.

She should have never made an issue about the kissing, she scolded herself. She should have pretended to be casual and experienced, to be the sort of woman he liked and was accustomed to holding in his arms. Now, with all that talk, she'd done about marriage and a family, she'd probably given him the idea that she was getting serious about him.

It wasn't the talking that gave him ideas, Isabella told herself. It was the kissing him as if there would be no tomorrow. She'd let him touch her intimately! Even now she could still feel his mouth upon her breast.

"Ross?"

"Yes?"

"I hope you're not angry with me."

Ross silently groaned. He wanted to be angry. She'd stirred him into a hot frenzy. His body was hard and aching for her, even though he knew there was no chance in hell of having her. Yet he couldn't be angry with her, when just the sound of her voice filled him with pleasure. When just the thought of her giving lips touched a spot deep within him.

"No. I'm not angry."

Her eyes focused on his back and the faint movement of his broad shoulders. "I want us to be friends. Are we?"

"As far as I'm concerned we are." Friends and more. But just how much more was the question, Ross thought. She wanted things he would never give her or any woman.

And he wanted from her what she would never give to just any man. The two of them were an unlikely pairing and he realized he should forget about any romantic notions he had toward her. But he couldn't. It was just that simple.

"Maybe I should…drive on up to Dulce and get settled in my own house. From what I can gather so far, I don't believe the D.A. is going to file charges against you."

He pulled up his horse and twisted his head around toward her. She stopped Trixie beside him and looked at him questioningly.

"What's wrong?" she asked, then immediately felt her heart turn over as he reached for her hand and brought the back of it to his lips.

"I don't want you to be angry at me, either," he said softly.

Isabella had never had a problem with vices. She'd always believed her willpower was strong enough to resist anything that might be harmful to her. But Ross was sorely testing it. Every nerve, every particle of her being, wanted to throw her arms around him and beg him to make love to her right here in the quiet shadows of the forest.

The wanton thought caused her voice to tremble. "I'm…not angry. I just think it might be better if I wasn't here on the ranch."

His thumb gently rubbed the back of her hand as his eyes probed hers. "There wouldn't be anything better about it. Even if you say I'm not in danger of being arrested, I still need you to find out who tried to kill Jess."

He needed her. It was ridiculous how much Isabella let that one little word sway her thinking. She didn't know why she was even letting herself believe it. Ross was a man who had most everything and what he didn't have, he could buy. If she wasn't here, he could easily hire another attorney, probably one more adept than her, from a big firm that had their own private investigators. She'd probably be doing him a favor if she did pack up and leave.

"Ross, did you ever think I might not be right for this job?"

Her question caught him off guard and he stared at her for long moments. "Why do you say that?"

Bending her head, she stared at the worn leather on the saddle horn. "I've had two years of assisting the D.A. in Dona Ana County, but that doesn't make me all that experienced. And besides, I think what you really need is a private investigator."

His fingers tightened around hers. "And I think because of what happened back there between us, you're running scared."

Of course she was running scared. Ross's track record with breaking hearts would be enough to send any normal woman scampering for safer ground.

"It's not exactly ethical for a lawyer to be…kissing her client," she said with disgust.

He chuckled. "It felt just fine to me."

Groaning, she lifted her troubled eyes to his. "I can't joke about this, Ross. I—"

Suddenly his hand was cupping her cheek, his expression turned solemn. "I'm not joking, Isabella. I need your help."

The touch of his fingers set her heart to pounding and she wondered if he could feel the rapid pulse in the side of her neck, feel the heat that was scorching her cheeks and spreading downward to her breasts. It had been a mistake to kiss him back there at the edge of the meadow, she told herself. Now every time she looked at him, she would think of those moments and remember all the ways he'd made her feel like a woman.

The Silhouette Reader Service™ — Here's how it works:

Accepting your 2 free books and mystery gift places you under no obligation to buy anything. You may keep the books and gift and return the shipping statement marked "cancel." If you do not cancel, about a month later we'll send you 6 additional books and bill you just $3.99 each in the U.S., or $4.74 each in Canada, plus 25¢ shipping & handling per book and applicable taxes if any.* That's the complete price and — compared to cover prices of $4.75 each in the U.S. and $5.75 each in Canada — it's quite a bargain! You may cancel at any time, but if you choose to continue, every month we'll send you 6 more books, which you may either purchase at the discount price or return to us and cancel your subscription.

*Terms and prices subject to change without notice. Sales tax applicable in N.Y. Canadian residents will be charged applicable provincial taxes and GST. Credit or Debit balances in a customer's account(s) may be offset by any other outstanding balance owed by or to the customer.

Get FREE BOOKS and a FREE GIFT when you play the...

LAS VEGAS
GAME

Just scratch off the gold box with a coin. Then check below to see the gifts you get!

YES! I have scratched off the gold Box. Please send me my **2 FREE BOOKS** and **gift for which I qualify**. I understand that I am under no obligation to purchase any books as explained on the back of this card.

335 SDL DUYG   235 SDL DUYW

FIRST NAME	LAST NAME

ADDRESS

APT.#	CITY

STATE/PROV.	ZIP/POSTAL CODE

(S-SE-03/03)

7	7	7	Worth TWO FREE BOOKS plus a BONUS Mystery Gift!
🍒	🍒	🍒	Worth TWO FREE BOOKS!
🔔	🔔	♣	TRY AGAIN!

Visit us online at www.eHarlequin.com

She drew in a deep breath and let it out. "You could hire someone else to help you. The best."

The corners of his lips lifted. "I've hired you. And Neal says you're the best."

"Neal is too kind to say anything else."

His fingers smoothed over her cheek, then into her hair. "The first day you came to the ranch, you insisted you could help me," he said in a soft, luring voice. "I expect you to hold to your word."

Closing her eyes, she told herself he was right. To back down from her promise would make her lose all legitimacy as a lawyer not only in Ross's view, but with the whole Ketchum family.

She opened her eyes and straightened her shoulders. "All right. I'll stay on a few more days," she finally agreed. "But what just happened back there between us...can't happen again."

A grin that could only be described as tempting suddenly curled the corners of his lips. "Whatever you say, Bella. You're calling the shots."

Dropping her hand, he nudged his horse on down the trail. Behind him, Isabella wondered why she didn't feel relieved.

Chapter Seven

For the next two days Isabella threw herself into the job of gathering as much information about the T Bar K employees as she could without being openly invasive about it. To accomplish this, she lingered around the work pens, the cattle barns and the horse stalls, catching bits of conversation here and there and simply observing their daily work routine.

Today the men were all working close by, so Ross had invited her to lunch with him and the hands at the bunkhouse. The outing had given her an even closer look at the men, who in Ross's way of putting it, rode for the T Bar K brand.

So far she'd not gleaned any suspicious activity by any of the cowboys. For the most part they were quiet, polite and hard-working. Only three—Steve, Tim and Jamie—had caught her attention. Mainly because they were the youngest of the lot and appeared to be cocky and a tad on the shiftless side. But she hadn't sensed any hostility toward Ross from any of them.

If she was making any headway into solving the case of Jess's shooting, she didn't know it yet. What was becoming evident to Isabella were her growing feelings toward Ross.

True to his promise, he'd left the boundaries of their relationship up to her. Other than a few casual touches of her arm and hand, he'd not attempted to kiss her or embrace her in any way. The fact that he'd stuck to his word both impressed and surprised Isabella. But on the other hand, she had to admit to herself that she was a bit disappointed that he hadn't tried something with her.

That day at the meadow, she would have sworn she'd felt a real need in his kiss and the touch of his hands. But she'd obviously been wrong about that. Even his desire for her must have waned, or else it had never been as hot as she'd first imagined and his behavior only proved how easy it was for a woman to misjudge a man.

Still, she couldn't deny it was a joy to have his company, and she had come to look forward to the evenings when his work was through and he would join her in the kitchen for the evening meal.

But that didn't mean she was falling in love with the man, she mentally argued, as she stood beneath the spray of the shower. It only meant that he'd become a close friend and there was nothing wrong with that. Except that it wasn't right to want to touch, kiss and make love to a friend.

With that degrading thought, she stepped from the shower and hurriedly blotted the water from her dripping hair with a thick towel.

Outside the sliding glass doors in her bedroom, sundown was painting the mesa with vivid hues of purples, pinks and magentas. Ross was probably in the house by now or perhaps he was already in the kitchen visiting with Marina while he waited for Isabella to join him. After a long day of physical work, he was always hungry. The last thing she wanted to do was hold up his meal.

She was jerking a pink-flowered peasant blouse over her head when a knock sounded on her bedroom door.

"Just a moment," she called as she snatched a pair of blue jeans from the bed.

Once she'd tugged them over her hips and pulled up the zipper, she scampered over to the door and pulled it open.

To her surprise, a grim-faced Ross was standing on the other side.

"Oh Ross, I'm sorry I'm late," she began as she swiped her wet hair away from her face. "I was working on my notes and time slipped up on me. If you'd rather start without me, please do. I'll be there in a couple of minutes."

She had to be the most beautiful thing he'd ever seen, Ross thought, with her hair wet, her face cleaned of makeup and her bare toes sticking from under the hem of her jeans. If he saw this woman every day for the rest of his life, it wouldn't be enough to suit him. But she wouldn't be here for the rest of his life, he quickly reminded himself. Once this thing with Jess's shooting was over, she'd be gone. And then what? Could he forget what it was like to have her here in the house, eating across the table from him, sharing a cup of coffee with him on the back porch as the sun slipped below the mesa?

Hell, even if he could forget all that, he could never cleanse his mind of the way it felt to have her in his arms, the taste of her lips, the soft touch of her hands against him.

"I'm not here to hurry you," he said. "I have something to tell you."

And it couldn't wait for five minutes? she wondered.

Uneasy now, she stepped back and motioned for him to enter the room.

Once he was standing in the middle of the bedroom, she asked without preamble, ''What's happened?''

He let out a long breath and she could see from his tight features that he wasn't pleased about something.

''I just got off the telephone. The sheriff's department wants to talk to me in the morning.''

Isabella's heart sank like dead weight. ''What did you tell them?''

He shrugged one shoulder. ''That I'd be there, of course.''

Nodding, she eased down on the side of the bed. ''You're right. You don't want to appear reluctant, as though you're afraid to talk to them.'' Her gray eyes studied his face. ''You aren't, are you?''

He grimaced. ''Afraid? Hell. The last time I can ever remember being afraid, I was three years old and I thought my daddy was going to whip me for letting his stallion out of the stall.''

''Did he?'' she asked curiously.

She watched him thrust a hand through his hair as he walked over to the sliding glass doors and peer out at the rugged land that belonged to him and his siblings.

''No,'' he answered. ''But I couldn't ride my horse for a week. That was much worse than any whipping and he knew it. Dad was sly. No doubt about it.''

Isabella noticed he appeared to be in a pensive mood and she wondered if the call from the sheriff's department had made him that way or if something else was occupying his mind.

''Was your father ever mean?''

He chuckled as though she'd asked a question that would be impossible to answer fully. ''Not to us kids or Mom.

But he could be damn mean if you riled him. And I'm not talking about just giving someone a cussing. Tucker was handy with his fists and he wasn't squeamish about using them.''

''People tell me that you're like him. Are you handy with your fists?''

Chuckling, he turned to look at her. ''According to Victoria I bloodied a number of noses when I was in high school. But that was a long time ago. I'm not nearly so physical now.''

Isabella very nearly laughed. She'd never seen a more physical man than Ross. And she wondered if that was part of her infatuation with him. Maybe she couldn't get his kisses out of her mind because he was so potently male, so big and strong and tough compared to the men she'd known in the past.

Who was she kidding? she wondered wryly. It wasn't just Ross's virility that had been keeping Isabella awake at night. She was taken with everything about him. His wit and charm, the hard work and devotion he gave to this ranch, the affection and care he gave to the horses and cattle, the obvious love he had for his family. Even the gentle way he treated Marina touched a spot in her heart.

Rising to her feet, she walked over to where he stood by the glass doors. ''I'm glad to hear you say that, Ross. It would be more difficult to prove your innocence if I had to defend a constant string of fistfights.''

As Ross looked down at her, he realized he very much wanted to kiss the faint smile on her lips. But he wouldn't. He didn't want to crowd her. Not when he had hopes that she would eventually reach out to him.

And then what, Ross? he asked himself. Isabella wasn't the sort of woman he was accustomed to having in his bed. He had the feeling she'd probably not had more than a handful of lovers. And she didn't want a bed partner; she wanted a husband. Jumping into that role just wasn't in Ross's cards. He needed to remember *that* instead of thinking of all the wild and wicked ways he'd like to make love to her.

"What do you think the law will be asking me tomorrow? I've already told them all that I know."

Isabella reached up and curled her fingers over his forearm. But whether her action was to reassure him or herself, she wasn't sure. Either way, touching him felt just as good as she remembered.

"It's impossible to guess. But we'll deal with the questions. Just make sure you look at me before you answer anything."

His brows arched. "You're going with me?"

Isabella's features wrinkled with disbelief. "Of course. What do you think I'm doing here anyway?"

Making a fool of him, he thought. If he wasn't careful, his heart was going to get all tangled up with his head. He'd start wanting to make her stay here on the T Bar K permanently, even though he had enough sense to know that wild horses couldn't keep her from returning to the Jicarilla.

Trying not to dwell on what that was going to do to him, he said, "You're my attorney. But…won't it make me look guilty to have a lawyer accompany me to the sheriff's office?"

"No. It will just show them that you aren't about to let them bulldoze over you."

Her blustery confidence caused his lips to twist with amusement. "You think you can prevent them from doing that—bulldozing over me?"

A firm resolution settled over her features. "I'm going to make sure they don't. So don't worry."

She was trying to reassure him, to make him feel better, and somehow that felt just as nice to Ross as if she'd risen on her tiptoes and kissed his lips.

Hell, he silently muttered, he was getting so soppy it was downright sickening. Is that what happened to a man when a woman got hold of him? Turned him as soft as putty?

No! Isabella didn't have a hold on him. And he wasn't going to let her get one, either. Everyone had always said he had Tucker's iron will. Ross figured now was a good time to put it to use.

Touching a fingertip to the end of her nose, he said, "It's going to take a lot more than Sheriff Perez to worry me. So brush the tangles from your hair and then we'll go eat before Marina starts yelling at us."

The next morning Isabella dressed carefully in a pale-green suit with a straight skirt and fitted jacket. After winding her hair into a glossy chignon at the back of her head, she finished the outfit with a single strand of pearls around her neck and pearl studs in her earlobes.

After dabbing perfume on her wrists and neck, she left the bedroom and walked to the front of the house where she'd planned to meet Ross. When she reached the living room, she discovered he was already there waiting for her.

Ross took one look at her and whistled softly. "Wow! Is that a diversionary tactic?" he asked as he gestured toward her skirt and jacket. "If it is, I have no doubt it will work."

In spite of her fluttery nerves, she couldn't help but smile at him. To have him insinuate that she was an attractive woman went a long way to heal the damage Brett had caused to her ego.

"It's nothing that drastic. I simply want everyone at the

sheriff's office to understand your attorney isn't a hay-
seed.''

He curved a hand around her elbow and guided her out
the door. ''I seriously doubt that notion will enter their
heads, Bella.''

On the twenty-five-minute drive to the sheriff's office in
Aztec, Isabella advised Ross as to what and what not to
say. And, above all, he was not to lose his temper. No
matter how annoyed he became.

But once they were seated in a conference room with
Sheriff Perez, Under-Sheriff Hastings and Deputy Redwing,
that counsel seemed to fly out the window.

The second the introductions between Isabella and the
three lawmen were concluded, Ross glared at his brother-
in-law.

''Jess, what in hell is going on here? I've been—''

The remainder of Ross's words halted as Isabella quickly
laid a calming hand on his arm.

''Ross, please let me handle this,'' she pleaded under her
breath.

His lips snapped shut. Tense moments passed as he
stared at her. Then finally he seemed to decide she was
there to do the talking for him and it would be better for
both of them if he allowed her to do her job.

Releasing a long breath, Ross settled back in his chair
and gestured for her to take over.

''Thank you,'' she silently mouthed to him, then turned
her attention to the three lawmen who appeared to be
closely watching the interplay between Ross and Isabella.

''Gentlemen,'' she began in a brisk voice. ''As I understand it, my client has already given you a statement. And
since he signed it without the advice of legal council, I
seriously doubt it would hold up in a court of law—''

Ross jerked upright. He wanted to let Isabella do her job. But she obviously didn't understand the way the cow ate the corn. He wasn't a man who beat around the bush. He was a straightforward type of guy. Just as Tucker had been. There wasn't any danger of him being caught in a lie. Didn't she know that about him by now?

"Damn it, Bella, I'm not worried about signing anything. All of that stuff is the truth and that's all these guys want anyway."

Her gray eyes turned on him and their dark stare warned him to be silent. Totally silent.

Snapping his mouth shut once again, Ross folded his arms against his chest and tried to slow his breathing.

"Look," she said to the three lawmen, "if you're going to charge Ross with attempted murder, then do it. But don't keep harassing him like this."

"Bella!"

She ignored Ross's outburst and continued, "I'm well aware of what little evidence you have. And as a former prosecutor, I can tell you right now it isn't enough to go to trial, much less garner a conviction."

A dimple appeared in Jess's cheek as he glanced at Sheriff Perez, a tall man in his mid-forties with a leather-tough face and a black Stetson pulled low on his forehead.

"Maybe you should tell them what they're doing here," Jess suggested.

Nodding, the sheriff cleared his throat. "Ms. Corrales, I appreciate what you're saying, and though I can't exactly speak for the D.A.'s office, I'm fairly certain they have no plans to arrest Ross. Unless, of course, some other evidence against him surfaces."

"That isn't going to happen," Ross muttered.

Relief poured over Isabella and though she wanted to

turn and throw her arms around Ross's neck, she had to conduct herself in a professional manner.

"Then what is this meeting about?" she wanted to know.

The sheriff gestured toward Jess. "Since he's your brother-in-law, I'll let you be the one to tell him."

Ross turned a skeptical eye on the three men. "Tell me what?"

"That we've received more information from the crime lab in Albuquerque," Jess stated.

Isabella watched Ross's eyes widen and realized he was just as surprised as she was about this new development. And what did it mean, she wondered. Did they have evidence against someone else in the family?

Her heart beating fearfully, she glanced at him, then over to the trio of lawmen.

"You're talking about the John Doe case now?" Ross asked.

Jess nodded, Sheriff Perez took a seat at the table, and Deputy Redwing continued to study Ross with a keen eye.

Jess said, "The remains found on the ranch have now been identified and Sheriff Perez wanted to talk to you about this person."

Grabbed by this news, Ross scooted to the edge of his chair. "Talk to me? Why? Who was this man?"

The under-sheriff motioned for Deputy Redwing to read aloud the information from a sheet of paper lying in front of him.

"'The remains were that of a Noah Rider. A white male, sixty-one years of age. Last known address, Hereford, Texas.'"

Sheriff Perez added, "Jess has the idea that he's heard that name mentioned on the T Bar K before. Is it familiar to you?"

Ross was clearly stunned; his jaw fell. "Noah Rider!

Why, he was Dad's foreman! Years ago—long before Hugh or Seth and I were old enough to run things.''

''Had you or any of your family been in contact with this man?'' Perez continued to question.

Ross glanced at Isabella then back to the sheriff. ''I can't speak for Victoria or Seth, but I haven't even thought of the man in a long while, much less been in contact with him. We were all just small children when Noah worked on the ranch. But we all liked him. He used to make little trinkets for us out of pieces of leather or wood. And once he talked Dad into buying an Appaloosa gelding for Seth. And believe me, getting Dad to buy an App took some doing.''

Ross's last bit of information came very near to putting a grin on the sheriff's face. But he just as quickly seemed to remember the seriousness of the moment and continued to question, ''How long has it been since Noah Rider worked on the T Bar K?''

Ross shook his head. ''I don't remember exactly when he left the ranch. All I can tell you is that it's been many years.'' He looked at Jess. ''Did you ask Victoria? She might remember.''

Jess frowned. ''Since I wasn't sure what connection this man might have been to your family, I wanted to talk to you before I broke the news to Victoria. She's…been pretty upset about this whole thing. But we'll speak to her this morning—as soon as she can make time between patients. Maybe she can give us some answers,'' Jess said hopefully.

It was obvious to Isabella that Jess was concerned about his new wife and wanted to protect her from any unnecessary grief or worry. Isabella could understand the lawman's feelings. She'd been experiencing the same protective concern for Ross. This was a somewhat normal feeling for a lawyer toward a client, but deep down Isabella had to admit that her desire to shield Ross had more to do with her heart than with any legal obligation—which only proved that she was sinking into a mire from which she couldn't climb out.

Still clearly stunned over the news of the old foreman's death, Ross took off his hat and scraped a hand through his dark hair.

"Noah Rider murdered. And on the T Bar K, at that. It's unbelievable." He looked around at the four other people in the room as though they could give him some answers. "What could he have been doing on the ranch?"

"If we knew that," Jess told him, "we'd probably have the killer behind bars before the sun set this evening. Right now we've got to find more pieces of the puzzle if we ever expect to see the whole picture."

Fifteen minutes later Isabella and Ross walked out of the sheriff's office and straight to Ross's pickup truck, which was parked on a street adjacent to the side of the brick building.

The sun was bright in a cloudless blue sky and Isabella realized the weather couldn't have been more beautiful on this summer day. And yet she felt chilled to the bone by all she'd heard in the sheriff's office. A killer was out there somewhere and she couldn't help but think that Ross might be his next intended victim.

Once they'd climbed into the vehicle, Ross stuck the key in the ignition, but made no move to start the engine. Instead, he looked over at Isabella, his expression dazed.

"Noah Rider. Killed on the ranch. My ranch!" He shook his head, still unable to accept the fact. "I just can't get over it. All along I'd been figuring the John Doe was just some transient, some stranger who'd met an untimely death by accident. But then the incident was declared a homicide.

And now I'm told the victim is an old acquaintance. Someone who once worked for my family! Hellfire, what's going to happen next?"

The distraught look on Ross's face prompted Isabella to lean across the seat and touch his arm.

"I'm so sorry about Noah Rider," she said gently. "It can't be easy to hear that an old friend has been murdered."

He heaved out a breath. "It's shocking, Isabella. The entire circumstances surrounding this incident are incredible." He glanced at her anxiously. "Do you think the person who shot at Jess is the same person who murdered Noah?"

She settled back in the seat and snapped on the seat belt. "I could only speculate, Ross. But one thing is obvious to me," she said grimly. "If they are the same person, then there's a killer among you on the T Bar K."

For the first time since she'd met Ross, a look of real concern crossed his face and she felt her own fears rise up to prickle her skin and cause her to grip the handbag in her lap.

"God help us," he murmured, then, starting the engine, he backed onto the street and headed the truck toward the ranch.

Throughout the drive, Ross said very little and Isabella didn't urge him to talk. She understood his head was reeling with the new developments he'd just been given at the sheriff's office. As for Isabella, she had her own things to think about.

The threat of Ross being arrested was more or less over. Legally, he didn't need her any longer. She could pack up her things and head to Dulce. Her mother would be relieved and happy to see her again. And she could finally begin to get the house she had rented in living order. But none of those things held quite the appeal they'd once had.

Once had! Why didn't she just admit it? she scolded herself. Those things were all she'd thought about, all she'd dreamed and wanted for the past ten years. Now a few days with Ross Ketchum had come along and changed her.

The realization sent a different kind of fear rumbling through her like a freight train with no brakes. She couldn't let herself fall for this man! He was a confirmed bachelor. To him, a woman was entertainment, a pleasant diversion and nothing more. If she fell in love with him, she'd be making the same horrible mistake her mother had made with Winston!

No, the best thing Isabella could do now was wind up this job as quickly as she could and head to the reservation where she belonged. It didn't matter that the crimes committed here on the ranch were still unsolved. She wasn't a law officer. She wasn't a detective. He could hire a better person for the job.

By the time they arrived back at the T Bar K, Isabella had decided to tell Ross immediately that she would be leaving the ranch tomorrow. The thought saddened her deeply, which only proved even more that it was high time she ended her stay here at Ross's home.

At the back of the house, Ross parked the truck. As they walked onto the porch to enter the kitchen, Isabella started to speak at the same time he caught her by the arm. The sudden contact of his fingers caused her senses to go on high alert.

"Bella, before we go in, I want to talk to you a moment."

She'd been so preoccupied with how she was going to tell Ross of her plans that the serious tone of his voice didn't register, until she looked up at him. Then her heart began to bang against her ribs. Something was on his mind.

And from the way he was looking at her she was beginning to believe that she might be that very something.

In a small voice, she said, "I—I want to talk to you, too."

His brows drew together. "About what?" he asked.

Shaking her head, she wondered why her breathing seemed to go haywire every time he touched her. Why just looking up at his face made her tremble with a yearning that threatened to consume her common sense. No man had ever made her feel so wanton, so much a woman.

"No," she finally managed to say. "You go first."

He drew her aside, to a spot on the porch shaded by the nearby branches of a cottonwood. As Isabella waited for him to talk, she watched the mottled light dance over his rugged features. He was so vibrant, so utterly male. His presence was so powerful she couldn't imagine the world without him in it. And yet a part of her understood he wasn't invincible. If someone wanted to kill him...

She inwardly shuddered and tried to focus her mind on what he was about to say.

"What is it you wanted to say, Ross?"

His green eyes suddenly grew as soft and tender as the spring grass sprouting beneath a snowbank. Isabella felt her heart quicken in response.

"I just wanted to tell you...how grateful I am to you. For sticking up for me in the sheriff's office."

Isabella's throat grew tight as a gentle tide of emotions ebbed over her heart. Maybe this man did respect and appreciate her in his own way. "That's my job, Ross."

His green eyes fell sheepishly to the toes of his boots. "Yeah. I know it's your job. But I'm difficult to deal with. You don't have to tell me that."

Surprised at his sudden display of humility, she said,

"You're a man who's accustomed to speaking for himself. I understand that, Ross."

He looked up at her then and smiled a crooked smile. "That's right. How did you figure that out?"

Isabella's heart turned over as his hand slid down her arm, then latched on to her hand.

"That's my job, too," she said thickly. "To know my client's way of thinking."

My client. Is that the way she thought of him? Ross silently wondered. To him, they were so much more. Especially since those reckless kisses they'd shared at the secret meadow. Since then, he'd spent most of his waking hours aching to touch her, make love to her. And the fact that he couldn't only made the wanting worse.

The sensual thoughts brought a smoky shadow to his eyes as they searched her lovely features. "Then maybe you can tell me what I'm thinking right now," he dared.

Shaken by the intimate look on his face, Isabella's eyes quickly darted to a spot in the yard. "I—uh—can't read every thought. Maybe you'd better tell me."

The tightening of his fingers over hers brought Isabella's gaze back around to his.

"I'm thinking how very glad I am that you decided to take this case," he said.

Up until now she'd believed he was nothing but rawhide. Now she was seeing for herself that he had some feelings beneath his tough exterior. And that was going to make it much harder for her to keep her heart distanced from this man, eventually to tell him goodbye.

"I haven't done all that much, Ross," she countered.

He shook his head. "The sheriff has backed off. I can breathe a sigh of relief."

And I can go home. But I don't want to. I don't want to leave this man.

She tried to ignore the little voice in her head. Or were the words really coming from her heart? Dear God, if that was the case, then she was stumbling, falling into the same trap as her mother had fallen into.

Drawing in a deep breath, she said, "I can't take credit for that. Sheriff Perez is a smart man. He doesn't believe you've committed any crime and he doesn't want to waste San Juan County's time and money trying to prosecute the wrong person. Plus, he doesn't seem the type that would ever want to accuse a person he believed to be innocent."

Ross didn't make any sort of reply and Isabella was surprised by the troubled frown wrinkling his face. "So what's the matter?" she asked. "You just said you could breathe a sigh of relief. Is something else worrying you?"

"A whole lot is worrying me, Bella. None of this is over. Oh, sure, the sheriff's department no longer considers me a suspect, but a lot of people around here still do."

Puzzled by his comment, she shook her head. "Ross, I thought you didn't care what people thought. You told me that knowing you were innocent was all that really mattered to you."

He squeezed her hand, then with a sigh, he dropped it and turned to face the piney bluff rising up some thirty feet away from the house. His shoulders were tense and she realized that he was carrying a great weight and probably had been ever since his father had died and left him in charge of the ranch.

"I did think that way, Bella. I believed it didn't matter about the gossip—what people were saying behind my back—my sister's back. But it does. My father was a hell of a man. Some people considered him an outlaw and others hated him because he was tough, hard-working and disciplined enough to make this place into something big. But to me he was a loving father and the T Bar K was his legacy to us children. I can't stand by and let this murder thing tear it all down.''

Isabella was touched by the resolution in his voice and the devotion he felt for his family. And she wondered how different things might have been in her own life if she'd had a father like Tucker, a brother who cared that he had a sister, a mother, a heritage of proud Apache blood.

Stepping to his side, she asked, ''What do you mean, tear it down?''

She watched his nostrils flare as he drew in a deep, weary breath.

''I hadn't said anything to you before.'' He shrugged as his eyes settled on her face. ''In fact, I haven't said anything to Victoria or Linc or anybody about this. But the ranch is beginning to suffer.''

Her brows drew together. Had she heard him right? ''Suffer? It appears to be thriving to me.''

''Oh, it is thriving. As far as the cattle and horse crop goes. But the T Bar K makes most of its money through private sales to ranchers both in and out of state. In the past couple of months, sales have dropped like a rock in a bucket of water. No one wants to do business with a ranch that's under a murder suspicion.''

Her heart ached for him. ''I didn't know. I've been so busy concerning myself over the legal part of things that I hadn't stopped to think how all of this might be affecting the ranch. And you never said anything. You've acted as though everything was going along normally.''

He grimaced. ''I didn't want to alarm Victoria. Or Linc. But Linc has already guessed what's happening. When horse buyers quit asking to see the stock, he pretty much knew something was wrong. As for me—well, I guess for a while there I didn't want to admit that something like this could touch me.''

Yes, she could remember back to the first day she'd met him. She'd gotten the impression he didn't need or want anyone's help. From his attitude that day, he'd seemed to be a man without a care. Obviously he'd been hiding a few things, Isabella thought.

She said, "I guess a lot of people don't believe in our judicial system. That everyone is innocent until proven guilty. Instead, they choose to believe gossip. But I really don't think this will last for long, Ross. Especially when they see that you're not being arrested or accused of shooting Jess."

He took off his hat and ran a hand through his dark, wavy hair. "It can't last long. Otherwise, we'll be working in the red. Since Hugh died and I took over the reins, that's never happened." He tugged his hat back on his head, then reached for both her hands. Once he was holding them tightly, he said, "That's why I'm so glad you're here, Bella. You can get to the bottom of this."

Her heart sank. He believed she was going to stay on and investigate this case. How could she tell him she had to leave? Especially now that he'd expressed how much he needed her?

"Ross I'm not a detective or a private investigator. And that's what you need now. Not a lawyer."

"You're an Apache. You have special tracking skills."

She made a noise somewhere between a laugh and a groan. "I'm only half Apache, remember? I couldn't track a bear in a snowstorm."

"You'd never make me believe that," he said, then tugged her toward the door. "Now come on and let's see if Marina has lunch ready. I've got to go to work."

Isabella didn't argue. Her heart just wasn't in it. And that was the whole problem. She'd gone from being attracted to the man, to liking then to caring for him. Which only enforced the fact that she needed to leave this place.

Ross opened the door leading into the house and gestured for her to pass in front of him, but the moment she started to step over the threshold, his hand came down on her shoulder. She paused to look up at him.

"I'm sorry, Isabella. You said you wanted to talk to me about something. What was it?"

Tell him now, Isabella. Tell him you've got to go.

The little voice in her head was firm. But it couldn't match the warm, needy feeling she got when she looked into his eyes.

"Uh—I was just going to—ask you a few things about Noah Rider. But we'll do that tonight. After supper."

He gave her a slow grin. "I'll try not to be late."

Chapter Eight

To Ross and Isabella's surprise, Jess, Victoria and their three-year-old daughter, Katrina, showed up just as Marina was about to serve the evening meal. The cook quickly added three more place settings to the table.

Isabella had already learned that Katrina was a child from Jess's previous marriage, but from the close interplay between Victoria and the toddler, anyone would have thought they were actual mother and daughter.

With the five of them gathered around the table, Isabella watched as Victoria filled the child's plate, and she could only think how lucky Ross's sister was to have a husband who obviously adored her and a child to call her own. A ready-made family.

For years now, Isabella hadn't been able to imagine herself with any kind of family. Oh, sometimes she'd dream that some bronze brave would come along and fall madly in love with her and she with him. And that the two of them would live the rest of their days together on the reservation, raising their children among their own people. But those dreams had been more fantasizing than anything.

In real life, she'd not been able to actually picture herself giving her heart, her trust to any man. She'd tried with Brett and she'd come close. But now she thanked her lucky stars that she'd not been deeply and profoundly in love with him. At least her heart, if not her ego, was still intact. She'd made a lucky escape. So why, all of a sudden, had she started envisioning herself as a wife and mother?

She didn't answer the question running through her mind. But then she didn't have to. Her eyes did it for her as they settled on Ross's face.

"I don't know about you, Ross, but when Jess told me about Noah this morning, I was shocked," Victoria was saying. "It's probably been twenty years or more since he left the ranch."

Realizing talk around the table had turned to Noah Rider, Isabella mentally shook herself and perked her ears.

"Yeah. I've been thinking the same thing, Sis. What would Noah be doing back here on the T Bar K? Especially now that Dad is gone."

Isabella looked thoughtfully from brother to sister. It was obvious that the two of them were equally perplexed about this new development.

"Could be the man didn't know Tucker had passed away," Isabella suggested.

"That's true," Jess spoke up. "Or he could have been coming to the ranch to see you kids."

Victoria glanced at her husband. "I thought that same thing, too, honey. But wouldn't you think he would have called ahead of time to make sure we'd be here?"

"We don't know that Noah was coming here," Ross

argued. "Could be he just happened to be in the area when he met up with whoever it was that killed him."

Victoria snorted. "Ross, that is plain stupid. This ranch is the only connection Noah Rider had in this area. And someone killed him because of it. His body was found on the T Bar K. Remember?"

Isabella cast a covert glance at Ross and wondered if he was thinking the same thing as she. Once news of Noah Rider got out, cattle and horse buyers might actually be afraid to come to the ranch to do business with Ross. The mystery of the man's murder had to be solved, all right. But she wasn't the one to do it. Maybe she had promised to try and find Jess's shooter, but that was before she realized she was headed straight for heartache.

Ross waved his empty fork at his sister. "Okay, so you're probably right. But it doesn't make sense, Sis. Why would anyone want to kill Noah? As far as I can remember, he was a quiet, easygoing guy. I can't think of anyone who didn't like him."

Victoria's expression turned thoughtful as she studied her brother's face. "You're right about that. I remember Daddy being upset when Noah quit his job here and left the ranch. In fact, I overheard him telling Mother that he was losing the best foreman he'd ever had."

Caught up in the mystery, Isabella spoke up, "Did Noah have a family?"

Brother and sister exchanged questioning looks.

"No," Ross answered. "He didn't have any wife or kids around here."

Victoria backed that up with an emphatic nod. "I don't remember any, either. I'm not even sure he had much family anywhere. He must have had some sort of family at one time, but how would we find them?"

Jess paused in the act of shoveling a bite of food into

his mouth. "So far the only thing we've been able to ascertain is that he lived in Hereford, Texas. Sheriff Perez is sending Redwing down there to search Noah's place. If there's any information there to be found, he'll find it."

"Well, in the meantime," Ross said, "the least we can do is give him a nice burial." He cast an inquiring look at Jess. "Can we do that?"

"If there's no family around to take care of things, I don't see why not. I'll find out if the remains have been released."

As the group went on to finish the meal, Ross and Victoria discussed the type of memorial service to give Noah Rider. Eventually dessert and coffee were passed around. After it was consumed, the men left the table to walk down to the horse barn, where Linc was sitting up with a foaling mare.

Once the men had disappeared from the kitchen, Victoria asked Isabella if she would mind helping her clear away the dirty dishes.

"I know Marina normally cleans everything up before she begins breakfast each morning," Victoria said, "but Jess and Katrina and I caused a much bigger mess. I don't want to leave all this for her to have to deal with."

"Oh, I wouldn't mind at all," Isabella said gladly. "So far Ross has insisted I stay out of the kitchen and I've been feeling guilty about causing Marina extra work around here. I'm glad to have the chance finally to do something for her."

Across the table, Katrina was still strapped in a portable high chair that Victoria had brought with them. As the youngster banged a fork on the tray in front of her, Isabella tried to hide an amused smile.

"Want more cake, Tori!" the child demanded. "More cake!"

Winking at Isabella, Victoria walked over to her daughter.

"More cake?" she asked with exaggerated dismay. "You've already had one big piece."

The little golden-haired tot wrinkled up her nose at her new mother. "It's good, Tori."

Isabella chuckled. "If you ask me, that's reason enough."

Victoria shared a quick grin with Isabella before she turned her attention back to Katrina. "All right. Since you ate all your chicken and vegetables, you can have a second piece of cake. But we're going to have to watch all this eating you're doing or you'll soon be growing taller than your daddy."

The little girl giggled loudly and Isabella was instantly struck by the musical sound. Except for seeing her god-mother's grandchildren on occasion, she hadn't been around babies or children all that much. She hadn't realized how much life one small girl could bring to a room or how special it was to see the joy and sparkle on her mischievous little face.

"Katrina is adorable," Isabella told Victoria as the two women carried dirty dishes to the cabinet counter. "You must be crazy about her."

Victoria's soft laugh bubbled with love. "She's a hand-ful. But I couldn't love her more. We hope we can give her a brother or sister soon." She cast Isabella a sidelong glance. "Do you want children? Or is that a stupid question since you're not married yet?"

Isabella shrugged as she tried to imagine herself caring for a child. A child with dark hair and laughing green eyes.

"Oh, I...suppose I'd like to be a mother. Someday. But I'm not sure I'd be very good at it. I never had any younger siblings. And I don't know very much about children."

Victoria waved away her words as she opened up the door to the dishwasher. "Believe me, you learn fast, Bella. I didn't have the luxury of learning as my baby grew, like a normal mother does. When Jess and I were married a month ago, I was thrown into instant motherhood."

"Yes. But you're a doctor," Isabella rationalized. "It couldn't have been all that hard for you to step into the role."

Victoria accepted the dirty plates Isabella handed her.

"Caring medically for a child is only a small part of it, Bella. And that doesn't come from being a doctor. It's just…maternal instinct, I suppose. Something I'm sure you'll have plenty of when the time comes for you to raise your own children."

Her heart wincing, Isabella glanced away from Victoria's smiling face. "Well, there's no need for me to worry about that now," she said. "It will be a long time before I have a family. I…have a career to get going first. And anyway, I'd have to find the right man before I could ever think about being a mother."

Rising up from the dishwasher, Victoria plugged the nearby sink and began to fill it with hot, soapy water for cleaning the counters.

"Speaking of men," she said, "Jess told me you really stuck up for Ross this morning at the sheriff's office."

Isabella blushed. "Jess and the other two law officials with him must have thought I was some radical idiot or something. I laid into them before they had a chance to tell us what the meeting was about. I'd just assumed they were planning to interrogate Ross again. I never dreamed they had information about the John Doe."

Victoria stopped what she was doing and turned to Isabella. As she leaned her hip against the cabinet counter, she said, "That part of it doesn't matter. What matters is that you were determined not to let anything bad happen to my brother. And I think that's wonderful.''

Victoria's praise brought another self-conscious blush to Isabella's cheeks. ''As I told Ross, that's what a lawyer's job is—defending her client.''

Victoria smiled slyly. ''Yes, but you've gone the extra mile by staying here on the ranch and trying to figure out who really tried to kill Jess. That means a lot to Ross, Bella. And to me and Jess, too.''

Unable to meet the other woman's gaze, Isabella walked over to the table and picked up a few more dirty dishes.

''You're giving me too much credit, Victoria. And I—'' She paused, a tea glass in her hand, as the rest of her words refused to come.

''Bella? Is something wrong?''

Victoria's questions brought Isabella's head around and with a heavy heart she looked at Ross's sister. The Ketchums had welcomed her into their home. And tonight, with the bunch of them sitting around the dining table, Isabella had been filled with a sense of belonging, of being embraced in something big and warm and loving. But she wasn't a part of their family and she had to remember that.

''No. I'm fine. I was just thinking—'' What was wrong with her? she wondered desperately. She couldn't even tell Victoria that she was leaving the ranch. The whole idea simply hurt too much. ''I was thinking about who might have been out there shooting at you and Jess that evening.''

Dark conviction suddenly gripped Victoria's features. ''None of us will rest until we find him,'' she assured Isabella. ''And that also goes for the person who killed Noah Rider.''

The next morning after breakfast, Isabella still couldn't bring herself to walk down to the barns, find Ross and tell him that she needed to leave the ranch. Instead, she decided to try to put the whole problem out of her mind for a few hours and drive up to the Jicarilla to see her mother.

The moment she pulled to a stop in front of Alona's house, she chided herself for not calling before making the trip. Her mother's pickup truck was gone from its usual parking spot. And since Alona sometimes filled in at the health clinic for nurse's-aides who needed a day off, she might not return home until late this evening.

Deciding it wouldn't do much good to hang around waiting, Isabella scratched down a short note on a small piece of paper and attached it to the screen door with a bobby pin. Before she climbed back into her car, she took a few moments to pet Duke and assure the dog she would stay longer the next time she visited.

As she drove away, she realized that she was disappointed. She'd wanted to see her mother. Not that she would have necessarily aired her troubled feelings to Alona. She'd simply needed to see the person who was always there for her, who would continue to be there for her no matter what.

A mile down the road, she decided the next best thing to seeing her mother would be to drive across to the other side of the reservation to visit her godmother Naomi.

The fifteen-minute drive over a bumpy dirt road wasn't done in vain. Naomi was home and met Isabella on the doorstep of her adobe house. The old woman was dressed traditionally in a long, colorful skirt topped with a long-sleeved green velvet blouse. Her silver braids hung from both sides of her head all the way to her waist. The happy smile on her face exposed a gap where the bridge for a missing eyetooth should have been.

Isabella smiled back at her.

''I'm so glad to see you, my daughter,'' Naomi said as

she gave Isabella a tight hug. "Come in out of the heat and tell me what this visit is about."

Isabella followed the woman into the small, crudely built house. The thick adobe walls had been built centuries ago and shielded the sparse interior from the June heat. As Isabella took a seat on a faded couch, she noticed the room was pleasantly cool.

"This visit isn't about anything special," Isabella told her godmother. "I drove up here to see Mother and she was gone. So I thought I'd stop by here before I headed back to the ranch."

Naomi settled her short, rounded form into a nearby chair and studied Isabella with black eyes. "I notice you say 'the ranch' like it was your home."

The comment brought Isabella up short. Had she said it that way? Surely not. Even though she'd been enjoying her stay on the T Bar K, she hadn't been thinking of it as her home, she mentally argued. Her home was here on the Jicarilla, not on a white man's ranch. Especially a white man who never planned to marry any woman.

"You're only hearing what you want to hear," Isabella told her.

Naomi smiled with gentle patience.

Isabella sighed. "Do you know where Mother is?"

"Working at the clinic. I talked to her yesterday and she told me she would be gone today."

"I should have called first," Isabella said with a grimace. Normally she had more forethought. But in actuality, she hadn't thought of calling. Her mind had been consumed with Ross and how to tell him that her stay on the ranch had to end. She'd been hoping a visit with her mother would put everything in the right perspective and she'd go back to the T Bar K assured that she was doing the right thing.

"And you were anxious to see her," Naomi stated.

Even though Isabella was long accustomed to Naomi's uncanny perception, it was always a little disconcerting to have the woman reading her thoughts. Marina and the old Apache would make quite a pair if the two women ever got together, Isabella thought wryly.

"Well, it's been a few days since we talked and I thought I'd surprise her with a little visit."

Naomi nodded. "How is the work coming on your office building?"

Isabella was glad the old house was dim and her godmother couldn't see the blush on her face. "I don't know. I haven't driven into town yet. I'll do that when I leave here."

The old woman peered at her. "Maybe you're not so excited about starting your law practice."

Frowning, Isabella made a helpless gesture with her hand. "Of course I'm excited about it. I've just been very busy with this case for the Ketchum family."

Naomi rested her hands on the arm of the chair and Isabella noticed she was still wearing the silver wedding band her late husband had given her more than half a century ago. It didn't matter that he'd been gone from this earth for years now. In Naomi's heart she was still married.

"And how is that going?" Naomi asked.

Isabella paused. Naomi had always been her confidante, sometimes even more so than her mother. But today she found herself reluctant to talk about Ross or the ranch and his family. Maybe that was because she was afraid Naomi would read what was in her heart. And she didn't want to worry her godmother with fears that she was going to make some of the same mistakes as Alona had made with Winston Jones.

"It's—going well. The law has pretty much decided that

Ross is innocent of the shooting. So there's no longer any danger of him being arrested."

The old woman's brows peaked with interest. "Then why are you still there?"

Isabella had been asking herself that same question over and over for the past twenty-four hours. And the only answer she could come up with was that she was a fool. A sucker for a man with dark hair and laughing green eyes.

"Well, Ross has asked me to stay on—to try to help the family find out who nearly killed his brother-in-law. And I promised him that I would."

Naomi studied her for long moments. "You're having doubts. Doubts that are making you sad."

The sight of her godmother's wise face caused something to suddenly break inside Isabella and all the feelings she'd been bottling up the past few days came out in one miserable groan.

"Oh, Naomi. I think—" Shaking her head, she rose from the couch and went over to her godmother, lowering herself to the floor at Naomi's feet and resting her cheek on the older woman's knee. "I've done something foolish. I've fallen in love with a rich white man. A man who doesn't want a wife."

Naomi's bony hand smoothed short, tender strokes over Isabella's black hair. "You've not done anything foolish, my daughter. You've looked upon the one you want for your mate. When that happens, you can't change it."

Troubled even more by Naomi's observation, Isabella lifted her head and stared miserably at her godmother. "But I have to change it, Naomi! Ross doesn't want to marry. Ever. And I could never lie with him—" she paused as her voice quivered, then with a hard swallow, she finished "—unless he was my husband."

Naomi closed her eyes and continued to stroke Isabella's

hair. "Your mother's pain has become yours and that is bad. You need to drive the pain away and trust your heart. This man will not be like Winston Jones."

Naomi might possess a sixth sense about a lot of things, but she couldn't know about Ross. She'd never met the man.

"He only wants me, Naomi. He doesn't love me."

The older woman smiled. "Sometimes a man cannot separate the two. Maybe if you told him how you felt it would help him understand himself."

Isabella shot to her feet. "No! Never! That would only make a bigger mess of things! I—I'd better go."

She hurried toward the door, but her godmother was spry on her feet and she caught Isabella by both hands and held them in a tight grip.

"What are you going to do, my daughter?"

Isabella shook her head. "I—I don't know," she answered miserably. "I promised Ross to finish the job, but—"

Isabella's words halted as Naomi's dark eyes suddenly took on a blank, haunted look.

"Naomi? Is something wrong?"

The woman shook her head and refocused her attention on Isabella's face. "As I held your hands I saw a knife," she said with dismay. "Cutting."

Apprehension shivered through Isabella. "Cutting what?"

Naomi shook her head once again. "I'm not sure."

"Who was doing the cutting?"

"I don't know that, either," Naomi said with regret.

Isabella did her best to smile and put her godmother's ominous vision into a better light.

"I'm sure you were envisioning someone cutting your

birthday cake. You'll be turning seventy-six in a few days.''

''Yes, you're probably right,'' she mumbled absently.

From the troubled frown on Naomi's face, Isabella could see that the image her godmother had experienced had nothing to do with a birthday celebration. And when Naomi pulled her into a tight hug, she said, ''Be very careful, my daughter and say your prayers to the Great Spirit. You've been living among danger.''

Naomi didn't have to tell Isabella that. From the very moment she'd walked onto the ranch, she'd been in danger of losing her heart to Ross. As far as Isabella was concerned, any other kind of danger was insignificant.

Isabella quickly exchanged goodbyes with Naomi, then climbed into her car and drove away from the old adobe house. Once she reached the main highway that headed toward Dulce or south to the T Bar K, she decided not to drive into town to see what progress the carpenters had made on her new office. At this moment the building didn't feel all that important to Isabella. Not nearly as important as getting back to the ranch.

As it turned out, Isabella didn't get to discuss anything with Ross that evening at supper. He sent word to the house that Linc was having trouble with another foaling mare and he would be staying down at the horse barn to help his cousin through most of the night.

Isabella went to bed early, plagued by the fact that a few hours without Ross's company left her feeling far more lonely and restless than it should have. For hours she lay awake, staring into the darkness, asking herself what she should do. Head home to the Jicarilla? Or stay and let herself fall a little bit more in love with Ross Ketchum?

Chapter Nine

When Isabella woke the next morning, she immediately climbed out of bed and walked over to the sliding glass doors, certain she would see that a rainstorm had swept through the area. But instead the red ground beyond the doors was dry and the early sun was rising in a clear sky.

The scene put a puzzling crease in the middle of Isabella's forehead and she reached up and rubbed the tiny frown with her fingertips. She would have sworn she'd stirred in her sleep to see lightning crackling over the mesa. Or had that been a part of her dream?

For long moments she stood there in her nightgown, staring out at the distant mountains as she tried to catch and hold the fragments of her dreams. None of the fleeting images were clear. Except for a fractured glimpse of galloping horses coupled with the urgent sense that Ross was calling to her for help.

Concerned that her nightmares might be some sign of

warning, she tried to shake the uneasiness away. She was getting worse than Naomi, she scolded herself as she reached for her robe. What she needed was hot coffee and a couple of Marina's homemade tortillas.

Moments later, she walked into the kitchen and came to an abrupt halt. Ross was sitting at the table, eating from a plate filled with bacon and scrambled eggs covered with ranchero sauce.

She'd never seen him in the house this late in the morning and the surprise of finding him here must have shown on her face because he chuckled and motioned to the chair at his left elbow.

"Come on and sit down, Bella. I'm not a ghost."

She pushed a hand through her tangled hair while thinking how pale and disheveled she must look to him. She hadn't even taken time to run a brush through her hair and her robe and gown were thin silk. Not the sort of fabric to hide one's nakedness. But she was already here in the room with him and there was nothing she could do about it now, except sit down and hope he didn't notice.

"Good morning, Ross."

"Good morning, yourself. Want Marina to cook you some breakfast?"

Isabella glanced around for Marina and found the woman was nowhere in sight.

"She's gone to the laundry room," Ross answered her unspoken question.

"Oh. Well, Marina never cooks my breakfast anyway. I usually just warm up a tortilla or two."

While she went to the cabinet and poured herself a cup of coffee, Ross clicked his tongue with disapproval. "That's not enough food for a bird. And surely not enough to start your day."

She carried the coffee over to the table and Ross immediately got up to help her into her chair. She murmured her thanks and for a moment he lingered behind her chair, his fingers playing with a strand of her hair.

"You're welcome, Bella."

The low spoken words were more like a caress and heat rushed to her cheeks as she thought about his big hands moving over her face, her throat and breasts. That day at the meadow his hands had scorched her and yet he'd touched her with a tender reverence she would have never expected. She'd not been able to forget that. Not for even one moment.

"You're—uh—getting a late start this morning, aren't you?"

Clearing his throat, Ross returned to his chair and picked up his fork, although the desire for food had left him the moment Isabella had walked into the room in her scarlet silk and bare feet. It was obvious she'd just gotten out of bed. Her eyes were still a bit puffy, her face bare of makeup, her black hair tangled around her shoulders. She looked earthy and sexier than hell. Not to mention beautiful. The chance to see her like this, with her hair down, so to speak, was definitely worth a few hours of missed work.

"I didn't get to bed until two. So I took the liberty of sleeping a bit later this morning," he told her.

For a man who'd gotten only a few hours of sleep, he looked fresh and alert. His dark hair was damp and fell in reckless curls across his forehead. His jaw was newly shaven and emitted the faint scent of tangy spices. He was the most masculine thing she'd ever seen in her life and just looking at him made her feel small and womanly.

Glancing from him, she sipped her coffee. "How is the mare? Did she finally foal?"

"Yes. About one this morning. A little colt. Black with a stripe on his face. He's going to be a dandy."

The smile she heard in his words brought her eyes back to his face and the sight of his joy over the colt lifted her spirits.

"Maybe he'll make up for you losing Snip."

He shoveled a forkful of eggs toward his mouth. "No horse could take Snip's place. Not even Juggler. And I'm not counting him lost yet."

From what he'd told her, the stallion had been missing for two or three months now. She couldn't believe he still held out hope to get the animal back. "Then you don't think he's dead?"

"No. I think someone stole him."

The conviction in his voice had her studying him closely. "To hurt you?"

He shrugged. "Maybe. Or maybe just because he's an animal worth a lot of money."

Isabella leaned forward. "I thought you said he couldn't be sold—something about the identification tattoo in his mouth."

"I said he couldn't be sold at a public sale. Privately— well, you can always find someone willing to buy a horse like Snip without asking questions about where he came from."

"I see."

The corners of Ross's mouth tilted upward. "That mind of yours is always working, isn't it?"

No, she thought. Sometimes it was dreaming. About him. About things she shouldn't be dreaming at all. "I'm just trying to put a few facts together. That's the only way I'll ever be able to help you."

Just her being here was helping him, Ross thought. Just having the house filled with her feminine presence had made his life so much richer, so much sweeter. It didn't matter that the agony of wanting to touch her was always with him. The most important thing was that she was here where he could see her face, hear her voice and know that when he came in for the evening she would be waiting for him.

Careful, Ross. You're starting to sound like you want a wife instead of a lover.

The thought creased his forehead with a frown and he turned his attention to cleaning up the remaining food on his plate.

Sensing his withdrawal from their conversation, Isabella rose to her feet and went to the gas range where she found Marina had laid out a plate of flour tortillas and a cube of butter for her.

She had switched off the gas burner beneath the skillet and was drizzling the heated tortillas with honey when Ross left the table and walked up behind her.

"Actually, I'm glad you came to the kitchen before I left the house this morning," he murmured. "I have an invitation for you."

Her heart beating fast, she whirled around and looked at him a bit skeptically. "An invitation? For another horseback ride?"

God only knew how much he'd like to have her completely alone to himself, Ross thought. But what good would that do, when he'd made that damn pact with her to keep his hands to himself? At the time, he'd held the notion that she would eventually break and invite him into her arms and possibly even into her bed. But so far that hadn't happened, and he was beginning to wonder if all the heat he'd felt that day at the meadow had been one-sided.

"No. It's something much more refined than that. The Cattlemen's Ball is tonight and I'd like you to go with me."

Surprise parted her lips. "You mean, as your date?"

Her disbelief amused him and he chuckled softly. "I'd rather introduce you as my date than as my lawyer."

She didn't know whether to feel flattered or used. No doubt he had plenty of women who'd be eager to be his companion for the evening. But maybe he figured squiring her would give the gossips something else to discuss besides the sinister happenings on the T Bar K. Or maybe he wanted everyone to think he didn't have her hanging around the ranch because he needed a lawyer, she was simply here as one of his love interests. The thought irked her. But she knew she would go with him. No matter what his reasons.

"I'm—you took me by surprise, Ross. I had no idea this ball was coming up. You haven't mentioned it."

"That's because I forgot all about it until Victoria reminded me a couple of days ago." He grimaced. "I'm not really into these sorts of social events. But since I am a local cattleman and I'm on the board of directors, I feel obliged to attend. And I sure as hell don't want people to think I'm guilty and hiding."

"No. That wouldn't be good at all."

His expression softened as his hand came down on her shoulder. "So will you go?"

Isabella realized she was trembling inside. Not because she was going to be his date for the evening, but because he was only inches away and his hand was like a torch against her skin.

She drew in a deep breath and let it out before she was finally able to answer. "Yes. Of course I'll go. What time should I be ready?"

"The dance starts at eight. So we'd better leave the ranch by seven."

"And what do the women wear to this event?"

His eyes slid sensually up and down the thin silk covering her body. Her rigid nipples were thrust against the bright material and just the sight of them was enough to make him hard.

Unable to stop himself, he moved a step closer and slid the palm of his hand to the side of her neck. "Oh—I don't know. Soft, frilly things. It doesn't matter. You'll look beautiful in whatever you decide to wear."

As Isabella watched his eyes darken with desire, she realized her breath was getting shorter and shorter. If he didn't move away soon, she was going to do something stupid, like kiss him. And then she would be lost, truly lost. He would know just how very much she wanted him and to him that was all that mattered.

"Ross, you don't have to charm me. I've already said I'll go."

His gaze focused on her lips. "Hmm. I'm not trying to charm you. I'm trying to tell you how beautiful you are."

She groaned. "I just got out of bed. My hair isn't brushed and my face is bare. I know how I look."

His fingers slipped beneath her hair to press against the nape of her neck. Isabella wondered how much longer she would be able to stand on her wobbly knees. If he continued to touch her she was going to have to grab hold of his shirt, grab hold of *him*. And that would never do.

"The way you look makes me want to pick you up and carry you right back to bed," he suddenly whispered. "It makes me want to bare every inch of you to my sight. To worship every part of you with my lips."

Just hearing him say the words aloud was enough to send blood rushing hotly through her body. In an unconscious act of defense, she placed her palms against his chest. "Ross! Please don't say such things to me!"

He pressed his aching manhood against her hips so that she could feel just exactly what she was doing to him. The pressure bent her backwards until the knobs of the range were gouging into her back, but it was Ross's body that was in danger of burning her.

His head bent, his lips hovered close to her ear. "I have to say them, Bella. Because I've never wanted any woman the way I want you."

Wanted. He wanted her. But there'd been no mention of love. He would never love any woman, he'd told her. And she had to remember that included her.

Glancing away from his probing eyes, she bit down on her bottom lip. "Other men have wanted me, too. But they didn't get me. And neither will you. I can't play that game, Ross."

"This isn't a game, Bella. Is that what it feels like to you?"

It felt dangerous, she thought. Dangerous and yet, at the same time, wonderful. "Ross," she said thickly. "You... promised—"

His hand came up to touch her cheek. "Yeah," he said huskily, "I promised not to kiss you...make love to you. But it's costing me, Bella. And I think it's costing you, too."

Insfantly, she thought of last night and how much she'd missed him when he hadn't returned to the house. And now she wanted him so badly that her whole body was aching. He was right. Fighting the desire between them was costing her. But giving in to it would be an entirely too high a price to pay.

Swallowing at the tightness in her throat, she looked up at him. "Maybe—uh, maybe you'd better find yourself another date for the ball tonight. And...maybe you'd better find another lawyer."

Her suggestion cooled his blood and he stepped back from her. Although he kept a hand on her shoulder, as though he expected her to bolt from the ranch right then and there.

His jaw tight, he said, "No. You've already said you'd go with me. And as far as getting another lawyer, you agreed to stay here on the ranch and help me."

Had she? She didn't remember saying exactly those words. But she supposed her silence had said it for her.

Groaning at the mix of emotions swirling around her, she eased away from him and walked to the middle of the kitchen. "Ross...my being here isn't doing either one of us any good."

He walked up behind her and threaded his fingers through her long, thick hair. The simple touch melted what little resistance she was attempting to hang on to.

He said, "Let me be the judge of that."

"All right. All right," she said crossly, hating herself for caving in to him so easily. "I'll go with you to the dance. I'll stay...a few more days. But—"

He tossed up his hands. "I know. I can't touch you. I can't kiss you. I can't tell you how much I want to make love to you." His lips twisted with sarcasm. "Tell me this, Bella, am I going to be allowed to dance with you to-night?"

She looked at him, her eyes full of pain. "I'm doing this for both our sakes," she said quietly.

He shook his head. "No. You're doing this because you're afraid. Why? I know that you're an intelligent woman. You can see for yourself that I'm not another Winston Jones. Or—" he stopped, his brows lifting as his eyes searched her face. "Maybe it's not Winston Jones who's made you so jaded toward men. Maybe one of those lawyers you worked for down in Dona Ana County broke your heart and now you're taking it out on me."

Isabel couldn't stand it anymore. She jerked away from

him and hurried out of the room. Ross's long strides caught up to her just as she was stepping into her bedroom.

As his fingers caught hold of her arm, she whirled on him. "What are you doing now?" she demanded. "Haven't you said enough?"

"No. It's you who hasn't said enough."

Her lips pressed together in a hard line. "I haven't exactly heard you airing all your dirty laundry to me," she accused.

His gaze traveled over to the queen-sized bed she'd slept in, with its tumbled covers and pink, tangled sheets. It was so easy, too easy to picture her beautiful body stretched out on those sheets, shamelessly waiting for him.

"What do you want me to say?" he asked gruffly. "That I've had lots of women and I didn't give a damn about any of them?"

She went still as she stared curiously up at him. "Is that true?"

He made a sound of disgust. "I have been a bit of a playboy, I won't deny that. But there haven't been *that* many women. And I can honestly say I never led any of them on. Is that what happened to you? Some man made promises and didn't come through?"

She pulled away from him and walked over to the glass doors where she'd stood earlier this morning and tried to make sense of her dreams.

"It doesn't matter, Ross. What happened to me down in Las Cruces has nothing to do with this…well, whatever this thing is between us."

He walked over and stood just behind her left shoulder. "So something did happen?" he asked softly.

She breathed deeply and tried to gather her scattered senses. Maybe she should tell him about Brett. Maybe then he'd understand why she couldn't give her body to him.

"Nothing as earth-shattering as you're thinking," she mumbled. "I...there was a man...a law officer. And for a while I believed he honestly cared for me."

"And you cared for him?"

She could feel him inching closer and then his hand was sliding up her arm, over her shoulder and finally stopped against her cheek. Her heart beating fast, she turned her head toward him, her eyes full of pain.

"At the time I believed he might be the man I was going to spend the rest of my life with. But once our relationship moved toward something more serious it—it all fell apart."

"Why? You refused to sleep with him?"

She grimaced. "Yes. No. I mean—that wasn't the reason we parted. It was something far deeper than that." Her gaze slipped to the middle of his chest. "He...uh...he wanted me to forget that I was Apache."

Ross stared at her, certain he'd heard her wrong. "What?"

Dusky pink color filled her cheeks as her eyes darted up to his. "It sounds so—well, I've never told anyone this. Not my friends back in Dona Ana County or my mother or godmother. It was just too humiliating. They wouldn't understand—or maybe they would," she added sadly.

"I don't get it, Bella. Surely this man realized you were part Apache from the very beginning."

Her head jerked up and down. "Yes, he knew. And he acted as though it didn't matter. But later, as I began to share my dreams for the future with him, he...well, everything changed. It made him angry that I wanted to return to the Jicarilla. He said I was stupid for wanting to live where there were nothing but goats and—" she paused and swallowed at the ball of anger and embarrassment clogging her throat "—and dirty Indians. He said that if I ever expected to be his wife I would have to stay in Las Cruces and live the white man's way.''

Ross's eyes narrowed with anger. "Why, the ignorant bastard! What did he think you were going to do? Grind corn and weave baskets? Didn't he understand you were going to practice law there?''

Shrugging, she glanced away from him and out to the mesa where the morning sun was streaking the desert mountains with pinks and purples.

"He argued that I was already practicing law in Las Cruces. There wasn't any need for me to set up an office on the Jicarilla—that the tribal police never arrested anybody anyway and that all Indians who lived on the reservation could basically get away with murder.''

"Sounds like a real nice guy," he drawled in a voice full of contempt. "What did you tell him?''

Realizing she'd been holding her breath, Isabella released the stale air in her lungs and pushed a shaky hand through her tangled hair. "I told him that my Apache godmother was clairvoyant, and she had told me I would someday marry a brave man. So I knew he wasn't that man.''

Behind her, Ross smiled, glad she'd put the lowlife in his place and glad, too, that she'd not promised to marry him and compromise her heritage and her dreams. She deserved better. No, he corrected himself, she deserved the very best. A husband who would adore her...the way he adored her.

The thought brought him up short. He couldn't think about marriage! Not after the lesson he'd learned with Linda. And it would be the very same way with Isabella. She was hell-bent on practicing law on the Jicarilla. It was her dream. She wouldn't give that up for him. He'd be crazy to think she would.

Suddenly she turned and, laying her hands upon the middle of his chest, looked beseechingly up at him.

"What are you thinking, Ross? That I was wrong? That I was selfish?"

His hand came up to stroke the side of her head. "Of course I don't think that," he murmured gently.

"I suppose...I can't expect a white man to understand this drive I have...this need to help my people." The corners of her mouth turned downward. "How could I expect it when my own brother has deserted his Apache heritage and chosen money as the main priority in his life?"

She didn't want money. Nor did she want fame. In those two ways she was very unlike Linda. But there was still the fact that she would eventually be on her way to the Jicarilla and Ross would be left in the dust.

"I understand it, Bella. You feel the same thing I feel for this ranch." And for you, he wanted to add. But he couldn't say that much to her. He couldn't be like that selfish jerk back in Las Cruces and ask her to give up her dreams.

Her eyes scanned his face for long moments. "I almost believe that you do."

An empty ache suddenly filled his chest, but he smiled at her anyway.

"You're still going to the dance with me, aren't you?"

The dance? In all that had just happened between them, she'd almost forgotten about the evening ahead.

Impulsively, she rose up on tiptoes and softly kissed his cheek. "I'll be ready."

A puzzled frown on his face, he rubbed the spot her lips had touched. "What was that for?"

She smiled helplessly up at him. "I don't know. For listening to me, I guess. And for understanding."

His lips twisted. "And do you understand I'd still like to toss you onto that bed over there and make love to you?"

Her nostrils flared as heat rushed to the most intimate parts of her body. Quickly, she dropped her hands from his chest and turned away from him. "Yes. But I won't let you."

He wished he felt as strong-willed as she sounded, Ross thought wryly. Then, heading toward the door, he tossed over his shoulder.

"You'd better go make yourself some more breakfast before I try to change your mind."

Chapter Ten

Soft and frilly. Ross's description for what she should wear to the Cattlemen's Ball was hardly enough information to tell her if the event was dressy or casual.

By that afternoon, Isabella had searched through all her clothing and decided she'd better give Victoria a call just to make sure she didn't embarrass herself or Ross tonight.

"Very dressy, Bella," Victoria told her. "Mostly long gowns. You'll see a few short cocktail dresses. But for the most part it's a glamour scene." She laughed softly. "If you can think of glamour around here. We're not exactly Hollywood or New York. But the women do like the chance to dress up, if you know what I mean."

"Oh, dear. I don't have those types of dresses with me. Is there someplace in Aztec I could find a dress at this late hour?"

"Why would you want to do that when there's no need? I have several dresses there at the ranch that would work,"

Victoria quickly assured her. "You're welcome to wear any of them you'd like."

Victoria's generosity took her by surprise. She'd known Ross's sister was a nice person, but she'd not expected the woman to treat her like family. The notion left her feeling both warm and sad at the same time.

"I couldn't."

"Why not? I won't be wearing them," Victoria replied.

Isabella frowned at this information. "Aren't you and Jess going tonight?"

"Yes. But I purchased another dress to wear. Those on the T Bar K have gotten…uh…a little snug."

"Oh. But what if I tear something or stain it?"

Victoria laughed. "I've done that myself a time or two. It's just a dress, Isabella. And I'd gladly give you a dozen dresses for what you're doing for my brother."

It wasn't exactly what Isabella was doing for Ross, she thought, it was what she *wanted* to do *to* him that had her worried. Her face pink even though Victoria couldn't see her, she said, "Well, if you're sure. Where do I find them?"

"Look in the closet in the bedroom next to the one you're staying in. I think Marina hung everything in there. And there are heels to match them somewhere. They might be stowed under the bed. I'm not sure. But the heels are all size seven, if that will work. And the dresses are eights."

Relief poured through Isabella. "That's perfect! I'll go look now. And thank you, Victoria."

"My pleasure, Bella..I'll see you tonight."

"Yes. Goodbye."

"Uh, Bella, just one more thing before you hang up."

"Yes?"

"I'm very glad you're going to be with Ross tonight. You're exactly what he needs."

Victoria's warm words touched her deeply. Yet she knew the woman was wrong. Ross needed a woman without inhibitions or fears. He needed a woman willing to share his bed without asking for a piece of his heart.

Emotion suddenly thickened her throat, making her voice husky. "I'll—I'll see you tonight, Victoria. And thank you."

Isabella hung up the phone before Ross's sister could say more and hurried into the bedroom adjoining hers. She found a closet full of clothes—very expensive clothes— and spent the next half hour trying to choose the most flattering dress from the dozen or so hanging on the rack.

Finally, she carried a red tulle done in a princess style and a full skirted organza in antique ivory down to the kitchen to get Marina's opinion.

The older woman was patting out tortilla dough, which she made fresh every day. Flour splotched her apron and a spot on her brown cheek. She smiled as she spotted Isabella coming into the room.

"What do you have there, *chica?*"

"Dresses for the Cattlemen's Ball tonight. Which do you think I should wear?"

Wiping her hands on her apron, Marina came over for a closer inspection of the evening gowns.

"Stand out and hold each one to you so I can see how you would look."

Isabella did as she instructed. First she held the red dress to the front of her body, then the ivory. Marina studied both garments thoughtfully, then finally pointed to the red tulle.

"That one. It makes your eyes sparkle."

Isabella smiled. "Okay. I'll go with your choice. Red is

a lucky color for an Apache. And I need all the luck I can get.''

Marina frowned at Isabella's logic. ''Now why do you need luck, *chica?* You'll be at the dance with the best looking man in San Juan County.''

Isabella's gaze dropped to her feet. ''Yes. Because I'm his lawyer and I just happen to be here. But that's okay. I need the luck for—well, everyone could use a little extra luck.''

Clearly disappointed at Isabella's attitude, Marina's head began to swing back and forth. ''*Chica,* don't you know by now that Ross loves you?''

Isabella gasped as she looked at the cook. ''Marina! Where did you get such a ridiculous idea?''

Waving a hand in the air, the older woman went back to making her tortillas. ''I have eyes. I can see for myself what's been going on around here. Ross is different since you came to the ranch.''

Of course he was different, Isabella concluded. His brother-in-law had been shot, almost fatally. He'd initially been accused of the crime, and then he'd learned an old acquaintance had been murdered on his own land.

That was more than enough to make a man behave differently. Love didn't enter into the picture. And as far as Ross was concerned, it never would.

''You'd better get those eyes of yours checked, Marina. You're seeing things that aren't really there.''

The dance was held in a large building on the outskirts of town that was used for civic affairs throughout the year.

Folding tables and chairs had been positioned at one end of the huge room, while the opposite end had been cleared for dancing on tile that had been sprinkled with cornmeal to make cowboy boots slide a little better. More metal chairs lined the walls and in one corner near the tables, a small buffet had been set up with snacks and drinks.

By the time Isabella and Ross arrived, the band was already playing a mix of old and new country tunes intermingled with popular classics. A few couples were already dancing, but Ross made no indication he was ready to join them. Instead, he took her around and introduced her to several cattlemen and their wives, who also owned ranches in the area. None of theirs would compare to the T Bar K, but Ross, she noticed, treated them all with equal respect.

She also noted that he didn't mention anything about her being his lawyer, and she wondered if he'd done that purposely because he didn't want his friends and acquaintances to think he was in need of legal defense. No. She didn't believe that was the case. Ross wasn't the sort of man to hide from anything, including gossip. The fact that they were here, mingling among the members of the local Cattlemen's association, instead of back at the T Bar K only proved that much.

"Well, here's a man who needs no introduction," Ross said with a grin that was reserved for his closest friends.

Isabella turned to see Neal Rankin walking up to them and she smiled at the handsome lawyer. "Hello, Neal."

He smiled back at her, then made a point of eyeing her from head to toe. "My, my, my," he drawled. "You look just like a piece of candy in that red dress with your hair all piled up on your head. You're just too beautiful for this little ole shindig, Bella."

She couldn't stop a thrill of pleasure from rushing through her as she felt Ross's arm slip possessively around the back of her waist.

"You're being kind, Neal," she said. "Especially when Ross didn't tell me about this dance until this morning."

Grinning slyly, Neal clicked his tongue. "Ross has never

understood women. He doesn't have a clue that you need time for preparation.''

Ross glared at him. ''Why are you here without a date?'' he asked crossly.

Neal shrugged. ''I'm just not as lucky as you, buddy. I couldn't find a date.''

''Well, if you keep flirting with mine, you're not going to be able to go to work tomorrow.''

The amused look on Neal's face said the last thing he felt was threatened. ''Speaking of work. I've noticed most of your hands have shown up tonight.''

Ross nodded. ''I encouraged them all to attend tonight. And I think everybody is here, except Linc. Another mare was showing signs of foaling and he wouldn't leave her.''

''Somebody needs to tell that guy that most mares have their babies just fine without any help,'' Neal remarked.

''Yeah. Linc handles each one of them like a queen.''

Neal inclined his head toward three young men standing near the entrance of the building. Isabella followed the direction of his gaze to see Steve, Tim and Jamie, the three T Bar K hands she'd mentally labeled as shiftless.

''It's too bad those three aren't as ambitious as Linc or Skinny. They'd be worth keeping.''

Ross frowned at his friend. ''I plan on keeping all three of them. They're just young, and each one of them came from a troubled family. They haven't really learned about work ethics yet. But I want to give them a chance. I believe they'll come around and eventually do things without having to be prodded.''

''Maybe one of them already has,'' Neal remarked.

Ross cut a sharp look at the lawyer. ''What is that supposed to mean?''

Neal glanced at Isabella as though to gauge her reaction to his comment. She raised her brows in helpless fashion.

His expression suddenly serious, Neal turned his gaze back to Ross, "Look, buddy, I know you don't want to think that any of your men tried to kill Jess and frame you. But let's face it, there were no visitors around that day on the ranch. You said so yourself."

"Angela Bowers was there for about fifteen or twenty minutes. She'd stopped by to talk to me about the fund-raising for this ball."

Isabella looked at him in surprise. "You never mentioned her being at the ranch before."

He shrugged. "I didn't think it was important. She's harmless."

Neal snorted at Ross's understatement. "Hell, I doubt Angela Bowers can ride a horse, much less shoot a rifle. She'd be afraid of breaking a fingernail. Besides, the woman thinks you walk on water. She'd hardly want to frame you for murder. No, I believe one of your men is out to harm you. And in my opinion, I wouldn't turn my back on any one of that trio standing over there by the door."

A cool shiver passed over Isabella's skin. She'd not thought of the three men in those terms. In fact, all of Ross's cowboys seemed incapable of such a heinous crime. So who did that leave as suspects? Someone who'd entered the ranch unseen? But that didn't make sense, either. The shooter had to have been at the ranch house in order to steal Ross's rifle.

"What do you think, Bella?" Ross asked her. "You believe Neal's on the right track?"

She glanced up at him and for a moment her heart was frozen with fear. If anything were to happen to him, her world would go black. It was that simple.

"I—well—" She pressed her hand to her throat as she tried to push the dark thought away. "I've noticed the

young men are a tad lazy and a bit cocky. And they tend
to run in their own little pack. But that's probably because
they're younger than the other men you have working for
you and they feel more comfortable with friends of their
own age. As far as I'm concerned, none of those traits
makes any of them a killer.''

Ross smiled at the same time Neal's lips pressed to a
grim line.

''I hope you're right, Bella,'' Neal said. ''But if one of
them isn't the shooter, then who is? One of Ross's long-
time, devoted cowhands? That's even harder for me to
swallow.''

Ross scowled at him. ''I didn't come here tonight for
this. Could you change the subject?''

The other man seemed to understand that Ross wasn't
bantering now and immediately he turned a brilliant smile
on Isabella.

''Well, Bella, since Ross is tired of hearing me talk,
would you like to dance?''

Neal had hardly gotten the words from his mouth when
Ross barked. ''Hell, no, she wouldn't. She's here to dance
with me. Go find your own partner.''

Isabella understood the exchange between the two men
was nothing more than jousting between old friends. Yet
to think Ross might feel even the tiniest bit possessive of
her, made her feel more special than she could ever remember. Especially when there was a bevy of young beau-
ties here tonight, the majority of which had their eyes on
the most eligible bachelor in the county.

''Ross! You're going to hurt his feelings,'' Isabella
scolded as he led her out onto the dance floor.

Ross chuckled under his breath. ''Hurt Neal's feelings?
The man doesn't have any.''

''You're joking, I hope.''

His hand tightened around her back as he drew the front of her up against him. "Yeah," he said, grinning down at her. "I'm joking. Neal has been my best friend since we were in kindergarten. He's more like a brother than anything."

"He's a good man," Isabella said, "But then, so are you."

His green eyes glittered down at her. "You wouldn't say that if you knew what I was feeling right now." The hand holding hers released her fingers and moved to the tiny diamond nestling between the faint cleavage exposed above the neckline of her dress. With his forefinger tracing a faint trail over her soft skin, he said, "You look so beautiful all I can think about is making love to you."

Even though the dance was a slow one, his intimate words caused her nearly to miss a step. "There are many gorgeous women here tonight," she countered.

"I've only seen one. And she's in my arms."

Her nostrils flared as she tried not to smile, but the corners of her lips tilted upward in spite of her efforts. "Oh, you are bad, Mr. Ketchum."

He chuckled. "So I've been told," he said, then as the music suddenly changed, he swung her into a waltz.

After that, the two of them danced several up-tempo dances before Isabella finally had to beg for a chance to stop and catch her breath.

Ross guided her over to the buffet of refreshments where they helped themselves to iced colas. While they were sipping their drinks, a tall young blonde with short moussed hair and a lethal black dress ambled up to them.

"Hello, Ross," she said, while casting Isabella a disinterested glance. "I've been looking all over for you."

From the corner of her eye, Isabella noticed Ross appeared to be mildly amused by the blonde's attention. As for herself, she wasn't amused at all. Not when she could see the woman was looking at him like a wolf studying a wounded lamb.

"Hello, Angela," he greeted, then quickly introduced her to Isabella.

"Angela is the one I told you about," he said to Isabella. "Her father is on the Cattlemen's board."

The woman who came to the T Bar K that day Jess was shot, Isabella thought. The one visitor he'd considered unimportant. Well, it appeared as though Neal was right. She looked too soft to be a killer. Not to mention the adoring looks she was giving Ross.

"Yes, I remember," Isabella said and politely held her hand out to the other woman. "It's nice to meet you, Angela."

The blonde gave her a limp handshake, then immediately turned to Ross and looped her arm through his.

"I'm ready for that dance you promised me," she said in a voice that Isabella could only think of as wheedling.

A tiny frown creased Ross's forehead. "Did I promise you a dance?"

The blonde giggled and whacked Ross's arm as if to punish him for joking her. "Why Ross, you're such a tease. Now come along. The band is playing a good song."

Yeah, good and slow, Isabella thought, as a wicked wave of jealousy washed through her.

Angela yanked on Ross's arm and he turned an apologetic look on Isabella. "Do you mind?"

As if it mattered, she thought again, then quickly scolded herself for having such nasty thoughts. Ross wasn't hers. He would never be hers. She might as well get used right now to the idea of him having other women in his arms.

"Go ahead. I'm going to stand here and finish my drink," she assured him.

Angela didn't waste any time leading Ross onto the dance floor and Isabella made a point of turning her attention elsewhere. But every now and then she couldn't stop herself from looking out and glimpsing the two of them as they wove their way through the other couples. The permanent smile on Angela's face made it a sure bet that Ross was saying all the right things to keep the woman infatuated.

"I guess it's just meant for Ross to get all the beautiful women."

The male voice behind Isabella startled her and she whirled to find Steve standing only a few inches away. The fact that the T Bar K hand had said anything to her was a surprise. He wasn't all that much of a talker. But then none of the other men were talkers, either, except for Skinny. Since she'd been staying on the ranch, Isabella had gotten close to the older man and when he wasn't busy, he told her stories of things that had happened on the ranch in years past.

"Hello, Steve. Are you enjoying the dance tonight?"

He glanced at her, then out to Ross and Angela as the couple continued to circle the dance floor.

"Sure am, Ms. Corrales. How about yourself? Looks like you lost your partner."

A wry smile touched Isabella's lips. "Oh, believe me, I don't have tabs on Ross."

Steve cast her a doubtful look, then as fast as a lightbulb switching on, a grin spread over his face. "Well, if that's the case, would you care to dance with me?"

She could hardly refuse without hurting the young man's feelings. And besides, what did it matter? Ross was preoccupied with the giggly blonde.

"I'd be delighted," she said and offered him her hand.

The dance with Steve must have broken the ice. Once it

was over, several more T Bar K hands came up to her with requests to whirl her around the dance floor. Isabella didn't refuse any of them and by the time the last man had led her to a chair and thanked her, Ross suddenly appeared in front of her.

"It's getting late," he said curtly. "I think we'd better go home."

Isabella stared at him as he took her by the arm and virtually lifted her out of the chair.

"Really? I was just getting warmed up."

He shot her a mocking frown. "Yes. I can see that."

Once she was on her feet, she discreetly pulled her arm from his grasp. "If that was meant in the context I think it was, then you're way out of line, Mr. Ketchum."

He glanced around at the people milling about them, then settled an accusing glare at her. "Why did you have to dance with every one of my cowhands?"

Her gray eyes widened. "Is this some sort of trick question?"

Ross's jaw tightened as his gaze slipped over her guileless expression. "You're the one who knows how to ask a trick question, not me."

She breathed deeply in an effort to stem her rising temper. "For your information, I danced with your employees because I was invited to dance. What was I supposed to do? Sit like a wallflower until you finished with your girlfriend?"

He cursed under his breath. "That was a duty thing."

The little laugh that passed her lips was totally mocking. "And what do you think my thing was?"

"Pure enjoyment."

Her brows lifted as she considered his remark. "Actually, you're right," she said coolly. "It was much nicer to have the attention of several men than to be totally ignored by one.''

He took her by the arm again and this time she didn't try to resist as he led her toward the exit of the building. There was no point in staying any longer, she thought miserably. The evening was ruined.

As they walked to Ross's truck, sadness fell over her like a heavy cloak. And throughout the trip back to the T Bar K, she remained silent and pensive.

It had been wrong of her to behave in such a jealous fashion. Actually, it had been stupid of her. She hadn't really been Ross's date in the true sense of the word. As she'd told Marina, she'd been more handy than anything. As for Ross's behavior, she was still trying to figure out his strange attitude. It shouldn't have mattered to him who she danced with. Unless he was worried about his reputation as a ladies' man. And that idea saddened her even more.

Isabella remained deep in her thoughts until the truck eventually came to a halt and Ross killed the motor. Looking around, she noticed they'd arrived at the ranch and he'd parked at the back of the ranch house.

Quickly, she reached for the door handle with the intention of getting out without his help, but then she realized she was still strapped behind the seat belt and fumbled with the snap for several moments before she finally got it to release. By that time Ross was already out of the truck and opening the door for her.

She looked down at his offered hand. ''You don't have to bother helping me out. I can manage.''

Although it was dark, there was enough light shed by a yard lamp several feet away to illuminate his face and Isabella was struck by the regret that suddenly twisted his features.

"I thought by now you'd be over being angry with me."

She stared at him, amazed that a thirty-minute drive could have transformed him from biting out accusations at her to apologizing.

"Ross, I don't understand—"

"Come down here," he said quietly as he took her hand in his.

Isabella carefully gathered up her long skirt and allowed him to assist her to the ground. Once she was standing beside him, he placed his hands on her shoulders and she looked up at him, while her heart waited and wanted him to say the things she knew she would never hear from his lips.

"I want to apologize for that…stuff I said to you back there at the dance. You were right. I was out of line. And I—well, I behaved like a jackass. But I was jealous, Bella. That's the only excuse I can give you."

Her throat tightened as emotions bombarded her from all directions. The evening had started so wonderfully and for a while she'd felt like Cinderella. She'd felt as though she belonged to Ross and he belonged to her, and that it would always be that way. Maybe it was a good thing Angela had come along and broken the spell Isabella had been under.

"Oh, Ross," she said, her voiced laced with regret. "It was just dancing."

His hands moved gently against her upper arms. "Yeah. Just dancing. But *I* wanted to be the one holding you in my arms."

"Angela—"

"Is just what I said. An obligation. Her father is on the board of directors for the local Cattlemen's association. I didn't want to insult him by slighting his daughter. And once the dance was over, I was coming straight back to you. But by then Steve had already stolen you."

She was probably a fool for letting his explanation make her feel better. After all, he was a playboy from his own admission. Yet everything inside her wanted to believe she was the woman who mattered to him. She was the only woman he desired. Dear God, what did that mean? That she was falling in love with him?

Shaken by her thoughts, she quickly glanced away from him. "It doesn't matter, Ross. And anyway—I was acting a little stupid myself."

His hands moved to her back and warmth spread from his fingers and tingled along her skin. "You mean you were a little jealous, too?"

The husky question brought her eyes back to his and she knew in that moment that she couldn't lie to him or herself. "Yes. Which was, as I said, very stupid of me."

One hand came up to the nape of her neck while the thumb and forefinger from the other hand tilted her face up to his. "I don't think it's stupid. I think it's very human," he whispered.

She felt herself melting to his touch and knew where they were heading. Yet as much as she wanted him, she couldn't let it happen. Her heart was already in trouble with this man. If she gave him her body, too, there wouldn't be anything left of her by the time she went back home to Dulce.

"I must have been out of my mind," she muttered, her voice self-deprecating. "You're not even my date. Much less my lover."

Groaning with embarrassment, she twisted away from him and covered her face with both hands. Behind her, Ross whispered, "You were my date," he countered. "And as for the lover part—we could change that right now. Tonight."

Shocked at how much she wanted to give in to his suggestion, she whirled back to him. "And then what, Ross?"

Her wide eyes desperately searched his face. "What happens after tonight is over with?"

Frustration caused him to lift his face to the starlit sky. "Damn it, why do you have to always think about tomorrow? Do you have something against living in the present?"

Isabella's lips spread to a thin line. "Living for the moment ruined my mother's life. I'm not about to make the same mistake."

His head straightened and he looked at her with mocking sarcasm. "Maybe you picked the wrong profession. Maybe you should have gone into a nunnery instead of the law."

Her heart was beating fast. Not just from the battle of their words, but because the front of his body was pressed against hers, heating every inch of her, reminding her of everything she was missing and everything she so desperately wanted.

"That's a nasty thing to say!"

His head bent downward until his face was hovering only inches from hers. "It probably is," he agreed. "But you're making me feel pretty nasty."

"Why?" she asked thickly. "Because I won't go to bed with you?"

His hands tightened against her back. "Would that be so bad? Would it ruin the rest of your life if we became lovers?"

"You don't understand," she whispered anguishedly, then groaned as his hands moved from her back to her breasts, where he cupped them in his palms and kneaded the sensitive flesh with his fingers.

"I understand all right," he said gruffly. "I understand I want you like hell. And you want me. You're just too damn stubborn to give in to it!"

There wasn't anything stubborn about it, Isabella thought

wildly. It was fear that was preventing her from flinging her arms around his neck and begging him to make love to her. Fear that, even at this moment, was beating in her throat like a trapped bird.

"Ross! I—"

He didn't give her a chance to say more. His lips came hungrily down on hers and the sudden, intimate contact caused her to moan and clutch folds of his shirt in her fists.

The coaxing movements of his lips took only seconds to persuade Isabella to close her eyes and open her mouth to him. Instantly, his tongue slipped inside and she felt herself going hot all over as an aching need built between her thighs and swelled within her breasts.

Her calves strained as she stood on tiptoe and leaned into him. Her senses whirled like the wind in a storm, yet somewhere in the back of her mind, she realized that if he didn't stop she was going to lose all control. And then nothing would matter but the burning, physical need to be his mate, his woman.

Just when she thought her knees were going to buckle and the need to breathe was going to burst her lungs, Ross broke the kiss and stared down at her.

"Do you know what I think?" he asked in a voice thickened with passion.

Dazed, she stared up at him as she struggled to regain her breath and clear the desire that was fogging her mind.

"What…what are you thinking?" she asked blankly.

His nostrils flared, his features hardened as he stepped back from her. "I think Winston Jones not only ruined your mother's life, he ruined yours, too."

His words hit her like the physical blow of a hand. For a few moments she was incapable of making any sort of reply. Then finally she opened her mouth to tell him how wrong and callous he was to twist all the fault of their situation on her. But he didn't bother to hang around and listen.

Before Isabella could utter a word, he turned away from her and quickly headed to the house. Stunned, she stared after him, until a wall of tears finally blurred her eyes and an empty ache filled the middle of her chest.

She'd been a fool for so many reasons. Now she had to decide what she was going to do about it.

Chapter Eleven

Isabella slept badly that night and tried to make up for it the next morning by drinking three cups of coffee in one sitting. This didn't do a thing to shake away her fatigue, but managed to make her nerves even jumpier than they were before.

She was thankful that Ross had left the house ages before she'd finally crawled out of bed, so at least she hadn't had to face him over the breakfast table.

She would have to face him eventually, though, and she didn't have a clue what she was going to do or say once she was in his presence. Last night, after she'd gathered herself together enough to get into the house, she'd quickly undressed and gone to bed in hopes that sleep would blot out his damning words. But her mind had been churning with all the ways he'd touched her, everything he'd said to her.

Was he right? she asked herself once again. Was she

allowing Winston's betrayal to ruin her chance for happiness? But right behind that question, she had to ask herself if going to bed with Ross would be enough to make her happy.

Of course it would. For a little while. Until his desire for her waned and his interest wandered elsewhere. Unless having a physical relationship with him made him somehow fall in love with her, made him somehow see that living with her, making a family with her, was all he really wanted out of life.

Oh get real, Isabella. The man is thirty-five years old. He's had plenty of women in and out of his bed and he's never fallen in love yet. What makes you think you'd be any different?

Because she wanted to believe she was special to him. She wanted to believe that the urgency she'd felt in his kisses wasn't just physical desire, but something far deeper.

Deciding she couldn't do any sort of work with this mental torture going on inside her head, she showered, dressed casually in a pair of denim capris and a yellow gingham shirt and headed to town with the excuse of dropping Victoria's evening gown off at the cleaners.

At the last minute, she decided to stop by the medical clinic and leave Victoria a thank-you card, just to let the doctor know how much she appreciated the use of the dress and the high heels.

Isabella was in the process of handing the card to Lois, the receptionist, when Victoria appeared from a door in the hallway and spotted Isabella in the waiting room.

Smiling with pleasure, she exclaimed, "Bella! What are you doing here? Don't tell me you're sick."

Sick at heart. That was all, Isabella thought wearily. Mustering the brightest smile she could manage for Ross's sister, she said, "Hello, Victoria. I'm fine. I just dropped by to give you a little thank-you card and to let you know I'm having the dress cleaned for you.''

''That wasn't necessary,'' Victoria gently scolded, then quickly added, ''Just a minute.'' After she pushed the manila folder she was carrying onto a shelf with several hundred others, she stepped through a door and out into the waiting room. ''Come back here,'' she urged, taking Isabella by the arm.

''Oh, no! I don't want to interrupt your work,'' Isabella whispered under her breath, so that the waiting patients behind her wouldn't hear.

''Nevada, my nurse, is setting up the next patient for an examination,'' Victoria explained. ''I have a few moments until she'll have her ready and I want to talk to you.''

''If you're sure,'' Isabella said uncertainly.

Victoria yanked on Isabella's arm, forcing her to follow the doctor down the hallway and into a brightly lit office filled with plants and books and a large, cluttered desk.

''I want to know what happened last night,'' Victoria quickly fired the request at her.

Isabella looked at her with raised brows. ''What do you mean? Nothing happened.''

Disappointment washed over Victoria's pretty face. ''Oh. I was so hoping—but then I saw this and didn't know what to think.''

The doctor turned, picked up a copy of the local newspaper and tapped her finger on a picture in the left-hand corner.

''Look at this! Ross always garners social attention wherever he goes and I guess the paper just couldn't resist snapping a photo of him last night,'' she said, handing the paper to Isabella. ''As far as I'm concerned, it's sickening.''

Isabella couldn't have described the sight any better as

she stared down at the black-and-white photo of Ross with a dreamy-eyed Angela Bowers in his arms. Just to see the image of him dancing with the woman was enough to send a fresh spurt of jealousy slicing through her.

"I thought he took you to the dance!" Victoria exclaimed.

Isabella drew in a deep breath and let it out. "He did."

Victoria rolled her eyes. "Then why was he dancing with Angela?"

"It was a duty thing, he said. Her father is on the board of directors."

Victoria groaned as if she'd never heard a more flimsy excuse in her life. Isabella was inclined to agree with her. But she wasn't going to. She didn't want Victoria, or anyone, to know how far she'd fallen for the biggest playboy in San Juan County.

"Oh, spare me. Angela is a piranha. She's been after Ross for ages. I'm sure she's going to frame that picture in gold!"

Her heart heavy, Isabella walked over and placed the paper on the corner of Victoria's desk. "Well, it doesn't matter. I didn't expect Ross to dance with me exclusively. I'm his lawyer, Victoria. Not—well, not anything else."

Victoria walked over to Isabella and placed a hand on her shoulder. "Maybe you don't think you are," she said softly. "But I've been seeing the way Ross looks at you. And I don't believe your feelings for him are all that indifferent."

Isabella was forced to clear her throat as emotions threatened to choke her. "Look, I wouldn't worry about him getting seriously involved with Angela. Ross isn't a dumb man. I'm sure he can see right through her."

"I'm not talking about Angela. I'm talking about you, and how you feel about my brother."

Isabella's gaze connected with Victoria's, then skittered awkwardly away to the other side of the room. "That doesn't matter, either. Ross is a bachelor. And I—I'm a career woman. The two don't mix."

"I'm a career woman and Jess is a lawman and we mix just fine."

Isabella gave Ross's sister a faint smile. "That's because Jess loves you."

Victoria picked up both of Isabella's hands and squeezed them tightly. "Did you ever stop to think that Ross might love you?"

Isabella's mouth fell open and she was fighting the mocking laugh bubbling up in her throat when a knock sounded on the open door leading in to Victoria's office.

Both women turned around to see Nevada, Victoria's young Hispanic nurse.

"Doctor, Mrs. Sutton is ready," she announced.

"I'll be right there," Victoria told her, then turned back to Isabella. "I wish we had more time to talk about this, but I've got to go. But before I do, I want to say that you're the first woman in Ross's life that's been good for him."

Isabella's heart winced with sadness. "I'm not sure there's a woman alive that's good for Ross," she said, then before Victoria could say more she hurried out of the room and out of the medical clinic.

To avoid running into Ross, she ate lunch at the Wagon Wheel before she finally drove back to the T Bar K. Once she got there, Marina was grumbling that no one had shown up to eat the meal she'd prepared for lunch.

"Where's Ross? Didn't he eat?" Isabella couldn't help asking.

Frowning, Marina shook her head. "He's gone today.

Him and the men are vaccinating cattle in the north meadows. He probably won't even be back for supper.''

Disappointment swallowed her up like a dark cloud.
Which didn't make sense, when she'd told herself all day
that she needed to stay away from the man.

''Oh. Then don't bother fixing anything for me, Marina.
I'll find something in the refrigerator.''

Marina shrugged as Isabella started out of the kitchen.
''Okay. I'll go home early. Before the storm hits.''

Isabella paused to look at the older woman. ''A storm?
Marina, it's clear as a bell outside.''

''Don't matter. We'll have rain tonight.''

''You've been watching the weather forecast on television?''

The woman snorted. ''Don't have to. There was a ring
around the moon last night. Didn't you see it?''

No, Isabella thought. She'd had other things on her mind.
Mainly Ross.

''I really didn't notice. And anyway, a ring around the
moon is just an indicator of rain coming in the next few
days. That doesn't mean it's going to storm.'' At least that
was what Grandfather Corrales had always told her.

Marina gave Isabella a patient smile. ''I'm going home
early just the same. I just hope Ross and the men get back
before it hits.''

Since it was still very early in the day and the weather
couldn't have been more beautiful, Isabella put Marina's
storm prediction out of her thoughts and went down to the
horse barn with a basket full of apples and carrots.

As she fed the treats to the few horses stabled there, she
didn't see anyone about the long shed row. After the visit
with her four-legged friends was finished, she walked over
to the cattle barn just to see if everyone was gone to the

north meadows, or if someone had stayed behind to watch over things here at the ranch yard.

The big barn was quiet and dim, the smell of hay and manure pungent as she walked through the maze of cattle pens situated along either wall of the building. Eventually, she found Skinny feeding two calves from bottles filled with specially prepared milk.

The old man glanced at her as she pulled up a wooden stool and took a seat a few steps away from where he was working. "What are you doin', Bella?"

"I've been feeding the horses a few apples. I came over here to see if anyone was left on the ranch."

The old cowboy's wrinkled face creased into a faint smile. "Just me. Well, that ain't exactly right," he corrected. "Cook is in the bunkhouse. And Linc is around here somewhere. He's strictly a horse man, he leaves all the cattle work to Ross."

She took a moment to digest Skinny's information. "It takes that many cowboys to do vaccinating?" she asked.

"Nope. Ross sent a couple of men to Farmington for a load of feed."

"Oh. I see," she said, then inclined her head toward the white-faced Hereford calves. Both babies were tugging on the bottles with an enthusiasm that made Isabella smile. "I haven't seen that breed here on the ranch."

"That's cause Ross don't raise Herefords, he raises Black Angus."

"Did their mothers die?"

Skinny's sun-splotched hand stroked the calf nearest to him between the ears. "Yeah. Poor little dogies. But we'll take care of 'em."

"I don't understand, Skinny. If Ross doesn't raise Herefords, what are those two orphans doing here?"

The older man chuckled. "It was sale day yesterday at

the livestock barns in Farmington. Ross always goes just to see if someone might try to slip Snip through the ring. He saw these little orphans and brought 'em home. That's just the way he is. He's got a soft heart when it comes to animals.''

But what about a woman? Isabella wondered. What about *her?* He'd made it pretty obvious that he wanted her physically. But was there anything in his heart for her that would even come close to love?

She was rubbing the frown marring her forehead, when Skinny asked, ''What's the matter, Bella? You look like you've gone a long way aways.''

Shaking away the questions pestering her mind, she focused her attention on Skinny. ''Nothing is wrong. I was just thinking.''

''You gotten any closer to figuring out who shot Jess?''

With a helpless shake of her head, she said, ''No. And I'm certainly not a detective by any means, but I've been doing a lot of thinking. And I—'' She paused, uncertain of how much she should say in front of the older man. Not that for a moment she suspected Skinny of ever doing anything to harm Ross. She knew the cowboy thought of Ross almost as his own son. But if he inadvertently said something to the other men about her snooping, it might not be so good.

Skinny didn't prod her to say more, he simply looked at her in the same way Naomi looked at her when she understood something was on her goddaughter's mind.

Releasing a heavy breath, she said, ''I've been worried, Skinny. The more I think about the whole thing, the more I'm certain it's not over. Like I said, I'm not a detective or a private investigator, but I have spent time around criminals and I can tell you that they rarely stop with just committing one crime. It worries me that the Ketchum family might still be in danger. Especially Ross.''

A shadow fell across Skinny's face. Obviously her words had disturbed the old cowhand, but she couldn't help it. If Skinny kept his guard up and his eyes open, he might help save Ross's life.

After a moment, he said, ''I wouldn't worry, Bella. Ross isn't the sort of man to lay down and let anyone roll over him. He might not be acting like it, but he's watching his back and he's ready to fight.''

Isabella cast him a wistful smile. ''I hope you're right.''

Skinny suddenly grinned. ''You kinda like him, don't ya?''

Isabella hadn't realized just how much until today. Yet that didn't solve the problem of what to do about her feelings.

''Yeah, I do kinda like him,'' she said softly, then rising from the stool she leaned down and kissed Skinny's cheek. ''I kinda like you, too.''

Once she raised up, she could see awkward color spreading beneath Skinny's three-day whiskers and she wondered how long it had been since someone had shown him a gesture of affection. He was obviously lost for words, so she quickly spared him.

''I've got to get back to the house. See you later, Skinny.''

For the next several hours, Isabella tried to put her tangled emotions for Ross out of her mind and make use of her time. In the study, she pulled out the notes she'd made over the past few days and went over the list of men who worked on the T Bar K.

Beside each name she wrote an age, a physical description, an attitude and a possible motive. Yet by the time she

reached the last man, she felt dissatisfied and no closer to
solving the crime than she had the very first day she'd
walked onto the ranch.

Tossing down the pen she'd been using, she left her seat
at the desk and walked over to the wide windows that now
only gave her a view of the mountains, but also a part of
the bunkhouse and connecting ranch yard.

Twilight was falling and from the looks of the activity
around the barns, the men were back from their work in
the north meadows. The notion lifted her spirits. Ross
would soon be coming up to the house.

In spite of her rush to get home early, Marina had left
him a meal on the kitchen stove. Isabella would warm it
for him and make him a pot of coffee. She'd sit down and
hear about all that he'd done today, and the sound of his
voice and the sight of his face would fill her heart with
gladness.

Because she loved him. Because being with him was all
that really mattered. When she'd exactly decided that, she
didn't know. But sometime between their kiss last night
and now, she'd faced up to her feelings and to Ross's ac-
cusation.

He was right—she'd allowed Winston Jones to wreck her
life, to shade all the choices she'd made since she'd become
a woman. Her father's rejection had made Isabella fear and
mistrust every man who'd tried to get near her. And Brett's
duplicity hadn't helped matters. But that was all over and
done with. She couldn't change any of it. Now it was time
she put the past in the past and started following her heart.

Quickly, Isabella locked her notes away in a file cabinet
that Ross had given her to use, then went to the kitchen to
wait for him.

Thirty minutes later, night had completely darkened the
landscape and Ross still hadn't returned to the house. Trou-

bled and wondering what could be keeping him, she walked through the house to the living room where a plate-glass window gave a full view of the ranch yard.

Through the darkness, she could see that the bunkhouse was brightly lit and another dim light was slanting out the open doors of the horse barn. Ross could be having supper with the rest of the hands. Or he could be helping Linc with a mare. Surely he wasn't avoiding her. He wouldn't do that to her just because she'd resisted having sex with him. No. He wasn't that sort of man, she thought. Besides, this was his house, he certainly wouldn't allow any woman to keep him from the comforts of his home.

Restless and edgy, she went back to the kitchen and made a pot of coffee. The brew had just finished dripping when she heard a rumble of thunder in the distance.

Shocked by the sound, she walked onto the back porch and stared out at the sky. A network of lightning streaks illuminated the western horizon, giving her just a glimpse of the roiling black clouds hanging low over the mesa.

It was the storm Marina had predicted, she thought incredibly. She should have known the old woman was far wiser about these things than she'd ever be.

Three minutes later, large drops of rain began to speckle the red dust out in the yard. For a few moments, Isabella watched as the drops gained momentum, then, realizing she was a lightning target, she hurried back into the kitchen and waited for the wind to hit.

When it did, it hurled a curtain of water against the windows with a force that made Isabella jump in her chair. Seconds later, the loud drumming of the rain drowned out the sound of the radio playing atop the refrigerator.

Clutching her coffee mug with both hands, she hurried through the house and walked onto the front porch. The lights were now off in the bunkhouse. So was the light in the horse barn. Had the electricity gone off?

She looked over her shoulder to see that the lamp she'd turned on in the living room was still burning. That meant the men in the bunkhouse had gone to bed. So where was Ross? she wondered. He couldn't be doing any sort of work in the dark.

What was she to do? she wondered as she stepped back into the house. Go to bed and tell herself it was none of her business if Ross was not in the house? After all, she tried to reason, there were a countless numbers of things he could be doing. He might even be gone from the ranch completely.

But she didn't think so. His truck was parked at the back gate and it hadn't moved from that spot all day. And he always let Marina know ahead of time if he was going to be gone.

An idea suddenly clicked in her head. There were telephones in both barns. Marina kept the number by the wall phone in the kitchen. She'd dial it and hope for an answer!

Anxiously, she headed to the opposite side of the house. She'd reached the end of the long hallway and was about to step into the kitchen when she heard a door click shut.

Relief flooded through her and she hurried into the room, expecting to find Ross shaking the rain off his clothes. Instead, she found the room empty.

Puzzled, she walked out to the mudroom to see if he might be there removing his boots or wet clothing. Yet the small space was dark and empty. Had she simply imagined she'd heard the door closing? Or maybe the wind of the storm had caused something to bump together on the porch.

Goose bumps danced along her skin as a creepy chill washed over her. *I see a knife. Cutting.* Naomi's vision unexpectedly crept into her mind and sent a lump of fear to her throat.

She had to find Ross. She wouldn't rest until she knew he was safe.

Snatching a plastic poncho from the mudroom, Isabella pulled it over her head and started to the kitchen door that led out to the back porch. She was contemplating searching for a flashlight, when she glanced down and saw muddy boot tracks on the tile.

Someone had been in the house! Had Ross come in and gone to his bedroom?

Urgent now, she rushed down to the wing where Ross's bedroom was located. All was dark and quiet. And slowly, as Isabella stood in the hallway trying to make sense of it all, the hair on the back of her neck began to stand on end.

Like a rabbit fleeing a hound, she raced out of the house and into the stormy night. The ground was uneven and wet from the rain, several times she slipped as she tried to run as fast as she could toward the horse barn.

The light she'd spotted earlier was gone. Apparently the storm had knocked out the power. To add to her frustration, Ross was not there among the stabled horses, so she hurried over to the big cattle barn.

As soon as she stepped inside the building she raised her voice as loud as she could and began to call, "Ross! Are you in here?"

Lightning flashed, briefly illuminating the dusty walkway between the metal pens. Isabella rushed several feet forward, then stopped abruptly as total darkness enveloped her.

"Ross! It's Isabella!"

Her frantic call was muted by the deafening sound of the rain drumming against the corrugated iron roof, but she must have been heard because the beam of a flashlight wavered in her direction.

"Bella!"

The sound of Ross's voice caused her nearly to wilt with relief. She wiped the rain from her face and stepped toward the light.

He was at her side in a matter of moments and she collapsed against the solid wall of his chest. "Oh Ross, thank God it's you!"

His arms came around her in a tight band. "Bella! What are you doing down here?"

She lifted her head and tried to discern his face in the darkness. "I was worried because you hadn't come to the house. And everything was dark down here. I was afraid something had happened to you. And then I heard the kitchen door closing and I thought it was you...but it wasn't and I couldn't find you anywhere in the house. But someone was there, Ross! There were muddy boot tracks and—"

"Bella, Bella, calm down," he interrupted. "I'm all right. And you're all right."

She gulped in a deep breath and waited for her racing heart to calm somewhat before she spoke again. "I was so worried, Ross. I thought you'd be back at the house hours ago."

"Worried about me, huh? Maybe you weren't as angry with me as I thought you were."

Even though she couldn't quite see him, she could hear a smile in his voice and the sound eased her heart. "Ross, I was never angry. I—well, I think there's some things I need to say to you. But I'll wait until we get back to the house. Are you finished here?"

"Almost. I was moving the orphaned calves to another pen. The barn leaks where Skinny had them and I didn't want them getting wet. It would be hard for the little things to shake off a bout of pneumonia.''

''I'll come with you,'' she told him. ''I'm not about to go back to the house without you.''

Sensing that she wasn't in the mood to be teased about a bogeyman, Ross took her by the hand and led her back to the opposite end of the barn where he'd been working when he'd heard Isabella call out to him.

''Just stand here,'' he said pausing beside a large stack of alfalfa hay. ''All I need to do is make sure there's water in their trough.''

''Okay.''

Only a few seconds passed before he was back at her side. ''All finished. Can you make it back to the house now?''

''Of course. I'm fine. Just a little wet.''

''A little wet.'' He flashed the dim circle of the flashlight over her. In spite of the plastic poncho, her pants were soaked. Mud was splattered on her lower legs and all over her feet, which were only protected by a pair of flimsy sandals. ''You're sopping. It looks like I should be worrying about you catching pneumonia instead of the calves.''

She reached up and twisted the long length of her hair into a tight rope. Water squeezed from the strands and dripped to the ground.

''Why didn't you call and let me know what you were doing?'' she asked with a measure of irritation. ''Didn't it occur to you that I might be concerned?''

''Not really. You didn't seem too concerned last night.''

She'd kissed him like there would be no tomorrow. Apparently he hadn't noticed or else he'd already forgotten those scorching moments she'd spent in his arms, Isabella thought dryly.

''I have been *concerned* about you from the first day I

became your lawyer. Someone doesn't like you, Ross, and with you wandering alone down here in the dark—''

''Come on, Bella,'' he interrupted, ''you're getting overly dramatic on me.'' He paused and the dim light of the flashlight showed a wicked grin had spread across his face. ''But I kinda like the idea of you worrying about me. And you came all the way down here—''

He paused as he started to reach for her and it was in that moment a streak of lightning lit the space around them and she caught sight of a huge object moving just above Ross's head.

''Ross! Look out!'' she screamed.

For a frozen second he hesitated as he tried to figure out why she was looking up at the hayloft and then it dawned on him that something was falling.

He jumped forward and took her down with him as heavy bales of alfalfa hay fell from several feet above. One of the large rectangles struck him in the shoulder, then rolled to the side. The others landed exactly in the spot where he'd been standing.

Dust from the ground and bits of hay from a bale that had broken boiled up in the air around them. Isabella coughed as Ross slowly sat up and looked at the mess.

''What the hell happened?'' he asked in a dazed voice.

Isabella scrambled to her knees and stared in horror at the hay bales. Weighing a good eighty or ninety pounds each, they could have been lethal weapons.

''My God, Ross, you were nearly killed!''

He flexed his shoulder in an attempt to shake off the fiery pain running from his collarbone all the way down to his elbow. ''I wouldn't go that far.''

''Are you hurt?'' She scooted closer and gently touched his arm.

"I'm okay," he said tightly. "One of the bales hit my shoulder. But I don't think anything is broken."

She gazed upward to where several tons of hay was stacked on a wooden platform. If she hadn't looked up and seen it falling, Ross's neck could have been broken. The notion left her trembling and tears gathered in her eyes.

"Oh, Ross! If you'd been hurt, I don't know what I would have done!"

The pain in his shoulder was forgotten when he felt the tremor in her hand as it moved up his arm.

"Bella, you could have been hurt, too. You're not, are you?" he asked urgently.

"No." The need to touch him, to feel with her own hands that he was well and safe, was all she could think about. She moved closer and circled her arms around his neck. "Just hold me, Ross."

Groaning, he clasped her close against him and buried his face in the side of her neck. "We need to get out of here," he whispered.

"I know—but—just give me a minute," she pleaded brokenly.

He could feel her whole body shaking and the notion that her fear was all for him stunned Ross. Women cared for his money and for his social status, but never really just for him. Not like this.

His voice husky, he mouthed against her ear, "Bella, don't be afraid. Everything is all right now."

She tilted her head back to look at him and he quickly framed her face with both hands.

"Ross..."

The impassioned way she said his name was like an urgent caress. It triggered a need in him so deep that the only thing he could do was bring his mouth hungrily down on hers.

Isabella responded by parting her lips and snuggling her body closer to his. At the same time, his hands delved beneath the wet poncho she was wearing, then slipped beneath her shirt until they were splayed against the warm flesh of her back.

Around and around her senses swirled as his lips rocked back and forth over hers, as his tongue plunged inside the warm cavity of her mouth. The tiny moan of need in her throat was drowned out by the distant thunder, but it didn't matter. He seemed to know what she was conveying to him. That she needed him and this time there would be no turning back.

Tearing his mouth from hers, he strained to see her face in the darkness. "Bella—we need to go. It might not be safe here."

A fresh spurt of fear caused Isabella to shiver. "You think those bales came down on us deliberately, don't you?"

Not wanting to panic her, Ross tried to play down the seriousness of what had just happened. "I don't know, Bella. But if someone did push the hay at us, he's probably already gone by now. Don't be afraid."

Isabella was afraid, but her desire for Ross was so strong, it overpowered her fear. "I'm not afraid—I just want you to make love to me."

"No," he said thickly. "Not here in this wet, dirty barn. Let's go to the house."

He got to his feet and pulled her up with him. Blocking out all sight of tomorrow, Isabella allowed him to take her by the hand and lead her out of the barn.

Chapter Twelve

Outside, the rain was tapering off and the rumble of thunder had moved on to the east. The two of them scampered, half running, half walking across the ranch yard until they reached the front porch.

Before they entered the front door Ross turned to her. "Stay right here while I check out the house. Someone could have come in while we were in the barn," he whispered.

Isabella didn't like to think someone might be after them, but she realized it would be foolish not to play it safe. Nodding, she whispered back at him. "Just be safe, Ross."

Inside the living room, the lamp she'd switched on earlier was still burning, casting a dim glow from one corner. Ross left her long enough to make a quick search of the house. When he returned to Isabella, he led her through the door and quickly locked it behind him. "It's all clear," he assured her.

She glanced down at her wet clothes. "My poncho. I need to take it off," she said softly. "It's dripping all over the floor."

"Do you think I care about the floor?" he asked roughly as he bent and picked her up in his arms.

She didn't argue. It was too easy, too wonderful to let him have his way. As he carried her down the hallway to his bedroom, she held on tightly to his broad shoulders and scattered kisses up and down the side of his neck.

Once they reached his bedroom, he didn't bother with a light. Instead his hands were busy with her clothes, first tossing away the poncho, followed by her shirt, then her pants and sandals. By the time he'd stripped her down to her underwear, his movements grew slower and more deliberate.

Isabella closed her eyes, luxuriated in the feel of his rough hands against her skin, and marveled at the strange leaps and jumps her insides were making in anticipation of becoming intimate with this man she had grown to love.

When he finally removed her bra and his hands cupped her breasts, she shivered as liquid fire raced along her veins.

"Am I hurting you, Bella?"

"No," she said on a breathless groan. "I just didn't know—I've never felt like this."

The awed note in her voice struck a spot deep inside him, shocking him with totally foreign emotions. To think that she'd never reacted to any man the way she was reacting to him now swelled his chest and filled him with a need to pleasure her, to love and protect her. Not just for this night in his bed, but for always.

"Bella! You're so perfect. So beautiful," he murmured as he bent his head and brought his mouth to her breasts.

Isabella had never considered herself perfect. Nor had she ever thought of herself as beautiful, but to think his eyes saw her that way thrilled every feminine part of her. Yet that pleasure was mild compared to the sensation of his lips and tongue against her nipple, tugging, tasting, sending ripples of excitement washing over her in wave after wave.

At some point when they'd entered the bedroom, he'd tossed his Stetson aside. Now she slipped her fingers into his thick hair and pressed them against his scalp as she instinctively arched her back and strained to have him even closer.

Her urgent movements fed the heat that had begun to build in his loins the moment she'd touched him in the barn. Wanting to go slow, but knowing it would be impossible, he lifted his head away from her and quickly tore off his clothes and boots.

Once he was undressed, he slipped away her panties and lifted her backwards, onto the king-size bed. When he was stretched out beside her, Isabella reached for him at the same time his hands searched for her.

Crushed in the circle of his arms, she sought his mouth in the darkness and sighed with sweet contentment when his lips opened over hers. Beneath her soft fingers, his shoulders were thick and broad. She explored their width and breadth, then moved on to the firm muscles of his chest and the flat male nipples that puckered instantly beneath the twirl of her fingertip.

Already throbbing and aching to have her, he tore his mouth from her velvety lips and pressed moist kisses along her throat and downward, to the rosy brown peak of her breast.

"You taste like honey, Bella. Sweet, sweet honey."

She quivered as his hands followed the track of his lips downward over each rib and across her belly until he reached the mass of dark curls between her thighs. Then he lifted his head and watched her face as he slipped a finger inside the warm moist folds of her womanhood.

Gasping, a shock of pleasurable sensations washing over her, she arched against his hand, desperately seeking the relief that only his body could give her.

The heated response inflamed him and he wrapped the fingers of his other hand around her breast and kneaded the soft mound.

Beneath him, she whimpered with need as her hands raced down his rib cage, his back and onto his hips. At the same time, the movement of his hand between her thighs was teasing her, burning her with such a lust she was certain she was going to die from the flames.

"Oh, please, Ross, please," she whispered shamelessly. "I can't wait any longer."

Her broken plea echoed the raging ache inside him and was all he needed to take her body and make it his.

Easing her flat on her back, he positioned himself over her, then bent his head and captured her lips in a deep, mind-drugging kiss.

As his lips continued to probe and tease, his hands delved beneath her hips and cupped around her buttocks to lift her upward toward the thrust of his erection. Her velvety heat instantly welcomed him, enveloped him in such overwhelming pleasure that he groaned aloud.

Dazed, but desperate to receive all of him, Isabella moved her hips, twisting them upward, recklessly urging him on. Ross pushed deeper, then gasped as he hit the barrier of her innocence.

Shocked, he instinctively eased back, but she held his hips tightly against her, determined to give him what they both so desperately wanted.

"Bella! You're a virgin! I—"

"You can't stop now," she said, her words a husky rush. "I won't let you!"

The fierce resolve in her voice convinced him that it would be futile to stop things now. And he wasn't at all certain he could, even if he wanted to. He wanted her like nothing he'd ever wanted in his life.

With a rueful groan, he pressed his lips to her damp temple. "Are you sure, Bella? If not, I swear I'll try to get off this bed."

She locked her legs around his and circled her arms around his neck. "I've never been more sure of anything in my life." *I love you,* she wanted to add. *I love you with everything inside of me.* But she kept the words to herself, certain that once she said them, she could never take them back. And certain, too, that once he heard them, he would surely withdraw from her.

"But you—"

"I want you," she murmured simply, then silenced any other protest he might have made by placing her lips over his.

Unable to resist, he responded by thrusting into her swiftly and completely. Fiery pain seared her, but as he began to move inside her, the pain fled and was instantly forgotten as incredible pleasure flooded her body.

Rocked by the intimate connection, she held on tightly and matched her movements to his. But it seemed only moments passed before she found herself climbing, climbing to a soft, sweet place where there was nothing but black sky and brilliant white stars bursting behind her closed eyes.

Above her, Ross felt every muscle in his body clench. Then his head fell back and a harsh guttural sound erupted from his throat as he felt his heart, his very soul, drain into her.

* * *

The next morning bright sunlight awakened Isabella from a deep sleep. She opened her eyes to see that she had slept late and that the storm from the night before had been replaced with clear, azure-blue sky.

Before she even bothered to turn her head, she instinctively knew that Ross was gone, his warm body no longer draped alongside hers. She immediately felt a sense of emptiness that he had not stayed behind to share the morning with her. But then he was a working man, she rationalized. He didn't lounge about for any reason.

Last night might have been life-altering for her, but she had to remember that making love wasn't anything new for Ross. She was just the latest in a line of women who had come and gone from his life.

Biting down on her lip, she recalled all the ways he'd touched her, kissed her, turned her body inside out with pleasure. Surely what they'd shared had been special, she thought desperately. Surely he'd never experienced that sort of connection with any other woman.

What makes you think that, you little idiot? He'd never said "I love you." He'd never said "I want you here beside me for the rest of my life."

Groaning at the goading voice going off in her head, she twisted onto her side and immediately went stock still. There on the pillow next to hers was a small branch of purple sage.

Scooting up to a sitting position, she reached for the blossoms and lifted them to her nose. Their scent was pungent and spicy, reminding her of the way Ross had made love to her.

Tears pooled in her eyes as she climbed out of bed and began to gather up her clothes.

Minutes later in her own bedroom, she showered and dressed in jeans, shirt and boots. Then she tied her hair back at the nape of her neck and dabbed on a bit of makeup. Her image in the mirror looked wan, her eyes cloudy from lack of sleep.

If Marina noticed her appearance, she didn't make any sort of comment. But Isabella figured the older woman had already concluded that she'd spent the night in Ross's room. And knowing that, Isabella had already decided she wasn't going to be embarrassed about it. She was a grown woman, after all. And what woman could resist Ross Ketchum? Certainly she hadn't been able to. Now she feared she was going to reap the consequences.

While she ate breakfast, Marina brought up the subject of last night's storm. Isabella made a few comments about the lightning and thunder, but she didn't go on to mention that she was certain someone had come into the house without making himself known to her.

If Marina had found the muddy boot prints on the kitchen tile, she'd probably thought they'd belonged to Ross and simply mopped them away. As for the accident down at the barn, Isabella was holding that close to her chest, too. She wanted to see with her own eyes just what might have caused those hay bales to fall out of the loft.

After breakfast, she pulled on her hat and headed down to the barns. As it had been yesterday, the ranch yard was unusually quiet. Most of the horses were gone from their stalls, and the outside pen, which normally held the working remuda was empty, except for Juggler. Since he was saddled and tied to a hitching post, she wondered if Ross might still be around somewhere.

Walking down the long shed row, she exited the building and discovered Skinny outside in the shade, tacking a loose shoe on Trixie.

The older man looked up as she approached. "Well, you're up early this mornin'. Goin' ridin'?"

Skinny was short on words, but long on manners. Since she'd been on the ranch, he'd gone out of his way to show her around the barns and help her with anything she might need. Through Ross, she'd learned that Skinny had been on the ranch almost as long as Marina, and from the devotion the cowboy put into his job, she knew he would be here until he died.

"Maybe later, Skinny. I want to have a look around first." She glanced over toward the cattle barn. "Where is everybody? Did they not finish the vaccinating in the north meadow?"

"Yep. They finished that job yesterday evening. There're two or three guys around here somewhere, but Ross has most of 'em out workin' the south flats. Had a bunch of steers to brand."

If she'd woken up when Ross had this morning, he might have lingered long enough to tell her of his day's plans. He might have even told her how much last night had meant to him. But she'd slept right through and now she could only guess what he might be feeling.

"Oh. Well, I think I'll go have a look at the orphans and then I might ride out on the mesa."

He dropped the mare's foot and straightened his back. "It'll be a while before I'm finished with Trixie."

Heading toward the cattle barn, Isabella tossed over her shoulder. "That's all right, Skinny. I'll wait. Or I'll ride another horse."

Except for a few mama cows penned near the entrance and bawling loudly, Isabella was relieved to see the big building was empty and quiet. She hurried down the dusty alleyway to the opposite end of the interior where Ross had moved the baby calves.

A quick glance in their pen assured her that the two little Herefords were dry and content, both of them curled up asleep on a bed of straw.

Leaving the calves, she walked over to the spot where Ross had initially left her standing last night when he'd gone to check on the water trough. Apparently someone had already picked up the fallen hay bales this morning and cleaned away the one that had broken and scattered over the ground.

A dark, shadowy feeling swept over her as she gazed upward toward the open loft running the width of the building. In the morning light, she could see that the overhead space was jammed with tons of hay. All of the rectangular bales were neatly stacked, the first row starting at least two feet away from the ledge. She didn't see how the bales could have fallen without someone deliberately pushing them. Ross must have known this. But she figured he must have played down the incident because he hadn't wanted to frighten her.

Had someone gone to the house, planning to do Ross harm, then left in a hurry when he'd heard her about to come into the kitchen. Had that someone then returned to the barn and found Ross there and deliberately waited for a chance to ambush him with the hay bales? It sounded too farfetched, too sinister to believe. Yet she couldn't dismiss the idea. In fact, the strange incidents made her even more determined to get to the bottom of this whole crime.

Leaving the barn, she walked back to where Skinny was working on Trixie's shoes.

"Skinny, were any of the cowboys out of the bunkhouse last night after the storm hit?"

He glanced up at her as he positioned a horseshoe on the nose of an anvil iron. "Yeah. Four or five of them were gone to town. Didn't come back 'til late."

She grimaced, then asked hopefully, "Were they all doing something together?"

Shaking his head, he reached for a small hammer. "Don't think so. Think they all had plans of their owns. Girlfriends, you know. The young ones can't go without their women for too long."

So that meant it would be hard to narrow down who might have been in the barn, Isabella concluded. Any of the five could simply say they'd gone to Aztec and not one of them would know the difference.

"Why you askin'?" Skinny wanted to know.

Isabella let out a long sigh. "Oh, there was a little accident last night in the barn. Some hay bales fell and came close to hitting Ross on the head."

The man rose up to his full height and leveled an anxious gaze on Isabella. "Ross didn't say anything about that happening this morning. Not to me or none of the other hands that I know of."

"Maybe he just wants to let things ride and wait for whoever it is to play their hand. I just—well, I'm very worried, Skinny. Please keep your eyes and ears open."

He patted her shoulder. "Now you quit frettin' about it, Bella. Just go out and have a nice quiet ride and let Ross an' me do all the worryin'."

She might as well, Isabella thought. Because right now there was nothing she could do about it, except try to piece all the clues together and hope something would click in her mind.

"How much longer will it be before you're finished with Trixie?" she asked him.

Skinny dug a pouch of tobacco from his jeans pocket and placed a hefty pinch in his jaw. "Probably half an hour. She's got a little chip in her toe that I want to rasp out. Why don't you ride Juggler?"

Isabella glanced thoughtfully in the direction of the re-muda pen. "I noticed he was already saddled. Why isn't Ross riding him?"

"He planned on taking him this morning, but at the last minute he decided he'd used him pretty hard yesterday and he needed to give the horse a rest today. Some of the boys were supposed to have unsaddled him and turned him out. I guess they haven't gotten around to it yet."

Frowning, Isabella looked back at the wiry old ranch hand. "If Juggler needs a rest, then Ross probably wouldn't want me riding him," she pointed out.

Skinny laughed. "A little thing like you isn't going to tire a horse like Juggler. Besides, you're not going to be cutting cattle or doin' any brush poppin'."

No, she was simply going to walk quietly out on the mesa, Isabella thought. Still, she hadn't forgotten that first day she'd seen Juggler throw Ross in the dirt. She was a fairly decent horsewoman, but she couldn't handle that kind of power if the gelding decided to put his back feet in the air.

"I don't know, Skinny," she said doubtfully. "Juggler is a spirited horse. I'm not sure I can handle him."

"Has Ross told you not to ride him?" the cowboy asked.

Ross had not only offered to let her ride Juggler, on several occasions he'd dared her to ride him, assuring her that the horse would never buck with a woman on him.

Isabella shook her head. "No, but—"

Skinny waved away anything else she'd been about to say. "Come on. I'll walk down and help you mount him."

Five minutes into the ride, she was thrilled that Skinny had talked her into riding Juggler. He was a beautiful, stout horse with a smooth gait. Plus, he was Ross's horse. Some-how that made riding him even more special. And so far he was acting like a complete gentleman.

Smiling to herself, she leaned up in the stirrups and patted the gelding's neck. "You're a true beauty, Juggler. I don't know why Ross is so obsessed with finding Snip when he has you."

The horse bobbed his head as if to agree with her. Isabella laughed softly then gave him an affectionate scrub between the ears. "Don't worry, ol' boy. We won't go very far before we stop and rest. I just need to do a little thinking."

Actually, she needed to do a whole lot of thinking. About herself, about Ross, and about what last night was going to mean to their relationship. She wanted to believe that every caress, every whispered word he'd given her had been done with love. It had certainly felt that way. Especially after he'd made love to her a second time, then tucked her exhausted body in the curve of his and ordered her to sleep. But of course, she hadn't slept. Not immediately. Instead she'd lain there basking in the warmth of his masculine body draped against hers, marveling at the rough yet tender way he'd aroused her to heights she'd never imagined. If she'd not already been in love with him, last night would have certainly pushed her over the brink. But knowing the depths of her feelings still didn't tell her what to do about them.

Ross was not a marrying man. He'd already told her so. And if she continued to stay here, she would no doubt wind up back in his bed, time after time. Would that be enough for her?

I could never lie with him…unless he was my husband.

The words she'd spoken to her godmother had pestered her all morning and now as she thought of them again, she groaned out loud. Thank God Naomi couldn't see her at this moment, Isabella thought. She would no doubt take one look into her eyes and know that she had spent the night in Ross's bed.

You have looked upon the one you want for a mate. And when that happens you can't change it.

Naomi's prophetic words seemed even wiser to Isabella now that she'd given her heart and her body to Ross. He was the only man she would ever want for a mate. And that could never be changed.

With a heavy sigh, she leaned back in the stirrups to settle her weight in the seat of the saddle. At the same time, a popping noise exploded from somewhere beneath her. Frightened by the sound, Juggler reared high on his hind legs and pawed the air.

The saddle listed violently to the right and Isabella screamed. Desperately, she clutched for a handhold and came up with a small clump of Juggler's mane. But the weight of her body, along with that of the saddle, were too much to hold upright and she found herself hanging sideways on the horse's body.

"Whoa, Juggler! Whoa, boy!"

The terrified horse ignored her commands and took off in a gallop, darting wildly around clumps of cacti and twisted juniper. Isabella's hat fell to her back and her black hair streamed out behind her as wind, branches and twigs slapped her face.

Horrified, Isabella continued to grip the horse's mane as she tried to lever herself out of the useless saddle. But each time she attempted to pull her boots from the stirrups, the movement caused her to slip even further toward Juggler's underbelly.

Oh God, she was going to die! She was never going to see Ross again! Any second the horse was going to slam her into a pine tree or the saddle was going to fall completely. And at this rate of speed, her neck would be broken on impact.

Praying desperately, she tried one last time to free her feet from the stirrups. She failed. And all hope inside her died. Now all she could do was hang on to Juggler's mane and even that lifeline was rapidly slipping away.

Across the wide mesa, Ross was cursing to himself as he glanced down at his burned palm. It wasn't like him to grab a hot branding iron too low on the handle. The heat had seared all the way through his glove and charred the major part of his palm and a portion of his thumb.

In spite of the injury, he'd tried to keep on working, but the rest of the work crew had insisted he ride back to the ranch and treat the burn with first aid. Not wanting to deal with a nasty infection, he'd finally agreed and set out toward the ranch.

Wasted time, Ross thought grimly. But then, he only had himself to blame. Only a portion of his mind had been on his work. The major part had been on Isabella. Since he'd left her asleep in his bed this morning, his thoughts had been completely consumed with her.

He'd felt badly about not waking her before he left the house. But when he'd slid out of bed shortly before dawn, she'd only been asleep a few short hours. And the truth of the matter was, he'd not been ready to face her with words.

Last night had shaken him to the very center of his being, and he still wasn't certain what had happened to him. No woman had ever made him feel the things Isabella had made him feel. No woman had ever burrowed under his skin and traveled straight to his heart. Even now, he still didn't know what to think. And this morning, he sure as hell wouldn't have known what to say to her.

She'd given him her innocence and in doing so, he knew she had also given him her heart. He wasn't ready for that kind of gift. He was a bachelor and he'd sworn to be a bachelor for the rest of his life.

But having her here on the ranch and now in his bed had given him dangerous ideas. Like how it might be to have her as his wife, a permanent partner in his life. How it would be for the two of them to have children together, to raise them here on the ranch, as Amelia and Tucker had raised him and his siblings.

But she was a career woman, just as Linda had been. Yet he had to admit there was a big difference between the two women. Linda had only wanted a career for her own personal gain. Isabella wanted to use hers to help others, not herself. And she was determined to move back home to the Jicarilla and do just that. So how could he ask her to give it up for him? How could he ever expect her to care for him that much?

With a silent groan of misery, he reached up with his good hand and wiped the sweat collecting on his face. The movement caused Ross to wince and reminded him of the black-and-blue condition of his shoulder. If something wasn't broken, it would be a miracle. And if Victoria could see the injury, she'd be zapping him with X rays and tying his arm up in a sling.

But he wasn't about to let his sister see what had happened to him. He didn't even want Isabella to see the injury. She'd already been terrified last night; he didn't want to scare her even more.

"Heeelp! Heeelp!"

The frantic call came out of nowhere and jerked Ross's head straight up. His eyes squinted against the hot summer sun, he quickly scanned the horizon until he spotted the white horse with a rider hanging precariously on his side.

Dear God, it was Isabella!

Icy fear thrust through him like a lance as he dug his

spurs into the sides of his horse and raced to intercept Juggler's path.

"Hold on, Bella!" he shouted out to her. "Hold on!"

Sage cracked and cacti popped as the horses busted wildly through the brush. With his injured hand, Ross steered his mount alongside the runaway horse and, using his other hand, reached for Juggler's bridle, missed, then reached again before he finally managed to catch the leather throat latch and jerk the animal's head toward him.

"Whoa, Juggler! Whoa now!" he shouted.

Juggler's head came around just enough to give Ross a chance to grab the bit shank at the side of the animal's mouth. Once he pulled it back, the horse came to a jarring halt.

The abrupt stop caused the cinch to break completely and dumped the saddle and Isabella onto the rocky ground. She landed with a heavy thud, the saddle twisted crazily between her legs.

"Bella!"

Jumping off his horse, fear beating like a wild bird in his chest, Ross raced around to where she was attempting to raise herself up to a sitting position.

"Careful now! Careful," he urged he as grasped her gently by the shoulders. "Oh God, Bella, are you hurt?"

Her lungs were heaving from exertion and fear. Gulping for air, she looked up at him, tears flowing from her eyes. "Oh, Ross! Oh thank God you found me! That you stopped Juggler! I—I was—I thought I was going to be killed! I thought I was never going to see you again!"

With shaking hands, he pulled her into his arms and buried her face against his shoulder. Above her head, he closed his eyes and tried to block out the image of her falling beneath Juggler's galloping hooves. If he'd lost her, he wouldn't want to live. It was so simple to see that now.

"Don't think about it, darling. You're safe. You're all right."

"Ross…Ross," she mumbled brokenly, "I thought—I was going to die out here alone! Without you."

His fingers meshed in her hair, then spread across her back as he tightened his hold on her. "Dear God, Bella, when I saw you—saw what was happening—my blood ran cold!"

His thumbs slid beneath her jaw and lifted her face. Tears had tracked twin trails down her dusty cheeks and he kissed them away as he attempted to assure her, and himself, that the danger was over.

As soon as his lips touched her face, heat spread through Isabella and chased away the cold shock of her terrifying experience. The strong circle of his arms around her was heaven on earth and the urge to be closer was the only thing on her mind as she turned her mouth hungrily toward his.

Groaning with need, he took her offered lips, letting his own express all the fears and longing and relief that had tangled up inside him during the past few moments.

The need for air was finally the thing that tore them apart and they both stared at each other, dazed and frightened by the depth of what had just transpired between them.

You've looked upon the one you want for a mate. When that happens, you can't change it.

Naomi's words leaped into her mind once again, reminding her that she had to be strong or she would never be anything more than this man's lover. Maybe that would be enough for some women. But not for her. Somehow, deep down, she'd always known that.

Slowly, she pushed herself away from his chest and nervously licked her lips. "I—uh—think I'd better get up from here. My legs are hurting from the strain."

Overcome with the need to keep holding her, Ross had to mentally shake himself before he could finally release her and turn his attention to pulling her feet from the stirrups.

"How in the world did all of this happen anyway, Bella?"

She winced as he helped her free the leg that was still trapped beneath the saddle. Her whole body was already stiffening, she realized. By tonight she'd probably be too sore to walk.

"Whatever you're thinking, it wasn't Juggler's fault. He was behaving perfectly and I stood up in the stirrups to pet him between the ears. The next thing I knew something popped. The saddle fell sideways with me in it. After that, the horse was terrified and took off galloping. I had no way to stop him."

His features tight, Ross helped Isabella to her feet, then squatted down on his boot heels to examine the saddle.

While he studied it, Isabella stepped over to Juggler to make sure the horse hadn't injured himself. Other than trembling and being wet with foamy sweat, the only thing she could find wrong with the gelding were a few cuts and scratches on his legs.

"It looks as though Juggler only has a few superficial cuts on his legs," she told Ross with relief. "I'm so glad."

When he didn't reply, she turned around to see he hadn't heard a word she'd said. He was staring in horror at the cinch strap in his hand.

"Someone tried to kill you, Bella!"

Chapter Thirteen

"Wh-what?" Dazed, Isabella stepped back to Ross and stared down at the piece of latigo he was holding.

Ross looked up at her, his eyes glittering with dark fury. "Who saddled this horse? I'm going to kill the bastard!"

Stunned and confused, she knelt down beside him and clutched his arm. "I—Ross, no! What are you talking about? What are you saying?"

"This latigo has been cut with a knife! He must have left just enough to keep the saddle upright until you rode away from the ranch."

Isabella swallowed as she remembered Naomi's vision the day she'd visited her godmother. *A knife. Cutting.* The Apache woman had foreseen this accident.

Shaking her head, she said, "But Ross—Juggler was already saddled when I went down to the barn. Skinny said you were going to use him this morning and then you decided otherwise."

The muscles in his jaw twitched as he digested her words. "Juggler was still saddled? That was hours ago. He was supposed to have been unsaddled and turned loose."

"Well, he wasn't. He was in the remuda pen. Skinny said the boys must have gotten busy or something. Anyway, I don't know who saddled him. And surely—surely someone didn't—why would they want to harm me?"

He lifted his eyes to hers and for a split second she thought she saw love in his eyes. Love for her. But that was crazy. He'd said he'd never love any woman. He was just emotional, she told herself. And so was she. Emotional. And scared.

"I was wrong, Bella. He wasn't out to get you. Whoever cut this cinch believed *I* was going to be riding Juggler this morning. He left him saddled, hoping I would come back to the ranch for a fresh mount." Lifting his injured hand to her, he tilted her face toward his. The scratches on her beautiful skin filled him with a murderous rage to get at the person who'd done this to her. "I'm not sure who saddled Juggler, but I have a pretty good idea."

"Who?"

His expression was suddenly sick. "Damn it, Neal was right all along."

Unable to follow his line of thought, she stared at him, puzzled. "What do you mean?"

"It's one of my men. I wanted to give him a chance here on the ranch. I thought he was my friend. I trusted him to work safely with the other men, to care for my livestock. I—" He looked away from her as his head swung back and forth with disbelief. "I never dreamed he had anything against me."

"How do you know that he meant this to happen?"

"Bella, you were almost killed just now! If I hadn't

come upon you—'' Closing his eyes, he breathed deeply through his nostrils and tried to calm the rage boiling up inside him. ''Oh, but he thought it was *me* that would be on Juggler,'' he continued, his low voice tight with fury. ''It was *me* he tried to frame with murder. And in trying to get to me, he came close to killing Jess and now you. It was probably him last night that dumped the hay out of the loft.''

Isabella looked at him as she tried mentally to assemble all the little clues she'd gathered over the past couple of weeks. Of all the men she'd met and tried to read through their actions and conversations, one had not stood out among them. She wanted to ask Ross who he suspected of this heinous crime. But she could see he was deliberately avoiding telling her the man's identity.

''The person who saddled Juggler might not be guilty. Someone else could have cut the girth without him knowing,'' Isabella reasoned.

''Maybe,'' he growled. ''But I doubt it.''

''Why? What does he have against you?''

''I didn't know he had anything against me. Until now,'' he added grimly.

Shaken by the hard resolution on his face, she grabbed his arm. ''Ross...what are you going to do?'' she asked desperately.

He reached for her hand. ''Can you ride double with me?''

She nodded numbly.

He said, ''We're going back to the ranch and I'm going to have a little squaring off with the guy. If he did this, I'll get it out of him.''

Isabella shivered with fear, yet she knew it would do no good to tell him to let the sheriff's department handle things from here on out. Ross had been wronged. He'd been targeted by someone he'd trusted, and he wouldn't rest until he had retribution.

She looked down at the saddle that had been meant to be Ross's death trap and had very nearly ended up being hers. "What about that?" she asked, pointing to the saddle as cold shock threatened to overtake her.

"It's evidence. We're going to leave it where it is and let the law do what they need to do with it."

Taking her by the elbow, he helped Isabella into the saddle of the sorrel horse he'd been riding, then gathering up Juggler's reins, he climbed up behind her and took a seat on the saddle skirt.

The unaccustomed weight of two riders caused the horse to go into a sideways dance. Since Ross had the job of leading Juggler, Isabella was responsible for the reins and though her nerves were already frazzled, she gritted her teeth and brought their mount under control.

Smoothing a hand over the back of her hair, he asked, "Are you okay? Or do you want me to go on to the ranch and come back for you with another saddled horse?"

She wasn't about to let him face the traitorous ranch hand without her. In his state of mind there was no telling what he might do. "I'm fine. I'll make it," she assured him.

"Good. He'll settle down in a minute," he said of the horse. "Just put him into a trot and keep him there."

"A trot?"

"Hell, yes! I want to get there as fast as we can. Before the guy decides it's time for him to fly the coop."

Fifteen minutes later, they trotted into the ranch yard and Ross directed her to head the horse toward the cattle barn.

"There's Skinny!" she cried as she spotted the older cowboy walking out of the horse barn. "Maybe we should ask him—"

"No! Don't bring Skinny into this. Ride on around to the front of the barn!"

She did as he ordered, while behind them she could hear Skinny calling out to them, "Hey? What happened?"

When they rounded the corner of the barn, they saw Steve and Tim spreading cattle cubes in a long metal feed trough.

Tim was the first to notice their approach. He nudged an elbow in Steve's ribs and pointed in her and Ross's direction.

The moment Steve lifted his head their way, Isabella knew with sinking certainty that he was guilty. Fear was frozen on his face as he took in Isabella's scratched, bedraggled appearance, Juggler without his saddle, and last but certainly not least, Ross, his expression that of a man on a dark and dangerous mission.

Since the two cowboys were inside a huge cattle pen, Isabella pulled their mount to a stop just outside the fence. Ross slid off and motioned for the two men to come to him.

Immediately, Tim dropped the sack of feed he was holding and sauntered toward his boss. However, Steve began backing up until his legs hit another feed trough and he staggered and nearly fell.

"Come here, Chambers. Or I'm coming after you."

Glancing wildly around him, Steve made a dash for the opposite fence and the pickup truck parked beyond it.

Like lightning, Ross bolted into the pen to race after him. By a fraction of a second, Steve managed to make it over the fence before Ross climbed after him. But he wasn't as lucky when he stopped long enough to jerk open the truck door.

Ross grabbed him by the arm and spun him around. "You're not going anywhere, you worthless bastard!"

Desperate to escape, Steve attempted to jerk away, but he was no match for Ross's strength or agility. His fist a blur, Ross sent a cracking right to the cowboy's jaw that put the other man flat on his back and sprawled in the dirt.

Ross stood ready and waiting as Steve sputtered for air and dragged himself to his feet.

"I'm gonna kill you for this, Ketchum!" he growled and made a staggering lunge for Ross.

Sidestepping Steve's grappling arms, Ross reared back and landed an uppercut to the cowhand's chin. The powerful blow landed Steve back in the dirt, and this time he didn't move.

Tim and Isabella reached the two men in a matter of moments. She snatched a hold of Ross's arm. "Ross, are you okay? Your hand—"

"Don't worry. I'll see to it later." His chest still heaving from the tussel with Steve, he glanced at her. "What about you? Are you okay?"

Although she was trembling with aftershock, Isabella nodded. "I'll be fine."

"Why, he's out cold!" He looked up at Ross, clearly stunned by this development. "What in heck did he do, boss?"

Ross circled his arm around Isabella and gathered her trembling body close. "He picked on the wrong man, Tim."

The next two days passed in a haze for Isabella. Once Ross had called to report the whole incident to Sheriff

Perez, Under-Sheriff Hastings and a number of deputies swarmed the T Bar K. Steve was arrested on the spot and charged with attempted murder, among other things.

The details of Steve's motives hadn't completely come to light yet, but this afternoon Jess had called Ross into town to the sheriff's department. She suspected that by the time he arrived back home, he would know more about the case.

As for herself, Isabella had spent most of the past two days answering questions put to her by Sheriff Perez and his men. And when she wasn't being questioned, she'd been trying to work the soreness from her bruised body.

Riding almost upside down beneath a horse's belly was not what her muscles were accustomed to. But Victoria had given her a prescription for an anti-inflammatory and she was beginning to feel more like herself, thank goodness. And just in time, too. Ross had planned a dinner party for tonight and already the house was filled with the good smells of Marina's special cooking.

Victoria and Jess would be coming, along with their cousin Linc, sister-in-law, Maggie, and nephew, Aaron, and the T Bar K attorney Neal Rankin. And, to Isabella's surprise, Ross had invited her mother and godmother, too. Not just to eat dinner, but to spend the night on the ranch so that the two women wouldn't be forced to travel after dark.

His thoughtfulness had touched Alona. It had touched Isabella that he would even think of her family on this special night. But then, he was a happy man, she reasoned with herself. Steve's arrest had solved a good deal of the ranch's problems, and that had been enough to put Ross in a celebratory mood.

With a heavy sigh, Isabella pulled a red dress from the closet and held it in front of her. As she'd told Marina, red

was considered a lucky color by Apaches and she certainly
needed all the luck she could get. But she'd worn red to
the Cattlemen's Ball, so she put the dress back and pulled
down a cream-colored sheath.

Ross might consider tonight a celebration, but as far as
she was concerned, she'd decided the evening would be the
final curtain call for her stay here on the ranch. Her job
was completely finished. Now all she had to do was find
the strength to tell Ross she couldn't hang around and have
an affair with him.

This was the way the ranch should be, Ross thought, as
his gaze took in the family and friends crowded around the
festive dining table. This was the way the T Bar K had
been while both his parents had still been living. Filled with
happy, laughing people, rich food and the sense that tomorrow would be good, as would all the tomorrows after
that.

From his seat at the head of the table, Ross turned his
gaze to his immediate right where Isabella was listening
intently to Neal's account of the day he took his bar exam.

The scratches on her face were beginning to fade, yet
the faint marks were a continual reminder to Ross of just
how close she'd come to having a serious or fatal injury.
Just the thought was still enough to put him in a panic, and
these past two days he'd found himself wanting to be near
her even more, wanting and needing to make sure she was
safe and close at hand.

He'd never believed that any woman could have such a
hold over him, but since Isabella had come to the ranch,
he'd not even thought of other women, much less wanted
to see one. She was changing his life, and there didn't seem

to be a thing he could do to stop it. Moreover, he didn't want to stop it.

"Ross? Everyone is waiting."

The impatient sound of his sister's voice finally reached his deep thoughts and he turned to look at her bemused face. "What were you saying?"

Victoria exchanged a knowing look with her husband. "We were talking about Steve. None of us can understand why he went so...crazy."

"Well, he never was one of the sharpest men I've known," Jess commented.

Ross shrugged, still reluctant to accept the fact that an employee and friend had turned on him in such an evil way. "No. I guess some people would call Steve a little slow-thinking. But he was a decent worker and I liked him."

The sadness in his voice prompted Isabella to reach over and touch his arm. He looked at her and smiled, grateful that she understood the mixture of anger and hurt he was feeling toward Steve.

At the end of the table, Alona said, "I can't understand why he shot Jess if it was you he had it in for in the first place."

Ross turned his attention to Isabella's mother. "Well, it turns out that Steve has done quite a bit of talking since he landed in jail. And as unbelievable as it might sound, he thought he was shooting at me instead of Jess."

"Couldn't he see the difference?" Naomi asked.

"I don't suppose he could," Ross went on to explain. "He saw Jess and Victoria from a distance through the sliding doors in my bedroom, and, thinking it was me and Victoria riding away from the ranch, he grabbed my rifle from the cabinet and followed."

Incredulous, Neal asked, "What were his intentions? To kill you?"

Ross shrugged. "I don't know. Whatever his plans were, he must have gotten scared after the shooting and threw the rifle down near the arroyo."

Victoria was completely floored. "He was in your bedroom? What was Steve doing in your bedroom?"

Ross arched a brow at his brother-in-law. "You haven't told her any of this?"

The under-sheriff shook his head. "No. I thought you should be the one to tell everyone the details."

Drawing in a deep breath, Ross glanced at Isabella and then at the other waiting faces around the table. "Well, I guess you could say Steve resented me for several reasons. One, he wanted Linc's job as head wrangler."

Linc's head jerked up in complete surprise. "My job? He said he wanted my job?"

Ross dismissed the notion by batting the air with his hand. "The guy was crazy. You're family. Plus you know more about horses than any man I've ever known. And that includes Tucker. There wasn't an ice cube's chance in hell that he could get your job."

"You said he resented you for several reasons. What were the others?" Isabella asked.

Ross grimaced. "He saw me as the rich guy who had everything. Including the woman he wanted."

Isabella's brows lifted with speculation. Victoria's lips pressed together as she leaned across the table toward her brother.

"Ross," Victoria said with a rueful groan, "don't tell me all this is because of one of your affairs!"

He held up both hands to ward off his sister's accusations. "Just stop right there, Sis. I'm not guilty. I'm only slightly acquainted with the woman—Angela Bowers. You all know her. She came here to the ranch that day you and Jess rode to the arroyo. If you remember, I'd just come in from my trip that day. When she came to the door, I was trying to have lunch and deal with a horse trader on the telephone. She wanted to talk to me about raising funds for the Cattlemen's Ball. We talked for about fifteen or twenty minutes and then she left. That's all there was to it, but apparently Steve saw her here at the house and thought something more was going on between us. From what Steve told the law, Angela apparently wouldn't date him because she had a crush on me. That's why he snuck into my bedroom, to see if she'd been in the room with me.''

Isabella looked at him with sudden dawning. ''That night—at the Cattlemen's Ball—Steve made a comment to me about you getting all the women. He must have been upset about you dancing with Angela. But I—I never made the connection.'' She shook her head. ''It sickens me now to think that I danced with the man.''

''Don't feel bad,'' Victoria told her. ''Steve fooled all of us.''

''In any case, he must have been a sick individual,'' Neal commented.

''Something in his head twisted off, all right,'' Ross grimly agreed. ''But at least he can't hurt anybody else now.''

With a satisfied nod, Neal lifted his wineglass. ''I'll drink to that. It's about time you Ketchums had things going your way.''

''I'll second that,'' Ross agreed with his old friend.

Everyone around the table reached for their glasses to drink a toast. From the corner of her eye, Isabella noticed

Victoria had turned an especially tender look on her husband.

"Don't you think it's time we told them?" she asked.

Nodding, Jess reached over and folded his wife's hand in his.

Ross's brows arched with curiosity as he looked at the two of them. "What now? You've found something new about Noah Rider's murder?"

Victoria's eyes were suddenly glowing with excitement while Jess smiled with unabashed pride.

"No," Victoria said with a smug smile. "It's nothing about that. Jess and I are going to have a baby."

Ross stared at his sister. He should have known Victoria and Jess would want a baby, a brother or sister to go with little Katrina. But he'd been a bachelor for so long, thoughts of babies were in the same league as washing dishes—he just didn't do them. That is, he hadn't until— Isabella had walked into his life.

"A baby," he repeated in wondrous fascination.

Victoria laughed at his dumbfounded reaction. "Yes, a baby. Isn't it wonderful?"

Ross glanced at Isabella to see if she was as stunned by Victoria's news as he was.

Isabella smiled at him, even while an empty hole was spreading inside her chest. How could she feel so happy for Victoria and still be so perfectly miserable? she wondered.

Rising from his seat, Ross went around the table, kissed his sister's cheek, then shook his brother-in-law's hand.

"This is the best news I've heard in a long, long time," Ross exclaimed. "A new little Ketchum in the family!"

Jess shot him a wry look. "Sorry to bust your bubble, Ross, but he'll be a Hastings."

Everyone laughed, and for the next few minutes congratulations were offered to the happy couple and talk focused on the coming baby. But as the meal progressed, the mention of Noah Rider came up again and the conversation turned to the problem of solving his murder.

"Are you having any visions about this case?" Neal asked Naomi.

The older woman with her silver braids smiled at the handsome lawyer. "No visions. But I'll let you know if I have any." She inclined her head toward Isabella. "My goddaughter will help you find the killer."

"That's right," Ross spoke up with happy confidence. "Isabella helped us flush out Steve. Maybe she can do the same on Noah's case."

Isabella looked around the table of people until her eyes settled on Ross. She couldn't go on letting them all think she was going to stay on the T Bar K. Especially Ross. It wasn't right. She had to speak out now. No matter how badly it hurt her.

"I—Ross, I'm not going to be here to help you with Noah's case. I—I'll be leaving tomorrow—when Mother and Naomi head back to the Jicarilla."

Ross stared at her as though she'd just struck him in the face. She couldn't leave. Not now. Not ever. He didn't know exactly when he'd come to that conclusion, but it was there in his heart. And letting her out of his life was no longer an option.

"Leaving?" he repeated as though he wasn't quite sure he'd heard her right.

She nodded, and the whole table went awkwardly quiet. Unable to keep holding his gaze, Isabella looked down at her half-eaten dinner.

Victoria was the one who eventually broke the silence

with another question for the Apache visionary. "Naomi, do you envision your goddaughter leaving the ranch tomorrow?"

Isabella looked up and was surprised to see her godmother smiling as though a rainbow had just arced over the dining table. *Naomi,* she silently thought, *can't you see my heart is breaking?*

"No," Naomi answered Victoria's question. "I have not had any visions of Isabella leaving the ranch. I think it is meant for her to be here." She paused and shrugged. "But maybe I need to do a bit of praying and chanting about it."

Isabella groaned with embarrassment. "Naomi, how could you say such a thing?"

Ross didn't wait for the other woman's reply; he scraped back his chair and reached for Isabella's arm.

"Don't mind us, folks, just go ahead and finish your meal," he said as he led Isabella away from the table.

Mortified, Isabella glanced back at the group of dinner guests and spotted several knowing smiles, especially on Naomi and Victoria.

"Ross, what—where are we going?" she asked as he led her through the kitchen, then out the back door onto the porch. "Your guests are going to think you're crazy. That we're both crazy!"

"We are. At least, I am, for not saying something before now." He stopped midway in the warm shadows and pulled her into his arms. Isabella wondered if she should resist, then didn't even try as his arms tightened and drew her against his chest. "I'm sorry if you think I've ignored you these past couple of days. But things have been crazy. I haven't had a chance to draw a good breath, much less talk to you. But talk isn't exactly all I've wanted to do," he added, his hands roaming seductively against her back.

Her eyes were troubled as they lifted to meet his. "Ross, I don't think you've neglected me. It's not that. It's…the other night…maybe you don't understand what it meant to me. I'm not like the other women you've known."

His lips twisted to a wry line. "That's an understatement."

"I, uh…I thought I could be. I thought being with you…that way…would be enough for me. But it isn't. That's why I can't stay here any longer. I'd only wind up back in your bed. You'd be satisfied with that, but I wouldn't. Don't you see?"

He studied her face for long sober moments. "So you want to leave. Go to the Jicarilla and forget about me."

Just hearing him say the words filled her throat with hot tears. Yet she knew she had to stand her ground with him. If not, she'd be following in her mother's footsteps. "Not exactly. But—"

His hands closed over her shoulders. "You said I didn't understand what the other night meant to you. Well, maybe you don't understand what it meant to me. I can't just let you leave, Bella. You're a part of my life. I thought you knew that."

She drew in a deep, bracing breath. "You haven't exactly told me that."

He grimaced. "I'm not good with words, Bella. Not when I need to be."

Isabella tried to swallow away the pain that continued to choke her. "You don't have to explain yourself. You made it clear from the start that you could never love any woman. I can't expect you to love me."

But he did. He loved her utterly and completely. If he hadn't known it before, he'd certainly known it when he'd seen her racing across the mesa, clinging desperately to Juggler's side.

"Bella, I was so wrong when I said that to you. I didn't understand—" he stopped as a groan of regret slipped past his lips. "I thought I could control my heart. I thought I would never have to love anybody unless I wanted to and I'd chosen not to."

"Because you were hurt," she said softly. "Because some woman with a career turned her back on you."

His eyes widened. "You figured that out?"

She nodded somberly. "You more or less spelled it out with some of the remarks you made after we first met. And then Victoria mentioned something about you not liking career women."

With another groan, he dropped his hands and turned slightly away from her. "Linda was a reporter for the Aztec newspaper. But she had high aspirations that didn't include me. I just didn't know that until a television station in Denver offered her a job writing the evening news."

Isabella tentatively touched his arm. "You must have loved her very much to have let her taint your life all these years."

He twisted his head toward hers, his expression wry. "The way you let Winston Jones taint yours?"

All of a sudden, his question peeled a veil from her eyes. He'd been hurt by a woman who'd wanted nothing but a career. And she'd been hurt by a man who was incapable of loving anyone. She'd once believed that Ross was like Winston Jones; he wanted only the pleasure of a woman's body. But now she knew better. That was all in the past. And this was their future he was talking about. Their future together.

With a little cry of joy she stepped forward and slid her

arms around his waist. "Ross, that woman—the one who hurt you—I could never be that way. I love you! And if it means keeping us together, I can give up my job. That is…if you love me."

"Love you? Bella, I adore you. Absolutely adore you. That day you were nearly killed—everything became clear to me. And I'm not talking about Steve now. I'm talking about myself and how I feel about you. I could see just how important you are to me. And I could see that I couldn't possibly survive without you in my life."

She trembled with hope. "Are you trying to say you want to marry me?"

His hands slipped into her long hair. With his fingers cradling the back of her head, he angled her face up to his. The position prompted her eyes to focus on his lips and she realized she was just now learning what physical hunger was all about.

"You're the only woman I'll ever want," he whispered huskily. "Say you'll marry me…soon! In the next few days!"

Ross wanted to marry her! Her, the half Apache daughter that Winston Jones had never wanted. Emotion overtook her, making it impossible for her to utter one word.

"Isabella, what is it?" he asked anxiously as he spotted tears building in her eyes. "Your job?"

She shook her head back and forth. "No. I mean, yes, I'll marry you! And for you, I'd give up my job. I'd give up anything for your love."

The fact that she could love him so unselfishly overwhelmed him, and he buried his face in the side of her hair.

"Never! I would never ask that of you."

Love, pure and sweet, began to pour through Isabella like a never-ending spring, and she knew it would always be that way for this man who now held her so tightly to his heart.

"If that's the way you feel, then I'll practice in Aztec," she told him. "That way I'll only be a few minutes away from you."

He eased her head back and gave her a lopsided grin. "I like the sound of you working only a few minutes away. But that isn't going to help your people on the Jicarilla. And that's the very reason you became a lawyer in the first place." His fingers stroked her cheek as his eyes promised a lifetime of love no matter what obstacles they faced. "What if you drove up to Dulce—say, a couple of days a week, then worked the remainder of the week in Aztec? How would that be?"

Laughing with sheer happiness, she snuggled her face against his chest. "Fine. Until we start to have our children. Then I'll gladly cut my caseload way back."

Smiling, he folded his arms across her back and rested his chin on the top of her head. "A few minutes ago, when Victoria and Jess announced they were going to have a child, I realized I wanted the same thing to be happening to us. Imagine—Ross Ketchum, a husband and father. When word of this gets out, my reputation will be ruined."

Laughing, Isabella reached for his hand. "Let's go tell them we have more news to celebrate tonight."

She made a move to tug him down the porch, but he stood in his tracks. "We'll go in a minute," he promised as his hand came up to tenderly smooth the stray hairs from her forehead. "Right now, I want to tell you just how happy you've made me."

"And I'm going to make you even happier by trying to find out who killed Noah Rider," she promised him.

He brought his lips down to hers and pressed a tempting

kiss against the moist curves. "You're going to be far too busy with your honeymoon to be playing private investigator, my little darling. I'm calling my brother, Seth, the Texas Ranger, to come up here. If anyone can get to the bottom of this thing, he can."

Smiling seductively, Isabella slid her arms around his waist. "A Texas Ranger, huh? Well, it sounds like I'd just be in his way. So that means I'll have more time to devote to my husband."

Behind them, the door leading from the kitchen to the porch opened and Victoria stepped out into the small shaft of light coming from the doorway.

"Hey, you two," she called, "do you need a referee out here?"

Chuckling, Ross led Isabella down the porch to where Victoria waited, and as the three of them rejoined the rest of the family, he realized the party had only begun.

* * * * *

Look for Seth's story coming in the summer, only from Stella Bagwell and Special Edition.

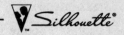

SPECIAL EDITION™

Three small-town women have their lives turned
upside down by a sudden inheritance.
Change is good, but change this big?

by Arlene James

BEAUTICIAN GETS MILLION-DOLLAR TIP!

(Silhouette Special Edition #1589,
available January 2004)

A sexy commitment-shy fire marshal meets his match
in a beautician with big...bucks?

FORTUNE FINDS FLORIST

(Silhouette Special Edition #1596,
available February 2004)

It's time to get down and dirty when a beautiful
florist teams up with a sexy farmer....

TYCOON MEETS TEXAN!

(Silhouette Special Edition #1601,
available March 2004)

The trip of a lifetime turns into something more
when a widow is swept off her feet by someone
tall, dark and wealthy....

Available at your favorite retail outlet.

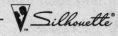

SPECIAL EDITION™

Delivering the miracle of life...and love!

EXPECTING!
by Susan Mallery
(Silhouette Special Edition #1585, available January 2004)

COUNTDOWN TO BABY
by Gina Wilkins
(Silhouette Special Edition #1592, available February 2004)

BLUEGRASS BABY
by Judy Duarte
(Silhouette Special Edition #1598, available March 2004)

FOREVER...AGAIN
by Maureen Child
(Silhouette Special Edition #1604, available April 2004)

IN THE ENEMY'S ARMS
by Pamela Toth
(Silhouette Special Edition #1610, available May 2004)

Available at your favorite retail outlet.

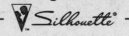